Protectors of the Crown

In pursuit of justice...and love!

As members of the Knights Fortitude of the Order of the Sword, Sirs Warin de Talmont, Nicholas d'Amberly and Savaric Fitz Leonard have sworn an oath of allegiance to one another and King Henry III. When faced with a new threat against the Crown, known only as the *Duo Dracones*, they must work together to find and bring the traitors to justice.

With each new lead they risk their lives to get one step closer to the truth... But the biggest danger these three men are about to face is the women who are about to open their minds and steal their hearts!

Discover Warin and Joan's story in
A Defiant Maiden's Knight

Available now!

Look out for Nicholas and Savaric's stories, coming soon!

Author Note

Henry III's reign of England in 1226 was a time of uncertainty since the young monarch had yet to gain his majority to govern. He ruled under the auspicious eyes of Hubert de Burgh, Regent and Justiciar of England, while other powerful men—earls, barons and magnates—frustrated by the situation in the kingdom, began to sharpen their knives against de Burgh. This created a climate of recalcitrance and instability, and it's against this backdrop that this book is set.

The hero, Warin de Talmont, is part of a small enigmatic group called the Knights Fortitude of the Order of the Sword, Protectors of the Crown who uncover a plot against the king by a shadowy unknown group in medieval London. Warin does this reluctantly with Joan Lovent, a spirited, astute maiden who is slowly losing her sight. She teaches him to trust his instincts and all of his senses. Their comradery and mutual respect create an unlikely friendship, but can this turn into something far greater? Can they find a way to trust in love as danger surrounds them at every corner?

I hope you enjoy Warin and Joan's story!

MELISSA OLIVER

A Defiant Maiden's Knight

HARLEQUIN®
HISTORICAL™

Recycling programs
for this product may
not exist in your area.

ISBN-13: 978-1-335-72327-7

A Defiant Maiden's Knight

Harlequin Enterprises ULC
22 Adelaide St. West, 41st Floor
Toronto, Ontario M5H 4E3, Canada
www.Harlequin.com

Printed in U.S.A.

Melissa Oliver is from southwest London, UK, where she writes historical romance novels. She lives with her lovely husband and three daughters, who share her passion for decrepit old castles, grand palaces and all things historical. She won the Joan Hessayon Award for new writers from the Romantic Novelists' Association in 2020 for her first book, *The Rebel Heiress and the Knight*. When she's not writing, she loves to travel for inspiration, paint, and visit museums and art galleries. If you want to find out more, follow Melissa on Twitter @melissaoauthor or Facebook @melissaoliverauthor.

Books by Melissa Oliver

Harlequin Historical

Notorious Knights

The Rebel Heiress and the Knight
Her Banished Knight's Redemption
The Return of Her Lost Knight
The Knight's Convenient Alliance

Protectors of the Crown

A Defiant Maiden's Knight

Visit the Author Profile page
at Harlequin.com.

To the lovely team at the RNIB
(Royal National Institute of Blind People),
who were so helpful and informative with
my research. This book is also dedicated to
anyone who has faced difficult obstacles
and managed to overcome them.

Chapter One

Westcheap, London—autumn 1226

Sir Warin de Talmont tugged his hood over his head and followed the man whom he had been trailing through the myriad of London's narrow lanes leading to the bustling thoroughfare of Westcheap. He caught the eye of Nicholas d'Amberly—a fellow member of a small select group calling themselves the Knights Fortitude of the Order of the Sword. *Pro Rex. Pro Deus. Pro fide. Pro honoris.*

Their motto was an apt reminder that they put King and country at the heart of everything they held sacred, unlike many other religious orders of the day. This they did foremost by working tirelessly to uncover and quash plots against the Crown of England.

Nicholas passed by him and made a single nod, which Warin returned. He continued to follow the man through the cobbled street famed for its row upon row of stalls of hustling market traders, selling their wares, giving Westcheap its distinctive vibrant spirit.

Completing their triumvirate was Savaric Fitz Leonard, who would be, at that very moment, manning nearby Ludgate, waiting to finally spy this man with any other possible conspirators he might happen to meet. This was what they were all waiting on before apprehending the man and finding out who it was that he was working for.

It had all been meticulously planned. And after weeks of uncertainty about the threat against the Crown, they had managed to gain this one lead to exploit. This one weak point that might be the very key they needed that could finally unlock the plot masterminded by an elusive group of traitors. Traitors known only by their insignia of the two entwined serpents or Duo Dracones.

Warin followed the man weaving his way through the crowds gathered around the market sellers and stalls where mercers sold silk, linen and fustian cloth and silver trinkets on one side of the street and the stretch of cordwainers, stitching and moulding soft leather deftly into footwear around wooden stumps, on the other. The smell of leather fused with that of livestock being sold in nearby Cattle Street and pails of milk and other dairy goods as well as barrels of ale in Milk Street, giving the air a distinct, pungent odour that mingled with the sweat and toil. But this was what Warin loved about London—the hustle and graft of a working city. A city he was determined to keep safe. A vulnerable Crown that had to be protected above anything.

The man he was following stopped abruptly and spoke to the cordwainer at the last stall, who nodded and retrieved a pouch from inside the sleeve of his cape, dropping it into his hand. The man then tucked this on his person and continued to mill his way through, this time with a little more urgency than before. Warin pursued the man, who turned into the noisy cobbled Bread Street where trade was seemingly busy that morning, with all types of warm baked breads, rolls and small crusty meat pies being sold along the long, narrow road.

Warin kept his eyes peeled on the man as he quickened his pace, glad that his towering height allowed him to follow the man expediently. But it was just at that very moment as the man slipped down a narrow alleyway between a wooden arched doorway when Warin heard a piercing scream on the other side of the road along Honey Lane, making him spin around on his heel and take in the scene before him. A group was gathering around a young woman who had fallen to the ground and, on her hands and knees, was groping around in the dirt and muck. A young woman Warin recognised instantly, Joan Lovent—the younger sister of the Knights Fortitude's leader, Thomas Lovent.

Damn!

He glanced back around at the retreating shadow of the man he had been pursuing for the better part of that morning and muttered another oath, cursing his bad luck. The blasted mission was about to end in disaster and for a moment Warin questioned whether to pursue the man or go to the aid of the woman who had just blundered into this mission.

He squeezed his eyes shut in frustration, knowing all that would be lost here and how the others in the Order might hold him accountable for letting the man go. But there was no question of what was expected of him—of what he had to do. Warin opened his eyes and turned in resignation, making his way towards the entrance of Honey Lane and the small crowd of bystanders huddled around the woman. Why in god's name was she even here, in this busy part of the city, seemingly alone? Especially with her brother away from London and on Crown business.

In truth, before Thomas Lovent had left London, he had asked him to look out for his unruly sister but Warin had thought he had meant to make a few courtesy visits, which he had yet to do. But never this—finding Joan Lovent unattended, friendless and sprawled on a dirty London road. He expelled an irritated sigh as he made his way through and knelt beside her.

'Are you hurt, Mistress Joan? What happened here?'

The young woman's head snapped up and she blinked several times, her eyes darting in every direction, not truly focusing on him.

'Sir Warin de Talmont?' Her dark strawberry-blonde brows furrowed in the middle as she absently rubbed her forehead, smudging a line of dirt across it, making him want to reach out and wipe it off for her. 'You are here?'

'I am and happy to be of service to you. Allow me, mistress.' Warin stood, reaching for her hand and pulling her up to stand in front of him. The contact shot a sudden warmth through his veins, which he dismissed, irritably. He dropped his hand as the small crowd began to disperse.

'Are you hurt?'

'No, I thank you, sir. I am perfect well.' She brushed her hands down the length of the stained brown apron tied around the waist of her kirtle.

'Good, because the pertinent question, mistress, is why you are here. Would you care explaining?'

She laughed softly. 'Ah, I see that you believe I should?'

'I do.' He shook his head and sighed. 'It is not safe for a maiden such as yourself to be here, in this part of London.'

'A maiden such as me?' Joan's back seemed to straighten as she tilted her head up. 'Heavens, but what could you possibly mean?' Her voice seemed to drip with disdain. He groaned to himself, knowing he had offended the woman.

Joan Lovent might be a notable beauty, with her creamy skin, delicate features and long russet and strawberry-blonde hair tucked beneath a dishevelled linen veil, which in truth made her lovelier and far more endearing. However, she also had failing eyesight that would one day lead to permanent darkness, once the blindness claimed her vision. And yet with Joan Lovent, Warin felt compromised between feeling empathy for her situation and annoyance since the woman was always such a damn nuisance.

The first time he had ever met her was two summers ago when Thomas Lovent had given him the responsibility of escorting his young sister at a perilous time for the man and, even then, she had made Warin feel wary. Since then, he had only seen her a handful of times and spoken to her even less. Yet he still felt the same about Joan Lovent. She was not only a nuisance but there was something far too perceptive about her that made him uneasy—that somehow managed to grate on him—as though she could see right through to his broken soul.

Which was why he tried to avoid the woman as much as possible.

He picked up her wooden staff and passed it to her. 'I hope you know that I intended no ill will, mistress. Only that a lady of your standing should not be on a jaunt to this part of London. It is not safe here.' He leant forward, whispering in her ear, 'Especially when you consider who your brother is.'

She smiled brightly. 'I thank you for coming to my aid just now, Sir Warin—however, my "jaunt" here can really be of no concern to you.'

He reached out and picked a twig that was stuck to her veil, tossing it to the ground. 'I beg to differ, Joan, and by and by I came to your aid because of the very fact that you found yourself in need of a knight.'

'You think so, do you?'

'Naturally.' He nodded. 'You screamed—I came.'

'You are excessively obliging, sir.' She turned to go. 'And are of great service to us foolish maidens who traipse on jaunts all over the wrong parts of the city. Now I really must go. Despite what you might believe, I did not come here alone and my young page will arrive with the provisions I acquired. Good day to you, Sir Warin, and thank you again.'

The woman spoke with such a light sing-song lilt to her voice that it seemed incongruent that she had been in such an aggrieved state only moments ago.

His hand reached out and cupped her elbow, stilling her. 'Not so swiftly, mistress. You have not still divulged to me the reason why you are here or even the cause of your distress that induced that…scream.'

She laughed softly again. 'I did not realise I had to disclose any such thing to you, sir.'

'Of course not, but in the absence of your brother, it behoves me to enquire as it does to ensure your safety.'

'So gallant of you, Sir Warin. You are an embodiment of brotherly concern.' It somehow irked him, the manner in which Joan Lovent boldly said the word *'brotherly'*. There was no doubt that he was nothing of the sort. His gaze fell to where his hand cupped Joan's elbow and he exhaled through his teeth, nettled that once again his notice of Joan was wholly inappropriate. He was a man who would never again be attached to a woman. No, once was enough and that had ended in heartache and pain. 'But if you must know, Sir Warin, I had been at the All Hallows Church where my patronage is hugely appreciated, enabling the good that can be done for the poor and sick of that small parish.'

'That is very commendable. I'm heartily impressed. It seems that you are all kindness and benevolence, mistress.'

She shrugged. 'It seems that way, does it not?'

'And I suppose your brother is aware that you come all this distance within the city gates to help at All Hallows?'

'Of course.' She bit her bottom lip, looking away.

He frowned, shaking his head at her. 'You know it is a sin to lie, Joan. And it is sadly just as I thought— Thomas Lovent is not aware of your jaunts,' he muttered. 'And since he is not here in London you thought to leave the safe confines of your home?'

They meandered through Honey Lane, which traded in exotic spices as well as food stalls just as in Milk and

Bread Streets. His hold of her tightened, safeguarding her movements as they walked along the narrow path, making sure that she would not fall down to the ground.

'Again I must wonder at how my movements can be of interest to you, sir?' she asked softly.

'Since your brother expressly asked me to look out for you, mistress, and as it happens your movements seem to undermine your safety.' Not to mention his mission, which had all but ended in disaster because of her. Not that Joan Lovent could know any of it. But it had been a great misfortune that their paths had crossed on this day. Yet, if they had not, the woman might have found herself in a more precarious situation than she already had.

'I thank you, but there is really no need. And I trust we shall keep this between us, sir.' She flashed him a warm smile. 'My brother, nor should I add my sister by marriage, really need to know about any of this, do they?'

Warin stopped abruptly and watched her for a moment, as he folded his arms across his chest, knowing he could make no such promises. And yet the concern furrowed on her brows made him soften a little.

He sighed. 'As long as you make an oath that this will be your last *jaunt* here without their knowledge.'

She huffed and continued to move down the busy cobbled road. 'But I do not know what I shall do with myself.'

'I am sure you will think of another cause. Somewhere far safer and far closer to your home.' Warin followed her and wrapped his hand around her shoulder, gently guiding her away, as she almost lost her footing on the uneven cobble path. 'What say you, mistress? Do you have an answer for me?'

She did not immediately respond, making him push her further on this salient point. With an unknown threat against the Crown, and with the woman's own brother away from London, it now annoyingly fell to him to keep her safe—and he would do it by having her as far away from him, his work and the machinations of Court as possible. Especially since Joan Lovent might become an impediment to all that he was trying to achieve.

'In fact, you need not do anything other than seek your own comfort within the safety of your house, away from the city, mistress.'

'How well you know me,' she muttered sardonically. 'In truth, I find I detest sitting idly by in the bower, spinning at the loom. Instead, I'd rather seek something worthwhile to occupy myself.'

His lips twitched. No, from their short acquaintance he was certain that was something Joan Lovent could not be described as, despite her limitations. 'I would never envisage you to be idle, but I am all agog that you cannot find a worthwhile occupation at home.'

'Sadly, I have not. I only seem to be good at being a benefactor and giving my patronage to a small insignificant church such as All Hallows and assisting them where I can. I dare say it gives me a purpose. But I suppose you would rather those poor souls seek another wealthy benefactor.'

'I do. But you have yet to explain what happened here for you to be crawling around in the dirt?'

'Well, in the interest of brotherly concern, I'm embarrassed to say that a scoundrel took advantage of me.'

'What?' He exhaled harshly. 'Hell's teeth, woman, why did you not say anything before!'

'There seemed so much more to say regarding where I had gone and why I was here.'

'This is no jesting matter, Joan. You could have been hurt. Tell me what happened.'

'You are right, Sir Warin. Truly I am fine and I only screamed out of frustration as the brigand snatched my gold necklace—snapped it clean off my neck!'

Hell's teeth.

'I am very sorry to hear this.'

'Oh, there is really no need.' She waved her hand dismissively. 'I feel rather indifferently about the necklace itself, but the little painted wooden cross that he tossed to the ground—for me that is worth all the silver in the land. And the reason I was on my hands and knees searching for it, but, alas, I could not find it.'

He frowned, not understanding her as he gently guided away from a group of rowdy young men walking towards them. 'What is so precious about it?'

'It's just a worthless trinket, really. But of great value to me.' She shook her head sadly. 'You see, my younger sister gave it to me, after painstakingly painting it for me, and…well, it is all I have left of her.'

Warin knew her story. He knew it well. And it was as marred by the same heartache and loss that he had experienced himself after the deaths of his beloved wife and child many years ago. It had left an unbearable pain that he still felt after all this time.

For Joan it had been a different heartache when she

had survived a horrific fire that claimed her home, her family and everything she held dear—including, it seemed, her beloved mother and young sister. It was after much time had passed before her brother, Thomas, returned from Aquitaine and felt the burden of responsibility of what had happened as well as the fate of his only living sister. God only knew what the man would say now if he knew about her coming to this part of London essentially alone.

'I will find it for you, Joan.'

'What did you say?'

'I said I will find it for you. On my honour.'

She raised her brows in surprise. 'You would do that for me?'

He looked down at her and sighed. 'I would, mistress, but only on one condition.'

She shook her head. 'Of course, there would be conditions attached.'

'Naturally.' He smiled. 'And it is this—if I happen to find this wooden cross of yours—'

'Don't forget that it is painted red, yellow and white,' she interrupted, 'although it's now a little dirty, I suppose.'

'*If* I find it,' he tried again, 'I want you to promise that you will cease coming to this part of London, however important the cause might be.'

He watched her intently as every emotion darted across her face before she exhaled a frustrated air of resignation. 'Only if you find it, Sir Warin.'

'Good, and you would swear an oath to that?'

'Must I?'

'I am afraid so,' he said softly. 'And by and by, I advise

that you become involved with something else that might provide you with purpose.'

Her shoulders dropped, but Warin would not be affected. He must not. This was for her own good. 'Do I have your agreement?'

'There is a pertinent word to describe what you're doing, but very well. Now I really must take my leave of you.' She looked straight ahead, her head held high, without turning to acknowledging him. It was clear that she was not happy with this and had difficulty hiding her displeasure. No matter, Warin could live with that.

He dipped his head. 'Allow me to escort you home.'

'Do I have a choice?'

'Certainly, but if you decline then I'll just have to follow you, mistress, so that I can be satisfied of your safety back home.'

She made a single nod as she moved with the aid of the wooden staff she used to meet the page who was waiting to assist her.

God's breath, but it was ridiculous that the woman had even ventured to this notorious part of London at all. Warin would have to make certain that he found this wooden cross of hers only to ensure that she never returned.

Chapter Two

Joan smiled at the gurgling baby sat on the strewn blankets under the apple tree in the orchard of her brother's walled garden. A brother who was at that very moment away on yet another mission that was deemed far too secret to tell her anything about. All for Joan's own good, apparently. To protect her. To safeguard her. She understood and appreciated it, knowing from where her brother Tom's concerns rose.

They had both lost so much in the fire so many years ago—their mother and beloved younger sister, whose memory sat heavily on Joan's shoulders as a constant reminder of those dark, dark times. A time where her father's rampant threats in the absence of Tom meant that Joan took the brunt of his extreme anger and sudden bursts of aggression. She was at the receiving end of her father's taunts and derisions and for good reason, as far as he was concerned.

He blamed everything—from his argument with Tom, which led to her brother leaving the family manor, to the failure of crops and even changes to their circumstances—on Joan. It was wrong. It was hurtful and undoubtedly irrational, yet it had never ceased to affect her, despite her best efforts to dispel his poisonous venom. Joan began to believe everything her father said about her, even when her mother tried to reassure her otherwise—his proof being that her gradual loss of sight was a sign, something which he never failed to remind her was due to her own wickedness. And her penance, her only salvation, had come in the form of prayer, which she was forced to do in the cold darkness of her chamber for hours on end, night after night.

Yet, everything changed on the night of the fire, when her father claimed that she was beyond redemption. It mattered not that she pleaded with him to spare her young sister. It mattered not that she complied with all of his wishes. It mattered not that her mother had tried to intervene. No, her father had been bent on destruction. And it happened so swiftly—the fire that he had started to rid them of what he believed to be impending evil, but which engulfed their manor, extinguishing his life, along with her mother's and young sister's.

Joan pushed the memories far away, wanting to forget that harrowing period in her life, and turned her attention to the infant who sat happily beside her. She looked down at her nephew and smiled, offering a slice of apple to the little boy, who grabbed it and proceeded to suck and rub his gums on the juicy piece of fruit.

Joan knew she was blessed to have the constancy of her brother's affection, his care and unconditional love. In the aftermath of that awful time, it had been Tom who had come to her aid and restored the safety she so desperately needed. And it had been Tom who had given her the faith and belief to start living again without bone-crushing fear—not that it had been easy. She still carried some of the insecurity from that time, however hard she tried to rid herself from its shackles.

Even so, Joan knew she was fortunate to have a permanent home with him, Brida—her sister by marriage—and their family. And although the events from the past had shaped her, she tried to resist being defined by her condition. It was a constant strain living with her sight slowly diminishing. Indeed, it made her feel a little vulnerable at times, not that she ever expressed her fears to another soul. In truth, she had little expectation for her future, but knew that it did not include marriage or even courtly love. How could it when she knew emphatically that no man would consider someone like her, with her limitations. She would live with her brother and his family and be grateful that she did.

Despite this, Joan was no longer that young maid whom Tom had sought after their ancestral home had been reduced to ash, once he had returned from Aquitaine. Yet she was still treated as one. And not just by her brother, or even Brida, but exasperating men such as Warin de Talmont who thought they knew what was best for her as well.

Lord, but Joan felt stifled from it all. The man had brought her home only yesterday and still everything that had passed between them swirled around her head as she had tried to sleep the previous night. It still vexed her that he had berated her for being in that bustling part of London as though she lacked sense and judgement. He would believe her to be a reckless, impetuous woman. Indeed, he had treated her as though she were a child, just like her little nephew who had dropped the slice of apple in favour of grinding his gums on his wooden toy.

Joan knew that Warin de Talmont viewed her as a nuisance. Especially after finding her in on her hands and knees and in 'in need of a knight' on a busy London street. God, how mortifying. It should not matter—it did not matter and yet Joan resented the man's censure and disapproval.

It had been the same two summers ago when he had provided her escort when her brother could not. And he had made it perfectly clear from the outset that he had begrudged the task given to him. It was not as though Joan had made such a request of a man she'd never met before. No, she had simply complied with Tom's edicts to leave where she had been staying for somewhere her brother had deemed far safer, until a time they could be reunited again. And now once again her brother had importuned Warin de Talmont to look out for her, while he was away from London. Much to her shame.

Joan closed her eyes and breathed the fragrant smells of the orchard as the leaves above her rustled in soft breeze, the sounds and smells so very different to the rowdy, dirty yet efficacious roads that she had wandered through to reach All Hallows Church yesterday. And though she loved the clean air and tranquillity that she found in her brother's walled garden woven with the heady perfume of the last blooms—indeed, the whole of this affluent tree-lined area along the Strand—she still felt far more alive in that hectic environment within the city gates. Especially the patronage and support she bestowed on All Hallows which cared for its poor and destitute. Her role far more than just a benefactor.

As Joan had explained to Warin de Talmont the previous day, it gave her purpose, but somehow also gave her life meaning. It allowed her not to be confined within these walls, however sweet the air and delightful the company. But far more importantly it made it possible for Joan to be more than someone with an impediment—which always, despite her best efforts, happened anyway. It was initially what most people observed and recognised about Joan—that her sight was poor—followed in its stead by the intolerable pity they would impart once they understood that her condition would one day lead to blindness.

The difficulties she faced with the gradual failing of her eyesight meant that her life was destined to be bound and constrained by it, however hard she fought against it. And although Joan hated being treated differently because of it, she had no choice but to accept her limitations. God knew that she lived with it daily, as it steadily plunged her further and further into darkness. She sometimes wondered whether it might have been a blessing if she had been born blind, then to cruelly have it ebb away from her gradually. To never again see the verdant shade of the meadows in spring, or the summer sky at dusk or after a rainfall. But of all the things Joan knew she would miss, it was her nephew's smiles as they changed from those of a babe to those of a man. Her chest clenched tightly at the thought. And just as quickly she dismissed it. Joan could not allow herself to wallow in self-pity, as it brought nothing but more pain.

On hearing Brida's footfall, Joan tipped her head

back and smiled at the heavily pregnant woman who had approached them and tentatively sat down on the blanket. A young maid had followed behind carrying a large platter of cold meats, cheese, warm bread and more fruit, while a page brought a large cushion for Brida to sit on.

'I thought to add a little more to this repast, especially as it's so unexpectedly warm today.'

'Splendid idea. This is a veritable feast, Brida.' Her eyes darted in every direction and found the hazy, blurred outline of the knife on the blanket. Joan leant forward, wrapping her fingers around the hilt of the knife, and brought it to her wooden plate, ready to cut up another of the harvested apples, when Brida's hand stilled her.

'Let me do that for you, Joan.'

She knew her sister meant well, the offer given only in kindness, but it also made Joan want to scream in frustration. It all but made her feel as though she couldn't breathe, as though she were suffocating from a world closing in on her.

'Thank you, but I can do it myself,' she muttered tightly.

'Of course. I thought to be of help.'

Immediately Joan felt guilt coursing through her.

'I know, Brida, I am terribly sorry for my rudeness. I really do not know why I have been so irascible and bad-tempered all day.'

Brida sat back and played with her son before glancing back at her. 'I hope that you were not put out by the manner in which Sir Warin provided you escort yesterday?'

'I do not believe I have given it, or rather him, much thought.'

Liar...

The truth was that Joan had thought of little else. The man intrigued, exasperated and annoyed her at the same time—all made worse by her own visceral reaction to him. From his enticing exotic clean scent that wrapped around her senses, even in such a malodorous environment where she had stumbled upon him yesterday, to his firm yet gentle grip of her elbow as he guided her through the narrow roads, the heat of his touch seeping through to her skin. The man was the epitome of a strong warrior knight with the breadth of his shoulders to that impressive height and dark, almost black hair. And even his features and countenance which Joan could recall vividly from two years ago, when her sight was a little better than it was presently, seemed most agreeable. From what she remembered, his eyes—grey—and his smile—smouldering—now those she could still make out. Handsome. Yes, very handsome. But far too knowing, far too infuriating.

'You're blushing, Joan.'

'Am I?' She bit into the apple and chewed slowly before swallowing. 'Only because I have sat outside in the sun for too long.'

'Of course.' Her sister grinned, shaking her head. 'But mayhap it is something else altogether.'

The truth was that Warin de Talmont was also exceedingly vexing, however handsome he might be. He had all but forced her to make an oath never to return to All Hallows Church or that *part* of London, something which she was cross with herself about.

In spite of all that she had said, Joan was not prepared to give up her patronage of such a small yet
worthy church. She could, as the man advised, find a
similar charitable venture outside the city gates, but it
would not be the same in the prosperous area such as
the one she resided in. Besides, she liked the parish and
the clergy of All Hallows, who actually listened to her
ideas and suggestions for the donations that she made.
It gave her worth, purpose, and made her feel useful.

But, alas, she might be thinking too much about
it—after all, the man might not find her little cross
which was the bargaining tool he had used. Not that
Joan wanted him to fail in those endeavours either—
she did not even want to contemplate such a grave loss.

'Or mayhap the man has made an impression on
you?' Brida raised a brow.

'Oh, yes, he made an altogether excellent impression
on me—his manners are so pleasing, do you not think?'
Joan muttered as she tapped her chin with her finger.
'I cannot say whether I like him best when he was just
scowling or scowling *and* scolding me at the same time.'

Brida shook her head and chuckled. 'It is only because he knows Tom is away from London. Personally,
I'm glad that Tom asked the very dependable Warin de
Talmont to check on us. Especially you, Joan. And why
did you not say anything about where you had gone? I
had not been aware that you had even left these walls.'

'Because it slipped my mind. But I promise you that
next time I leave, I will inform you of my movements.'

'Next time? No, Joan, there cannot be a next time.'
Brida brushed her fingers through her son's hair before

looking up at her. 'I know that Tom would never allow it. Not while he was away from London.'

'You are only presuming that. Surely you can trust me to be safe.'

'I might trust you, but not everyone else in that busy part of London.' She bit her lip and frowned. 'Besides, there are certain things that you are unaware of—that render the situation even more dangerous, with your brother away.'

She frowned. 'Which you cannot tell me about, I assume?'

'No, that I cannot do.'

Joan split a bread roll in half and stuffed some cheese inside irritably. 'I see that you are unable to trust me after all.'

'That is neither fair, nor true.'

'Is it not?'

Brida stilled her by placing a hand over hers. 'Tell me why this is important to you?'

How could Joan explain it? How could she make her sister understand what it meant to her to have just that little freedom, just enough to make a small difference, in whatever way she could in that small church?

'It is not something that I can explain easily, Brida. Yet I can say one thing.' She took a deep breath. 'It gives me peace that I have seldom found elsewhere.'

'I see. But why there?'

'Because… Because it is a small insignificant church—so insignificant and forgettable that many pass by it for the more illustrious religious sites nearby—St Mary le Bow for one and St Paul's for another. And yet there is so much more to All Hallows than what one observes from its façade.'

Joan felt her sister sniff before grabbing her hand and giving it a squeeze, making her smile.

'This matters deeply to you, does it not?'

'Yes,' she whispered. 'More than I can say.'

Joan hoped it would be enough—that she had been persuasive enough to convince Brida that she would support her continuing to venture to All Hallows.

Just then she heard more footfalls getting nearer before a booming voice spoke, alerting them to his presence.

'Good day to you, ladies.' Warin de Talmont crossed over the pebbled pathway and made his way towards the area where they sat beneath the oldest apple tree in the orchard. 'I was told that I might find you here. No, no, please do not get up.' The man held out his hand as Brida tried, but failed, to get up.

'Good day to you, sir. To what do we owe this pleasure?' Brida beamed at the man. 'You may hardly countenance it, but we were discussing you only moments ago. And now here you are.'

Joan felt her cheeks growing warm as her sister continued with her hurried prattle. The man was now close enough for her to notice his lips kicking up at the corners, clearly amused.

'Yes, here I am.' He dipped his head in a perfunctory bow. 'And a bearer of good news, I dare say.'

'Oh, and what news might that be?'

'Here, I have managed to locate this after all.' He held out Joan's little wooden cross. 'Is it the one you lost? The colours are as you described.'

The unexpected dart of heat shot up the length of her arm as her fingers grazed the palm of his outstretched hand.

'Oh, yes, Sir Warin, it is.' She smiled up at him. 'How can I ever thank you?'

Joan realised her mistake as soon as a slow smile spread across the man's lips—and, really, how was she even noticing his lips? Again. Mayhap it was her imagination, since the man rarely smiled. And yet he had definitely raised a brow in a challenge, as if to test her very resolve—something she understood very well. What he wanted was her thanks given by keeping to the terms of the promissory oath. But shouldn't her oath to care for the unfortunate parishioners of All Hallows mean more than any promise made to this dour man who would insist on interfering in the business of a grown woman?

'I had no idea that you had lost it, Joan.'

'Oh, I had merely misplaced it—had I not, Sir Warin?'

How well the lies slipped off her tongue. She followed it up by giving the man a pointed look, hoping he would not divulge the truth to Brida by telling her how he stumbled upon Joan screaming as a man had yanked her necklace from her neck.

'Yes, that is right, mistress. It was exactly where you believed you had *misplaced* it. And really, your thanks are not necessary. It was my pleasure to have been of service. And, of course, now you have your trinket returned, you have no need of returning to that place.'

'Of course, I have no intention of doing so, sir,' she muttered, annoyed at having to placate his mild threat.

He made a single curt nod. 'Good, I am glad we understand each other, Mistress Joan.'

'As am I,' she said, biting into the crisp apple.

Brida glanced from one to the other before settling on Joan. 'Forgive me, but I thought you said that you wanted to—'

Joan snapped her head around quickly, giving her sister the smallest shake of her head, hoping Brida understood not to disclose her intentions of continuing her patronage of the small church on Honey Lane. God, but she did not welcome any more of his disapproving rebukes. And although Sir Warin de Talmont had no authority over Joan, he could make matters rather difficult for her, especially since he could inform her brother of everything that she had been up to.

'Wanted to…? Do what, exactly?' the man ground out, his voice suddenly suspicious.

'I wanted to…ensure all of our guests had a chance to try these delicious apples.' She placed a few on a pewter and held it out. 'Would you care for some, sir?'

Joan felt the weight of his stare as he grabbed the fruit and muttered his thanks, biting and chewing the juicy fruit.

'Of course, where are my manners?' Her sister rubbed her brow. 'Please do help yourself to our repast, Sir Warin. Can I offer you a mug of wine? Or some ale to fortify you before you return back within the city gates?'

'Thank you, but, no.' He bowed stiffly. 'I ask only to refill my flagon and then I will leave you ladies to your leisure.'

'Yes, by all means, sir.'

He made another awkward bow before turning to leave.

'Thank you again, sir, for returning my little cross. As I said before, it means a great deal to me.'

'And as I said before, it was my pleasure and an honour to be of service.' He turned a little and glanced back in her direction. 'And it will be best, mistress, if you were to take heed of what I also said yesterday about turning your attention to a different endeavour than the current one you're pursuing. Especially when you consider how you came to *misplace* your cross in the first instance.'

God, but the man was insufferable.

'I shall certainly heed those wise words, sir. Good day to you.'

And good riddance.

Chapter Three

The woman was going to be the death of him! After every warning, every caution, Warin knew in his bones that Joan Lovent would not take heed of anything he had said, after all. Not one bit. She would come back inside the city gates and make her way back here to Honey Lane and All Hallows Church despite her empty promises.

'Remind me again why we are loitering around here?' Nicholas d'Amberly frowned, leaning against a stone wall.

'We are here to witness someone breaking their word. A betrayal of trust.'

'As much as that?' he drawled, raising a brow. 'I thought it was to be on guard for the possible arrival of a certain woman—a woman who scuppered our mission only a few days ago. I have a good mind to ask her what she was about.'

'By all means see if you can instil a little more sense into the woman. But do not forget that she is also related to one Thomas Lovent and knows nothing about what we, or her brother, do for the Crown.'

'Either way, it was unfortunate that you collided with her at that crucial time, my friend. It took us so much time, so many weeks just to track the bastard and attach him to the traitors—the Duo Dracones.'

Warin knew the frustrating truth of that, understanding well how the nefarious shadowy group were bent on creating uncertainty in the climate of corruption, fear and uneasiness within the kingdom. Even at that very moment, his liege lord, Hubert de Burgh, had rushed out of London with Tom Lovent in an attempt to quash unsubstantiated rumours that he had ordered the poisoning of the Earl of Salisbury, no less. And with the two senior members of their secret Order away, it fell to Warin and the others to press ahead and unravel the rising threat manifesting in London.

'Yes, I do know, d'Amberly. I know how valuable the man would have been to us.' Warin sighed deeply, feeling guilty again about his part in the failure of the mission. 'Did either you or Fitz Leonard manage to find out anything about the cordwainer he had spoken to?'

'No, just like the man himself, there's now no trace of the cordwainer—it's as if they both disappeared into thin air.'

'Wherever they are, I believe that they're still somewhere hidden within the city.' Warin took his hat off and ran his fingers through his hair. 'Before I returned that troublesome maiden to her home I gave word that every gate in the city from Ludgate to Aldersgate must be manned and no one fitting our man has left.'

'Then some way or another we have to find a way to drag them out. In the meantime, we must continue to decrypt and decipher the flow of the messages we're seizing through our usual methods in the hope it might lead to the source of these threats. I do not know which of them is real and which is not.'

Warin nodded absently as he watched the flurry of activity from across the road. 'That is their intention, d'Amberly—their main aim. They want us to be on our guard and not know the real threats from those that are not. It is the way the Duo Dracones seemingly operate.'

It was a frustrating situation, not least because their best chance at uncovering the truth had now been thwarted by Joan Lovent...

And just when he had been thinking about the woman, there, directly in front of him on the other side of the road, emerged the misguided object of his frustration herself.

Nicholas d'Amberly followed the direction of his cold glare and whistled low as he pushed off the wall to stand beside him. 'I take it that is the lady in question?' Warin nodded as his friend continued to add, 'Although not attired exactly as I would imagine.'

No. Not at all how Warin would imagine her either—since she was there walking alongside her page, using a long wooden staff for support as before, but this time dressed as the young boy, while the page in question was in all likelihood the maid walking beside Joan Lovent—wearing his mistress's attire.

God give him strength...

How this ruse was supposed to keep the woman any safer, had she been attired in her own clothes, Warin could not even fathom. But he had to admit, begrudgingly, that it was all rather inventive. She was determined if nothing else. In fact, he was torn between congratulating Joan Lovent on her ingenuity and marching up to her to demand an explanation.

'Well, I can see why the woman is such a distraction, my friend.' Nicholas d'Amberly grinned, slapping his shoulder with his hand as Warin ground his teeth together in response. 'Very comely little maid.'

Rather than actually throttle his friend, Warin added a reminder. 'Who happens to be the sister of our leader, Thomas Lovent, less you forget.'

'No, I have not forgotten, but I do have eyes that can appreciate a fine figure of a woman and such exquisite, graceful features, even if she does happen to be under the guise of a young lad.'

'Well, look all you like, but no more beyond that.'

'We are testy this morn, are we not, de Talmont.' His friend smiled, shaking his head. 'And does Lovent know what his sister is doing in his absence?'

No. The man was probably unaware that his nuisance of a sister had surreptitiously slipped away from the safety of their home to this blasted part of the city.

His friend took his lack of response as a confirmation. 'Ah, I did not think so.'

Warin started to move towards Joan Lovent and her page as they turned into Honey Lane with Nicholas d'Amberly following beside him.

'And what if she refuses to listen to your counsel? What if she continues to do precisely as she pleases despite your best intentions?'

'I shall endeavour to be more convincing.'

'More than usual, do you mean?' Nicholas d'Amberly shook his head, chuckling. 'Your irascible brusqueness isn't the usual way to charm a woman into doing what you want, you know. But I suppose I will be on hand to show you the way.'

He was beginning to regret inviting his friend along with his keen observations and all too teasing tone. And frankly they both had better things to see to. Far more important ones then dealing with one aggravating maid.

'What would I do without you?' Warin retorted dryly.

'I dread to think.'

They crossed the road passing the stationary wagons of traders and intercepted Joan Lovent and her page, who had no choice other than to halt on the pathway, since they stood in their way.

'Will you allow us to pass?' she muttered beneath the hooded cloak.

'I think not, mistress. I see that we meet once again.'

Joan blinked several times before slowly raising her head and looking in his direction, but not quite meeting his eye.

'Sir Warin de Talmont?' The woman had the temerity to grimace at him. 'It seems that once again you have somehow found yourself in this part of London that you have a great dislike for.'

He smiled. Joan Lovent certainly had a spark of humour laced with her obvious irritation in finding him here again. 'Ah, but I only dislike it when I happen upon *you* here, Mistress Joan.'

'You put me to the blush, sir, by singling me out with these attentions. Truly—you honour me.'

'I very much doubt it,' he said wryly. 'May I introduce my friend, Sir Nicholas d'Amberly?'

'Of course. It's a pleasure to make your acquaintance, sir.'

She turned her head around, but something in the manner in which she spoke must have raised d'Amberly's curiosity in her. The man's brows shot up as he darted a quick quizzical glance in Warin's direction before returning his attentions to the woman. Ah, d'Amberly had not been aware of Joan Lovent's impaired eyesight and he had forgotten to inform him. After all, for Warin it was neither an important nor a pertinent fact about her. The woman was vexing with or without her diminishing sight.

'Enchanted, Mistress Joan.' D'Amberly caught the woman's dainty hand and lowered his head over it. 'I have heard so much about you.'

'Have you indeed, sir? I am surprised.'

'I do not see why. For once my friend has not been excessive in any way when describing your lovely appearance.'

Her lips curved into a real smile—one that she had never bestowed on him. 'I thank you but I'm sure Sir Warin has grossly exaggerated.'

Nicholas d'Amberly flashed his devastating smile. One that had usually amused Warin at the absurdity at the impact it had on women—but not this time. This time it irritated him in a wholly unexpected manner.

'I assure you that he has not.'

'Thank you, sir, but I think it might be prudent to release my hand from yours as it might raise a few suspicions about your attentions to just an unassuming *page*.'

D'Amberly let go of her hand and tilted his head. 'You see, mistress, how your beauty and graciousness, even dressed as you are, make me forget myself. In truth, I have quite forgotten where I am.'

This time Joan Lovent actually giggled, making Warin grind his teeth together. And not because he had never managed to make her laugh. Not that he cared about such trifles—the woman was nothing to him. Even so, it was irksome that she was actually enjoying this discourse with Nicholas d'Amberly. But then most women did.

'Then allow me to enlighten you, sir, for I would hate for you to get lost.' She grinned. 'You are on the corner of Honey Street in a part of London considered so terrible, so very bad, that our friend here has resorted to following me in an attempt to intimidate me into never returning back here again.'

'That is very poor form.' D'Amberly shook his head. 'However, I can vouchsafe that he does mean well.'

'I do.' Warin was beginning to get more and more aggravated with the mild flirtation between his friend and this woman. 'And by and by, there was never an intimidation, rather an agreement that was made, Mistress Joan. An agreement, I might add, which you have soundly broken with this little outing.'

She had the good grace to blush before tilting her head up defiantly. 'I'm afraid to say that when I thought about it at length I came to the conclusion that my prior vow to the souls of All Hallows must prevail.'

Warin's face was like thunder. 'Is that so, mistress?'

'I'm afraid it is. But you will be heartened to know that my visit here is not entirely unsanctioned, since I informed my sister by marriage of it. Indeed, Brida acquiesced to my *little outing* here.'

Warin's patience was becoming raggedly thin.

He moved a little to shield the woman from a moving cart, before responding.

'You might believe that these jaunts might meet Mistress Brida's approval, but be assured that they would not meet her husband's—your brother's.'

Warin noticed a muscle flick in her jaw. 'Then it is good thing that Thomas is none the wiser, sir, and can only hope that it would remain so. I bid you a good day. Sir Nicholas, it was a pleasure to make your acquaintance,' she muttered, turning to leave.

'Wait one moment, if you please.' Warin reached out and caught her wrist, preventing her from moving away. 'As I have maintained before, this is not some jest, Joan. Nor is it a game.'

'Have I said that it was?' she whispered, looking up, hurt filling those pretty blue eyes of hers.

He needed to make the woman understand the situation far better. He needed her to cease being so bloody obstinate.

'You must understand that I mean you no disrespect. I am only looking out for your safety, as I have reiterated time and again, mistress.' He looked her up and down. 'And this guise falls short of offering you any kind of protection.'

'Which you seemed convinced that I need. Let me assure you that the incident that you witnessed a few days ago was very much out of the ordinary. Despite your reservations, it is as safe here as my own home, Sir Warin. Now if you would be good enough to remove your hand from my wrist, I would be much obliged.'

Warin flicked his gaze to his hand still wrapped around her wrist and felt as though she had delivered a blow to the stomach.

'I am afraid that you still do not seem to appreciate the situation, mistress.' He sighed, letting go of her wrist. 'There are things that you are unaware of. Things that make these expeditions of yours in this part of the city quite dangerous.'

Her blue eyes were now icy cold. 'Strange, but that is the second time that I have heard this.'

He stepped towards her. 'Then take heed of the advice you have been given and cease returning back here.' Cease being a damn nuisance, he had wanted to add, but just about managed to hold his tongue.

'And I assume that you cannot tell me what this perceived danger is?'

'Your assumption is correct.'

'As I thought.' It was Joan Lovent's turn to step towards him, a flash of temper in its wake. 'Allow me to remind you, Sir Warin de Talmont, that I am neither a child nor an invalid, despite the fact that I am treated as such.'

'That, mistress, would never be my intention.' He dragged his fingers irritably through his hair. 'And nor do I view you as such. But you have to understand that I cannot allow these jaunts.'

'You *cannot* allow them?' she bit out, clearly incensed, but this was for the woman's own good. It mattered not that his manners had all but deserted him. Just as it did not matter that he was being an insensitive, unyielding boor. Joan Lovent had to cease being such a hindrance to their mission. She might not know anything about what it involved, but it was imperative that she was kept within the safe confines of her home and its environs.

'No, I'm afraid I can't. Let someone else do your bidding here at All Hallows Church. Now please allow me to take you back home, mistress.'

Joan had always been considered a congenial, kind, happy sort of maid despite the cruel circumstance of her situation. Not that she was given to bouts of self-pity. Nor did she ever give in to fits of temper or show any ill feeling to another person. But at this very moment, she wanted to rage and scream at this man who, although unrelated to her, felt that he somehow had the authority to prevent her from going about her business. He thought to disallow her from visiting All Hallows in person.

Yet Joan knew very well that he did. The man's status as a knight of the Crown meant he could prevent her from doing just that. Not to mention that he could inform her brother as he had threatened many times to do—and Tom, being the overprotective brother that he was, would soon put a stop to her movements in any case. But how dared Warin de Talmont belittle her patronage and the vital work they did? How dared he think to restrict her movements just because he could? How dared he?

'May I be so bold as to intervene here?' In her anger, Joan had forgotten that they were not alone, but in the middle of a busy pathway and in the presence of Warin de Talmont's handsome friend. 'There might be another way that could provide a truce of sorts that should result in a resolution of this unfortunate impasse.'

She smiled at the man. At least he could appreciate that his friend was being unreasonable. 'I would be happy to hear it, Sir Nicholas.'

'Well, since de Talmont is adamant that you cannot

travel to this part of the city unaccompanied, a notion that I wholeheartedly agree with, mistress, I would like to offer to escort you whenever my services might be required.' He bowed again over her hand, grinning as he rose. She realised with a jolt that the man was manipulating his friend and received affirmation of it when Warin de Talmont next spoke. Irritation laced his words.

'If you are to be escorted to this part of the city, and to All Hallows Church and back to your abode again, then I must be the one to provide it, Mistress Joan.'

'Should you indeed?'

'Yes…' he inclined his head and gritted his teeth '… I would be happy to oblige you. Your brother entrusted your protection to me after all.'

Joan might have impaired sight, but could tell that the man was not at all happy to offer any such thing. And for the first time since she bumped into Warin de Talmont and his friend this morning, the man's annoyance for having this thrust on him felt…rather gratifying. It might be insufferable to be forced to endure his presence as he provided her escort every time she needed to venture to All Hallows Church, but it was better than nothing.

'Well, in that case I find I have no other choice but to accept your kind offer. Thank you,' she muttered, pasting a smile on her face.

Oh, yes, Joan would have to make certain that if she were to tolerate the inconvenience of having the man's company, then it would be as painless and fleeting as possible.

Chapter Four

It had been over a sennight since Warin de Talmont had
begun to provide Joan escort to All Hallows Church at
dawn and then returned her back home again at dusk,
ensuring that a guard was posted outside the church
while he went about his business. But in that whole period, the man uttered only a scant few words to her. And
while he treated her with courtesy, Warin de Talmont
made it patently obvious that he would rather be anywhere than in her company with his obvious resentment
of having this obligation thrust upon him. Not that she
had actually demanded anything of the man, yet Joan
could not help but feel a little guilty now for being such
an inconvenience.

Still, after more than a week of being largely avoided,
Joan knew she had to make amends. It was not in her
nature to hold on to any ill feeling against anyone—
even this surly, brooding man who now walked beside
her. Nor was she able to go without conversation for
this long and it was high time to cut through this unnecessary tension between them.

'I hope you have been keeping well, Sir Warin?' The man snorted and gave her a sideways glance, or mayhap a frown would be an apt description. 'I believed I asked after your health, sir?'

'Did you?' He smiled, shaking his head. 'After being in my company for over a week, almost every day, you enquire after my health only now? Tell me, is there something that has prompted these queries? Mayhap some foul, rotten malaise or a skin rash that I am unaware of.'

'You need not be so facetious, Sir Warin. I was just making polite conversation that has been sadly lacking on these jaunts into the city, but I can see that it is of no use. You are as ever...' *irascible, sullen, churlish* '...a man who prefers to be singular and keep to himself.'

'I admit I do.' His hand wrapped around her elbow, strong and assured as he guided Joan across the busy street, where horse riders, carts and wagons passed by. 'I find I work better on my own and apologise that my escort is sadly lacking in the usual polite discourse that is expected. I shall endeavour to do better.'

'And while you attempt to do that, sir, I feel I should offer an apology that you were forced to escort me.'

He came to an abrupt stop and turned to face her. 'No one forced me to do anything, Joan.'

'That may be so, but I am certain that you have more important matters to see to.'

'I do...as in I did.' He ushered them to resume walking side by side along the narrow path that led to Friday Street.

'Well, at least you are nothing if not forthright.'

The corners of his lips curled. 'And at least you are nothing if not...'

'A bother?' she offered.

This time he did chuckle, his whole demeanour changing, making him seem a lot younger and so much more appealing. 'I would never dream of saying that.'

'Ah, then it seems that you're not that forthright, after all.'

'Naturally. I would always aim to spare a maiden's blush.'

Her lips twitched in the corners. 'Are you jesting with me, sir?'

'Nor would I dream of doing *that*, mistress,' he added, making her laugh.

'It seems there is much you would never dream of doing or saying.'

'Quite. I do try for gallantry now and again.' He grinned, shaking his head. 'And what I had wanted to say was that you are far more loquacious than I remember from the last time I provided you escort, mistress.'

How strange that the man's smile somehow made the little butterflies unfurl inside her stomach. 'I was much younger then and probably afraid to be. Besides, one of us has to provide some discourse.'

'Then it would seem my assessment of you is correct.'

'As a bothersome babbler?'

'I could never utter such asinine things, mistress.'

'That is a blessing. Though I am inquisitive as to what your assessment of me might happen to be.'

'I am sure you are, but I think I will disclose that mayhap at another time.'

'I can hardly wait.' She smoothed down her veil with her free hand, feeling somewhat lighter than before. She was enjoying this teasing and repartee between them. It made her forget the strain that she felt at the back of her eyes this morn. 'But I think I shall part with my assessment. And it is that you, Sir Warin, are a man of mystery.'

'A man of mystery?' he repeated, frowning, pulling her gently out of the way as a man unloaded hay from a wagon.

'Indeed.' She nodded. 'After making your acquaintance over two years ago I can still attest to knowing very little about you.'

'Mayhap that was by design.'

'Then it would seem that my assessment of you is correct.' She shrugged. 'Since you are cloaked in secrecy, you must be a man of mystery.'

'Nothing so interesting as that, I'm afraid. Just a man going about his daily business, without much vainglory, I hope.'

'Of course.' Joan lost her footing as her long staff caught on a slab of stone that was jutting out. It sent her unceremoniously hurtling to the ground, wrapped with a good dose of humiliation.

'Hell's teeth! Are you hurt, Joan?' he ground out, coming expediently to her aid.

'No, no but once again you find me in the dirt and on my hands and knees.' She tried, but failed to make light of her fall. But before she had time to shake the dust off her hands, bigger, more powerful ones belonging to Sir Warin de Talmont reached out, scooped her from the ground and into his arms without much effort.

'Oh, I… I thank you,' she declared, not knowing what else to say.

Joan could not remember a time when she had been held in anyone's arms, least of all a huge, brooding warrior knight such as the man holding her, so closely now as this. It felt intimate. It felt…safe. Her cheeks heated up with this sudden awareness, with his very nearness.

'You may put me down, sir. I promise that I'll try to refrain from falling on my face again.'

'And if you do, I shall do better to catch you.' He sighed as he carefully put her back on the ground before bending to retrieve her stick. 'Are you sure you are unhurt, Joan?'

She rubbed her forehead, trying to smooth away the growing tension in her head. 'Yes, I thank you.'

No. The backs of Joan's eyes suddenly ached from the tumble, which made her sight a little worse and hazier than usual. And as well as that, her head throbbed with the usual pain from having to focus and concentrate. The stark truth of her condition was becoming more and more a reality. Where once she could see details, she now mainly saw hazy outlines of shapes, which depended on the light and brightness of the day, forcing Joan to use her other senses. For one thing, she was now rather good at gauging anyone's emotions from the tone and expression of their voice, the way they held themselves and even their small movements, which informed her where eyes could not.

'What is it, Joan? Are you unwell?' All mirth drained from his eyes, to be replaced with concern.

She tried smiling. 'No, no. It is just that my eyes can be a little tiresome on bright days such as this, which could explain why I did not see where I was going. Although I admit they are far worse in the flickering low light set in candles.'

She chuckled, hoping that it might diffuse his concern.

But the man continued to watch her for a moment before responding, 'Mayhap you might want to consider forgoing All Hallows and returning home for some rest, mistress.'

Rest... In truth, that was what she needed to do—lie down, close her weary eyes and rest. But Joan could not give in to her affliction. It might hold her back and cause her pain from time to time, but if she did not persist through this, then she would truly become an invalid—which she would be one day, in any case.

She tightened her grip around her long wooden staff. 'No, I thank you. I wish to persevere, if I may, and I promise I am unhurt from the fall.' Only a little mortified from tumbling in front of this man, but she would live through the embarrassment. She would endure as she always did.

'As you wish. But know this—there is no shame in curtailing your endeavours on days where you find yourself in more discomfort than usual.'

His gentleness surprised her—not that Warin de Talmont was unkind, yet the tenderness he showed her was something she had not expected from him.

'I shall be well, thank you. Besides, we are almost there.'

'Very well, but before we do, allow me to procure some honey bread for both of us. That is, if you'd care for some? I find that the smell of warm bread never fails to entice me.'

'Thank you…' she nodded '…that would be most welcome.'

They approached a wagon that had stacks of breads, rolls and pastries of various sizes piled high. Sir Warin purchased a handful of soft, warm rolls dripping in honey and two mugs of goat's milk, as they resumed their journey on foot. He offered her some of the sweet bread and milk which she gladly accepted. Mayhap a little repast might help lessen the pain as it sometimes did.

'Tell me why you do this, Joan?' he muttered, taking a sip of the milk. 'I do understand your patronage, but this undertaking to help in person seems a little unnecessary, if you do not mind me saying so.'

His question was not one that was so easily explained. At times, even Joan could not fathom why it was imperative as it was to be so diligent in her attentions to All Hallows.

'All I can say,' she pondered, biting into the soft sweet roll, 'is that this city has been my home for the past few years. It has given me everything…well, after everything that happened to my mother and sister.' Joan stopped again and looked up, wondering how much Sir Warin knew surrounding the demise of her kin.

'Yes.' He gave her an encouraging smile. 'I know a little from what your brother has divulged.'

Thank goodness. It meant that she did not have to revisit the horrific time again. Joan closed her eyes momentarily and rubbed her clammy brow and tried to form the words she needed to answer his question.

'What I do, Sir Warin, is a way for me to bestow a

little back to this city that somehow breathed life back into me again.'

'I see.' He studied her before making a single nod.

'As to why I chose such a small parish as All Hallows…?' She paused a moment before continuing. 'There was a priest at the church whom I was introduced to by my brother—a Father Paul de Hazlett. He was afflicted with a similar condition as me—by the time I met him, he was all but blind. And yet he was the kindest, most selfless, benign soul I had ever met.'

'He sounds like a good man.'

'He was. You see, when I came to London, I was still so bitter and angry with everything that had happened to me, but Father Paul taught me so much. He made me understand that I did not need my sight. I did not need to *see* using my eyes—that I could use other ways. He told me to stop blaming everyone around me or myself and start living my life. And so, I began to—I tried to see without my eyes. I used sounds and scents and everything around to comprehend the world around me. And after Father Paul's death I decided to continue his good work at All Hallows.' Joan lifted her head with a faint smile on her lips.

'There is also another reason, Sir Warin. My mother was forced to spend her confinement here in London and it was to All Hallows that my mother went after birthing my sister. It was also there where I remember being allowed to hold my infant sister for the first time. It might seem rather ridiculous, but I feel somehow connected to that memory of her there, especially as nothing now remains of our manor, our home or even the chapel that once stood on that small part of England.'

No, nothing now remained of her young sister...or her mother.

Oh, dear, she had not meant to share as much as she had about her past.

'There is nothing ridiculous in that, Joan,' he whispered. 'In truth, I believe I can understand your experience far too well.'

Warin knew very well the haunted, grief-stricken look in Joan Lovent's eyes, since he had lived and breathed it himself for so long. And to find it now enveloped within this young lively woman made his heart clench in sadness. He knew, too, how easily it could consume the very heart and soul of a person and wished to God that it had spared her. That somehow she had endured the desolate bleakness of that time in her life when she'd almost perished and come through the other side unscathed. But that was doubtful for someone who had lived through what this woman surely had, not that Warin knew every detail.

She looked up then and gave him a small smile—one that he felt all the way to the bottom of his feet. 'I believe you must have, sir, after all the dangerous things that you have seen...and done.'

'Yes. And more besides.' He shook his head. 'Do you know my true assessment of you, Mistress Joan? That you are brave to withstand all the challenges that you have faced.'

'No more than anyone else.' She shrugged her shoulders, looking decidedly uncomfortable at his compliment.

That made him smile despite himself. In truth, they might have both shared the experience of loss, yet for

Warin there was this inexplicable connection—an understanding that he felt every time he spent time with the woman ambling beside him.

He had felt it again when he instinctively drew her closer, as he held her in his arms only moments ago. And it had nothing to do with the woman's fall, but Joan Lovent herself. So much so that he had been glad when she had reminded him to put her down. In fact, his hand had shaken as he had done so, not that she had noticed, thank the Saints!

'Would you allow me to show you something, Sir Warin? There is something I would like you to see, if you'd oblige me.'

His curiosity roused, Warin guided Joan along the pathway in companionable silence before they reached the arched gateway of All Hallows Church. Pushing through the wooden door, he sidled beside her as they made their way inside the small church.

He watched as Joan dipped her finger in the holy water stoup and used it to make a sign of the cross on her forehead before entering the nave of the church. Warin followed behind her while she forged ahead, dropped to her knees and said a wordless prayer in front of the altar before turning around to face him. Not for the first time he wondered why in God's breath he had agreed to follow her. He had other, more important matters that needed his attention.

'Come, this way.' She motioned, leading him out of the small nave, under a stone archway and across the aisle to another doorway that opened out on to a small enclosed churchyard with a modest cloister and an area for contemplation on the far side. There, half a dozen young children were busying themselves by tending to the various parts of the outdoor space, while a young man whom he assumed was a priest, wearing robes and a close-fitted coif, supervised them.

'So this is where you escape to every day?' He gave her a ghost of a smile as he glanced around at the orderly way the children, who were no older than six or seven, milled around the place.

'Yes, this is where I "escape to", as you so eloquently put it. And this is where I am most needed. The children here are largely foundlings from close to the parish. They come to us when they are destitute and have nowhere else to go.'

'But they're so very young.'

'Yes.' She nodded. 'They're too young to go to larger monasteries and nunneries, so they remain here first, where we give them shelter, food and comfort in a place they can belong, before they move on.'

'It is impressive, Joan.'

'For a small insignificant church, we do our best even if it can be a struggle at times.' The way Joan Lovent spoke about the place, her contribution and *being needed,* attested to the obvious pride she had attached to All Hallows Church. Here, she had the purpose she had often spoken of.

'Do you see the young waif yonder with the long golden hair? She is only five or six in years, Sir Warin, and bears the weight of an anvil on her young shoulders.'

His brows drew close together. 'How so?'

'I found her ragged, dirty and starved, trying to feed meagre scraps to an infant who might or might not have been related to her.' Joan sighed, shaking her head. 'I brought them here, but sadly the younger child died and my golden girl there stares out with that anguished, hollow look on her face from dawn to dusk, never uttering a word, however hard I try. I do not even know her given name. If she has one.'

'Poor little maid.'

'But I know this—if there is one who is brave to withstand all the challenges that they have faced—it is that child there, not me. I...well, I have been more fortunate than most.'

'As has that child,' he murmured, stepping towards her. Without thinking he cupped her jaw and tilted it upwards. 'Because you found her, Joan. Without you she might also have perished.'

'Yes, I suppose she might, although I am not certain whether the poor child will ever stop blaming herself for being the one who survived.'

Warin swallowed slowly as he glanced at the child again, wondering whether Joan Lovent realised that her observation disclosed as much about her as it did about the young girl. It reminded him that it applied in equal measure to how he felt every time he thought about his late wife. How he had failed her and their child, when they had needed him the most. The guilt was something he could never quite erase.

'One day she might. After all, you will show her the way.'

He had spoken so softly and bent his head so close to hers that he could see the small breaths she took and the different shades of slate, cornflower and borage in her eyes when she stared intently back at him.

Warin pondered on how well she could really see him—how well she could sense the growing conflict within him, at this very awkward visceral connection that somehow pulled him towards her, even when he knew he should sever all connection. He could ill afford getting close to Joan Lovent—and neither did he want to. All manner of trouble lay down that path.

Warin dropped his hands to his sides and took a step back. 'I have tarried too long, mistress. I bid you good day, until later.' He made a perfunctory bow and turned on his heel to leave.

It had been a mistake to come here. Just as it had been a mistake to look into the depths of Joan Lovent's eyes. In truth, Warin was not sure that he wanted to know what was hidden there. No, for it might prove too difficult to claw his way out.

Chapter Five

Warin knew he was being far more withdrawn and re-served than usual with Joan Lovent. He could not help but fall back into the awkward silence that had charac-terised the first week he had escorted her before *that* morning at All Hallows Church. That particular morn-ing had unsettled Warin more than he cared to admit, reminding him of his past in a manner that left him feeling uneasy and agitated.

And he might feel a little guilty about his lack of providing the usual *polite discourse* that Joan Lovent had mentioned, but it was better than acknowledging this growing attraction that he also felt for the woman. Which was not only wholly inappropriate, but damna-bly inconvenient, especially since he actually enjoyed Joan's company—far more than he should.

She was spirited, witty, kind and had the uncanny ability of being able to subtly comprehend him. It was unnerving, but also reminded Warin that they did have much in common and knew too well the heartache of losing loved ones. And it was this connection with Joan that made having the usual perfunctory conversation with her, however polite, seem inconsequential. He was drawn to her in a manner he could not readily understand, making her just so intriguing—at a time when he could do without more intrigue in his life. Indeed, Joan Lovent tempted him in a way that, if he was not careful, could pose as a real threat to him in more ways than one.

Added to this was a different threat and the problem of having no further information regarding the Duo Dracones and the man whom Warin had followed through the narrow twisting streets of the city more than a sennight ago. No one had any sighting of him or his apparent accomplice, the cordwainer. Not one of his fellow brethren of the Knights Fortitude, the guards at the city gates, or the many informers they used as lookouts, all over the city as well as the area of Westminster, had any sightings of them.

But Warin knew the men who would provide more insight into the Duo Dracones had to be somewhere in the city. They must be hidden and given shelter to be this inconspicuous. Unless he along with the other Knights Fortitude had overlooked their movements somehow. Which would be all the more frustrating and dangerous at a time when his liege lord, Hubert de Burgh, along with Joan Lovent's brother were not even present in London—leaving it exposed to the machinations of mercurial groups such as the Duo Dracones.

All of which rendered Warin's awareness of and attraction to the woman walking beside him all the more unseemly.

'You seem quite preoccupied, sir, if you do not mind me observing.'

'I admit to being so, mistress.' He sighed deeply. 'There is much that demands my attention and much that confounds me presently.'

All at once he could see that he had piqued her interest. He almost groaned out loud for divulging as much as he had.

'If I may, I would offer my assistance to this quandary that confounds you, Sir Warin.'

'And I would gladly solicit your opinion, Joan, but I am afraid that my problem is one of my own doing.'

'Then all the more for having it shared?' She looked up so expectantly at him that it made him want to laugh despite himself.

'Not this particular problem, I dare say. We men of mystery must, after all, keep the oath of our epithet.' He hoped that she would now drop the matter, but then this was Joan Lovent, after all, and she was nothing if not inquisitive.

'Yes, I can understand that, Sir Warin, but I have often found that if a problem penetrates and takes root then it will grow wide spindly shoots, becoming far harder to shift. Another's perspective might help cut the shoot from the ground.'

'Very well.' He scratched his chin, wondering how much he could reveal. 'I have, in truth, misplaced… something that I must seek and find expediently.'

'I see.' She came to a halt, her brows pulled together, evidently deep in thought.

'You do?' he bit out before he could take the words back. The last thing he wanted to do was to inadvertently offend Joan Lovent again.

'Ah, because my sight is poor you presume that I cannot *see* in other ways?'

'No, of course not, and I apologise. That was badly done of me.'

'No insult is taken, Sir Warin, and there's really no need for an apology.' She shrugged. 'After all, it's what is perceived of someone like me.'

Damn! The words were like a punch in the stomach. *'Someone like me...'*

The woman seemed to believe that her affliction made her appear weak and helpless, when the opposite was true. And yet, what did he actually know of the difficulties Joan faced? Nothing...nothing at all. And why did that notion make him want to take up arms for her and slay anything and everything that might cause her harm?

He looked down to find that the woman had tilted her head up towards him. She then shook her head, speaking softly. 'But I believe that initial perceptions can be wrong at times, sir.'

Warin knew the truth of that better than most, being involved with the type of work that he did. He put into practice his years of experience, raw talent, judgement and canny instinct just to survive in the dangerous sphere he inhabited, when trust and allegiances could be broken in a blink of an eye. And the only men he could readily trust were his Knights Fortitude brethren.

'I believe they can, too. But you need to understand, Joan, that I have no such perceptions about you.'

'I am glad to hear it.' She nodded, happy with his answer. 'So, can you tell me what you have lost?'

God's breath, but she was determined, much to his consternation. And it had not escaped his notice that she had said *'lost'* and not *'misplaced'* as he had. Mayhap if he ignored her query, she might drop the matter.

'Come, Sir Warin, you can share your woes with me, can you not?'

Then again, mayhap not.

'There is really nothing to share,' he muttered inanely, wishing he had kept his mouth shut. 'Shall we resume our walk to All Hallows?'

'Very well, but I want you to know that I shall also be happy to return the favour and help you find whatever you have lost—after all, you found my little cross.'

'You cannot help me find him.'

'Ah, so it is a *him*…interesting.'

God, but the woman was vexing.

'It is not at all interesting, I assure you.'

'Will you allow me to help you find your mysterious person, Warin? May I call you Warin? You have, after all, called me Joan on many occasions.'

'Yes, you may and, no, there is really no need. Ignore this whole conversation, if you will, *Joan.*'

'Come now, this is all far too intriguing for me just to ignore.' She walked briskly, keeping up with him. 'And you know I might be an asset to you. After all, I am good at seeking what needs to be found.'

Not strictly true since the woman had never uncovered anything regarding what her own brother did, nor what his work for the Crown actually encompassed. And Warin knew with certainty that Thomas Lovent would want that to remain the case.

He looked down at her as she continued to make her case. 'After all, I managed to find and gather the children that come to us at All Hallows.'

Just then, a few horseback riders trotted past them along the narrow street, giving Warin much-needed inspiration. It was Friday after all and many would be making their way to the fields near the priory of St Bartholomew, commonly known as Smythfeld, outside the city gates.

'I am sure that must be true, but I will require no such help, sadly. Now I must escort you to All Hallows and return swiftly to Smythfeld.' He bent his head, giving her a benign smile. 'I thank you, however, for your offer of help.'

'Oh, I am very happy to give it.' Her brows knitted as she bit down on her lip, a picture of thoughtful concentration. 'I know what I can do—I shall come with you to Smythfeld and provide you with much-needed aid.'

Saints above, but the woman was doggedly relentless.

'I assure you that will not be necessary. And will not you be missed at All Hallows? Think about all the children—the poor young, helpless children who rely on you, Joan.'

'Thank you, but I believe that they can spare me for one day. I would like to return the favour you gave me and assist you.' She smiled brightly, clapping her hands together. 'And you know I have never visited Smythfeld on market day.'

Now what in heavens could he say to that?

He sighed in resignation, guiding her to the other side of the street. 'In that case I would welcome your

company, Joan. Come, let's not tarry here. We'll need
to change course and exit Newgate.'

'How exciting. Then lead on, sir.'

Joan could not remember the last time she had been
this impulsive and insistent that she accompany anyone anywhere. And she was still not completely certain
why she had done it—only she was glad that she had.
Smythfeld on Market Friday had been a marvellous
spectacle to behold and she would not have missed it
for the world. How had she never ventured here? The
place was a marvel.

And all because the market was primarily a place to
trade in horseflesh. God, even the smell of the magnificent creatures was just wonderful. She felt like bursting
with excitement at being here. From the sights, as much
as she could make them out, to the smells and the bustling noise that enveloped her, market day was unlike
any place she had ever experienced.

Big crowds of people—from barons, knights, noblemen and women, to ordinary working peasants—
gathered to watch the display of horses and other cattle
within the wide clearing that made up the flat, smooth
field that accorded Smythfeld its name. People bartered
with one another with gusto and verve as sums of coin
changed hands for prime horseflesh—from magnificent destriers, palfreys, coursers to rounceys and even
humble packhorses—all jostling for position.

'Come, let us partake in a mug of something. I find
that I am parched after all the walking.'

'Yes, let's.' She flicked her gaze at the passing palfreys trotting past, their coats glistening with sweat.

They strolled to one of the stationary carts that offered refreshments and procured two mugs of ale.

'I have to express my gratitude in allowing me to accompany you here, Warin. Smythfeld is a true wonder!' A pang of longing for those days when she could easily ride darted through her, which she damped down just as quickly. 'I had no notion of it being so.'

'Truly?' He raised a brow. 'Have you never come here in late summer, when the Bartholomew Fair is in progress?'

'Oh, yes, I have attended that many times and, while a lovely distraction, it's nothing quite like this splendid spectacle.'

'You surprise me, Joan. I would have thought that, as a young maid, you would have delighted far more in everything that the fair would offer.'

'Oh, no, I take far more delight *here*—the thrill of this place.' She could see from the man's bemused expression that he did not quite comprehend her. 'Horses... I have always adored horses. From the first time that I was put on the back of the animal as a child, I have revelled in every aspect of horseback riding—a pursuit that used to afford me a huge amount of pleasure.'

He frowned. 'It used to?'

She nodded. 'Yes. I have often been told that I learnt to ride before I could even walk. And in time my enjoyment was derived from the dizzying speed that I would put my horse through.' She smiled at that longago memory. 'The faster I rode the more thrilling and unfettered the feeling was. Yet...yet it was more than just the riding that enchanted me—I loved everything about those big, majestic creatures.' She inhaled before continuing. Not that this part of her story was easy to revisit. 'Then one day, when I was eleven years or so, my horse jumped clear of a bushel that hid an uneven ditch behind it. I took a bad tumble, which may or may not have attributed to my poor eyesight, as I was bed-ridden for more than a sennight, slipping in and out of cognizance.'

'God's breath, Joan, that's dreadful.'

'Indeed.' Along with everything else that she had faced.

'And yet you rode on horseback when I escorted you two years ago?'

She took a sip of ale and nodded. 'I did, but that was the beginning of the end unfortunately.'

Even to her own ears she sounded a little unmoved by these circumstances, when the reality had been quite different—the very opposite had been true. It had dev-astated Joan when she had been resigned to forsake the one thing that had given her so much pleasure. And it was the first of many, with many more changes that she would eventually be forced to accept as her condi-tion would worsen.

'I am sorry, Joan,' he murmured, shaking his head. 'That could not have been easy to accept.'

'No,' she muttered, unable to say more. Her life had not been easy and she had sacrificed many things. She exhaled and even managed a smile as she lifted her head. 'But this is welcome, so I thank you.'

'No need to thank me.'

'Of course I do! I practically forced my company on you.' She chuckled. In all honesty, her behaviour had been quite unbecoming even if the sentiment behind it was a good one.

'Never mind that.' He took her empty mug from her, setting it back down on the cart, and held out his hand. 'I have an idea. Something that I hope might also be equally welcome. Come.'

Joan took his offered hand as it closed around hers, strong, warm and strangely intimate. Warin led Joan along the path that wound through the area where horses were being traded.

'Where are you taking me?'

'You shall find out soon enough.' He continued leading her away from the main area of the market until he stopped in front of the last horse trader and possibly the most inconspicuous, tucked away as he was at the periphery.

'If it ain't Sir Warin of Talmont, as I live and breathe. I 'aven't laid eyes on yer since Lent, my good man. What brings you 'ere?'

'Same as always, Asa of Bath. Same as always.'

'If that be the case, then I might or might not have information that you might be searchin' fer.'

'Good to know, Asa, we shall discuss *that* later. I come bent on a very different matter altogether.'

The other man nodded, clearly understanding Warin. ''Appy to oblige. What can I do fer yer?'

'Well, I was wondering whether you might just happen to have a young, docile palfrey suitable for a lady.'

The trader grinned a toothless smile and made a single nod. 'I might have just the thing, as it 'appens.'

In no time at all, Joan was amazed to find herself atop the very young, docile palfrey Warin had requested, while he led the young horse at the rein as they gently ambled away from the crowd. In truth, it felt wonderful to be on horseback again—something Joan had never believed she would ever experience again. And she had Warin de Talmont to thank for that.

'I hope you realise how much this means to me.' She beamed down at him as he led the horse at a slightly quicker pace.

'And I hope *you* realise that I do it with pleasure.'

She held on with one hand on the pommel of the saddle and the other holding the reins. It felt just as it had ever done, simply stupendous. Something as ordinary as riding. 'Well, it is certainly a day that I will never forget.'

'Glad to hear it.' He slowed the animal to an eventual stop. 'Shall we make it all the more memorable?'

'What do you propose?'

What Warin de Talmont suggested was made evident in the following moment when the man managed to mount the horse, swinging his leg, so that he was now sat behind her.

'Are you ready to go a little faster?' The warmth of his breath from behind brushed against her skin.

She felt a little hot. A little breathless being this close to him.

'It is your choice, Joan, but know that I have you. I will never let you fall.' Warin's hand came round her waist, anchoring her to him. 'So, the question is whether you would like to ride like the wind again?'

Oh, God, how could he comprehend what this meant to her? The unparalleled joy it would give her to ride *like the wind* again? Somehow, he knew how unbelievably welcome this was for her.

'Yes,' she whispered. 'I would like it above all else.'

Without uttering another word, Warin used his spurs

to nudge the palfrey to trot and then to canter before finally the horse broke into a long swinging gait, galloping at speed. The thrill of the rush quickened her blood, making her feel alive—more vital than she had in years. But it was more than that. Joan was acutely aware that her back was pressed against the hard strong wall of Warin's chest. With his huge arms wrapped around, enveloping her, she felt safe. She felt protected. Indeed, she knew that he would do as he promised. He would not let her fall. His closeness, his scent and even his steady rhythmic breathing sent a frisson through her— one that she had never experienced before. In fact, Joan had never been this close to or this aware of a man.

'Is this how you remember riding on horseback?' he whispered softly in her ear.

'This is so much more than that.' She closed her eyes and let the cool breeze whip up and kiss her skin. 'It is magical. I cannot recall the last time I enjoyed myself more.'

'Well, then, I'm glad to have been of service.'

As was she. This was the most wonderful balm to the heartache of not being able to ride on horseback again, and in the arms of another. Another who imparted small quivering sensations that danced along her skin. She exhaled slowly, pulling her mind to other matters. 'But coming to here to Smythfeld was never about being of service to me, Warin. The intention was to seek your missing person, if you recall.'

'It can wait, Joan,' he murmured in a low voice, sending a shiver through her. 'It can wait.'

They rode away from the bustle of Smythfeld, away from the noise and the crowds, until there was only the

pounding of hooves on the dry grassy plains. They gal-
loped in complete enraptured silence, gliding through
the night, soaring far and, yes…like the wind. She
closed her eyes shut and smiled to herself, savouring
the breeze whipping up against her skin. It felt marvellous. Stupendous. Astounding. There were no words to
describe the rush of this giddy feeling. In that single moment as they rode just as she once used to, Joan could
forget and let go of all that she had lost and still stood
to lose. All that would never be the same in her life.

She opened her eyes and wondered how long it had
been since she had been on horseback, like this, for the
sheer enjoyment of riding. The enjoyment and delight
of being unfettered just as she once sought to be from
the constraints and difficulty of living under her father's roof after her brother, Tom, had left to be a squire
many years ago.

Those were not particularly good memories to dwell
on. No, they were dreadful, hard and bitter recollections
that ended in such terrible tragedy when her family perished in a fire—a fire she had survived. God, but why
did Joan do this to herself? Turning a glorious moment
such as this into one that she felt penitent, and remorse,
reminded of a harrowing time she tried to forget. She
should turn her thoughts instead into savouring this
one precious moment.

'We should turn back.' She felt Warin's warmth
against the back of her neck, bringing her back to the
present.

'Yes…' she smiled weakly '…I dare say we should.'

Just as quickly as it began, Warin turned the horse
and reduced the pace to a trot as they returned back to

the main crowd in the market. This unexpected surprise that filled her with a sudden burst of exhilaration was over. And a good thing, too, as it was time to get back to reality.

Chapter Six

Warin did not know what prompted him to offer Joan Lovent a ride on horseback with him, but her excitement at being in Smythfeld on market day, when he had initially wanted to be rid of her, made him reconsider. The look of glee on her face as they meandered through the tracks and she darted her head in every direction made him comprehend her situation with stark clarity. The woman clearly adored the cattle here, especially the equine.

But it was her attempt at insouciance when she brushed off the fact that she could no longer ride due to her dwindling sight that really tugged at his heartstring—whatever *that* was. He felt guilty that he had ever thought the woman so exasperating, when it struck him again how much difficulty and hardship she had endured in her life. In truth, it humbled him—her tenacity, her courage. And it was then that Warin knew that he wanted her to have the thrill of riding once more. And he wanted to be the one to give it to her.

Yet, what Warin was not prepared for was a wholly

different kind of thrill to course through his veins once he was sat snug behind Joan Lovent on the saddle, much to his shame. The fact she had happily reclined in his arms meant that the woman was now lodged firmly against his chest. Her backside tucked perilously close to his loins, where he could feel her curves, her softness, and glory in her gentle floral scent. Her linen veil brushed against his chin as her head was nestled under his chin. In truth he wanted to bury his head just there in that spot of her neck.

It felt wonderful, peaceful even, and yet it was playing havoc on his senses at the same time, God help him. Yet even when he made the decision that they should return back to the thrum of the crowd, he was reticent about letting her go. Which was all the more reason to do so.

He jumped down, ready to help Joan dismount, holding out his arms. God, but he would have to hold on to her again, when in truth this whole encounter had been far more than he had bargained for. His body was still humming to the lingering heat from her closeness.

Damn...

He had to fight it—this unwanted attraction to Joan Lovent.

'That was very pleasant. Thank you.'

'My pleasure,' he muttered gruffly, wishing that she would stop continually thanking him. 'Come down, mistress, we must be away.'

'Of course.'

Warin tore his eyes away as she arranged her skirts about her and it was then that he saw *him* in the crowds. There, in the distance, the man he had lost through the twisting lanes of London over a sennight ago ambling along without as much as a care in the world. Warin blinked several times, frowning as he glanced at him again. Tall, gormless, with a distinct scar that ran diagonally from his temple to his chin, wearing a simple cream-coloured coif covering his head. Yes, it was most certainly the man who was involved with Duo Dracones, here in Smythfeld, outside the city gates, of all places.

How in God's name was it even possible that he was here? The Knights Fortitude had secured the city's gates, ensuring that they were impregnable for a man fitting his description and likeness. And yet here he was, outside the city, after breaching those very gates. It was more than disconcerting that this had happened here when Warin was all but alone save for Joan Lovent.

'May I ask for your assistance to dismount?' He looked up to find Joan's inquisitive gaze directed at him. What she saw, he could not readily tell. But a small perceptive smile spread on her lips. 'You have seen him, have you not? The man you were seeking?'

Warin reached out, his fingers flexed around her small waist as he helped her down briskly without answering her query. He had far too much on his mind such as making certain that this time he did not lose the man in the crowd. He stood perfectly still, watching the man's movements as he planned the best course of action.

'I can help you,' the woman beside him muttered. Naturally, it had to be a plan that did not include Joan Lovent.

It was damnably unfortunate to encounter the blasted

man again with Joan in tow. And once again he had to put her safety first before embarking on any perilous Crown work.

'That,' he said, shaking his head slowly, 'is simply not possible.'

'I don't comprehend why that should be. For instance, I might possibly be able to—'

'Joan!' he interrupted abruptly. 'Please. I want you to stay here with Asa.' He nodded at his old informant. 'He can show you other horses in his stable.'

'Nah, 'fraid that wouldn't be possible. I must go and see a lord who wants to buy 'alf a dozen of my prime horseflesh for his retinue.'

Hell's teeth! He could hardly leave Joan Lovent alone at the mercy of the dubious crowds here.

'Fat lot of good you are, Asa.'

The man glanced down, prodding his rotund belly, looking hopeful. 'Do you think so, Sir Warin?'

'Never mind.' Warin grabbed Joan's hand and started ambling away.

'Wait. My staff.' She pulled back, trying to grapple for it.

'No need, Joan. Use me as you would your staff.'

'But I… I never walk anywhere without it.'

'I promise you will not need it. You can lean on me. Now come, I would not want to lose him again.'

'Very well, if you are certain.'

Warin held on to her hand tightly as he watched the man intently, not letting him out of his sight. They strode in his direction, allowing a measure of distance between them so as not to rouse any attention.

'Try not to appear so agitated,' Warin muttered from the side of his mouth.

'I am not as much agitated as I am excited.'

'Well, damp down your *excitement*, mistress. You give yourself away far too easily.'

'I shall try, but I want you to know that this has been the most incredibly exciting day. One that I will hardly forget.'

Dear Lord...

'I'm very glad to hear it, but let's please try for some semblance of mundane normality,' he hissed. 'Otherwise, our prey shall...'

'Fly away?' she offered as a rejoinder.

'Precisely. And pull your hood over your head, Joan. I would not want the man to be able to recognise you later.'

'When exactly should he recognise me?' She blinked before lifting her head. 'This, Warin, is becoming far more intriguing than I had anticipated. I take it that we are following that spindly tall man yonder with the white coif tied around his head? Which begs the question...who, pray, is our missing, er...prey?'

'A dangerous man,' he responded in a low voice. 'And this is not a game, Joan, so please refrain from thinking of it as such.'

They continued to pursue the man as he wound his way through the track, viewing the different traders. The man seemed agitated, but strangely he did not seem in the least bit interested in the cattle on offer. In fact, he appeared to be looking for someone himself. *But who?*

The possible significance of this, however, was not lost on Warin as he comprehended the man's present predicament—that he might actually lead him to other potential members of the Duo Dracones.

'In what manner is he dangerous?' she whispered, barely able to conceal the excitement that she spoke of.

'In the manner that does not concern you.'

'You sound like my brother,' she hissed. 'Tom also dismisses my interest in any given matter.'

'Mayhap for good reason, Joan.'

He held on to her hand, wondering how his good manners had deserted him and why he was suddenly so irritable. It was not Joan's fault that she was here at Smythfeld, but his. Warin knew the grave mistake he had made in bringing her here and felt the enormity of this error wrapped in the guilt at having embroiled her in this, however *exciting* it might seem to her. Yet this was not the time for regrets. After all, had he not brought her here, he would not have uncovered his quarry.

'I am not a child who constantly needs to be humoured and looked after,' she whispered as she kept pace.

'What is your complaint, mistress? That your brother cares for you? Wants to shield you from the drudgery of life?'

'Oh, believe me, I do not need shielding from *that*. I know very well about the drudgeries of life, as you so eloquently put it.'

That might be true, yet that was no reason for her to know anything further about the man he was following, the reason for it or anything else for that matter.

'I have no time for this, Joan.' Warin expelled an irritated breath as he looked down at her fleetingly. 'This, as I explained earlier, is a particularly dangerous situation. And I would rather you were not involved or, better still, far away from here.'

'For goodness sake. I am merely accompanying you because I happened to be with you when you spotted this man here.'

'Just so.' He gave her a single nod. 'I would be obliged to you if that is the extent of our conversation regarding the matter. And, please, no more questions.'

She returned his nod. 'And just so you do not believe me an ingrate, I want you to understand that I do hold my brother in high esteem for all that he has done for me.'

'I know,' he muttered softly, reminded again of Joan Lovent's situation. 'You do not need to explain.' But he also knew that her brother would also not thank him for exposing his innocent sister to the work they did.

They continued to follow the man, as Warin noted with curiosity that he stopped at different stands and spoke briefly with the traders. He frowned, wondering again who it might be that he sought. Was he then a trader and, if so, what possible connection could a cattle merchant have to do with the Duo Dracones? Not that much was known of this secret group which threatened the balance of power in England.

Two years prior when Joan's brother, Tom, had initially uncovered the group's existence, they had been nefariously putting all their efforts into undermining a fragile peace treaty between the Kingdom of England and Wales. The deaths of two priests who had been conspirators of the attempted treason in question had been the only link to this new group—the Duo Dracones. They had managed to infiltrate the Bishop of Hereford's retinue at the time, but their deaths had also severed all lines of inquiry, with any further information regarding the group at an impasse. That was until the Duo Dracones began to re-emerge once again more recently.

'Do you know whom he seeks?'

'No,' he hissed under his breath. 'But I had hoped that he might lead me to the person or persons connected to him.'

Warin realised he had divulged more than he had intended, almost forgetting that it was Joan Lovent walking beside him and not one of his Knights Fortitude brethren. But thankfully she remained silent and did not probe any further. He narrowed his eyes, his gaze following the man's every move. Whoever it was that the blighter sought, they did not seem to be presently here in Smythfeld, much to the man's apparent chagrin. Which could imply that the man might then be on the move again and possibly depart soon.

'Do you believe that the man might be unsuccessful in his quest?'

'Yes,' he agreed. 'I do.'

Which begged the question of what Warin should do next, especially with Joan Lovent walking beside him, making his current predicament all the more difficult. He could hardly leave Joan on her own in Smythfeld on a busy market day while he continued to follow the man and yet this was the first real sighting of the brigand. And it would not be a good a plan for Warin to catch and reprimand the man here either, as it would expose him to anyone who might have accompanied him to Smythfeld. Indeed, it would prove disastrous, since the Knights Fortitude had to maintain their integrity and anonymity.

God's breath.

If only Nicolas d'Amberly or Savaric Fitz Leonard were with him here. They would be able to easily spread the net far, between the three of them, pulling the fellow in. And then finally, they would be able to get somewhere with this damnable mission. God, but it was Warin's own fault for taking his mind off and casting it in a different direction. One that might plunge him in equally difficult waters.

'Would it be possible to slow our pace?' Joan murmured.

No, it would not. The man might very well slip through his fingers. Again.

'Of course we may,' he mumbled, hoping that he had not shown his disappointment. It had not worked as Joan tugged on his sleeve.

'Go. I shall be safe enough here by this particular trader's wagon, Warin.' She nodded at the woman who was sat on a wooden stool. 'At least this man has brought his wife. Is that not so, sir?'

'Indeed, mistress. My wife Meggie, 'ere, goes wherever I goes.'

'How lovely. And I hope you don't mind if I wait with you a short time while I rest my weary feet?'

'No. 'Ere, you can sit on my stool, mistress. Budge up, Meggie.'

'Thank you, but I shall stand.' Joan pasted a benign smile and turned to face him. 'Now go, Warin. Do what you need to. I shall be perfectly safe with these good people.'

'That she will.' The older man nodded. 'We'll look after her.'

It bemused him, the speed with which Joan had managed to orchestrate this arrangement. But it also provided Warin the opportunity to follow the man un-hindered and without the responsibility of her company, as she had clearly intended.

'Very well, make sure that you do.' He leaned in to the trader so only he could hear. 'And I shall make it worth your while for your troubles. Do not let this woman out of your sight.'

Warin gave Joan a small smile of appreciation and hoped that he also conveyed that she must stay put while he continued to pursue the man. He gave her one last lingering glance before following him through the thick of the crowd which had gathered around a vendor trad-ing in magnificent destriers. The interest in these beau-tiful warhorses was heightened with high-stake bidding transactions that were being made vociferously. So much so that Warin was surrounded by the clamour-ing noise of men bellowing over the top of one another excitedly. Yet throughout, he keenly kept his eye trained on his mark, never letting him out of his sight, lest he attempt to slip away. He still seemed to be searching for whomever it was that he was due to meet. With the person or persons unknown failing to appear, the man stopped abruptly and turned around slowly.

It was then that his eyes fell on Warin through the narrow gap that had suddenly opened as the throng of men between them jostled and shifted. And in the man's startled gaze, Warin initially saw confusion that gave way to wide-eyed recognition. Hell's teeth, he knew exactly what the braggard would now do. Make haste and run! Which he did. Damn, but he began to sprint back in the direction he had come, as Warin gave chase. Yet there were so many people in his way as he wove around to get to the bastard. The man made his way past the wagon that Joan had settled herself in, making Warin feel uneasy. But thankfully, in his hurry to get away, the man failed to notice anything or anyone, other than his need to flee the area. By the time Warin had caught up to where Joan was waiting, the man had long gone, having made his way to a tethered horse, which he had probably secured earlier.

Warin muttered an oath under his breath in frustration, understanding the magnitude of the missed opportunity to gain more regarding the Duo Dracones. Furthermore, the man had damn well recognised him from before, which made Warin's situation even more precarious. But there was one thing for it—the man had been unsuccessful in meeting whomever he had sought here.

He turned and flicked his gaze at Joan, relieved that she, at least, was safe and had been spared from being entangled more than she already had.

'I am sorry that the man got away from you,' she muttered as Warin went to her.

'As am I.' He held out his hand, which she tentatively took. 'Did he notice you in any way?'

She shook her head. 'I do not believe so. He had no notion of me being associated with you, as I did what you asked and pulled my hood low, covering my head.'

'Good. And as far as the man is concerned, at least I found out something about him.'

'What was that?'

'That he sought a person or persons who, although he was unsuccessful at finding, might be either a horse merchant or breeder.'

'That seems a sound reasoning.' She nodded, smiling.

'I am glad you think so, but I wish there was more that I had uncovered. I'm still very much in the dark.'

'Then step out in the light, Warin, because I might be able to help you.'

He frowned, unable to comprehend how on earth she believed she could help him. 'Oh, and how would you do that?'

'My sight might be impaired and deficient, but, in its stead, my sense of smell is exemplary, if I may say so myself.'

'I'm happy to learn that, Joan, but cannot think how it can help enlighten me in any way.'

'Ah, you still do not see.' She tapped her nose. 'The man you sought moved past me, you know. And as he did so I got a very strong scent of oak bark mixed with…animal hide.'

He shook his head in an attempt to unclog the fettered impediment that seemed to be lodged in his head. 'And are you entirely sure that it was the man I followed who carried this unique…er, odour?'

'Oh, yes, without question.' She threw him a winsome smile that managed also to convey a mild pitying look—since it was still quite obvious that he had difficulty comprehending her meaning. 'My sense of smell is strong. I dare say it compensates for my lack of sight. And this man's odour—well it was quite out of the ordinary, as I said. And I know it was him, you see, as he hurried past me, leaving his scent in his wake.'

'I see.' And suddenly he did, quite clearly. 'And you are certain the smell was of oak bark mixed with animal hide?'

'Yes.' She nodded. 'Mixed with a floral note, although, I dare say, that might have been from the woman I sat with.' She frowned, considering this, and then shook her head.

His eyes suddenly widened.

'Ah, I believe that you have considered something.'

'I have, yes.' He lifted his head and met her gaze. 'Thanks to you, Joan.'

'Think nothing of it. The horseback riding more than made up for any help I might have given.' She sank her teeth into her bottom lip. 'So, is it of any significance?'

He inclined his head. 'Indeed. Oak bark is the traditional substance used for tanning—a process tanners use to turn…'

'Animal hide into *leather*!'

'Precisely.'

'So, this man might be involved in some way with tanners? Could that be significant?'

'Again, yes, it might just.' And the leathers produced by the tanners were invariably used to furnish shoes made by…cordwainers. Indeed, this new discovery was more than merely significant.

Chapter Seven

The significance of Warin de Talmont ensconced within the safe stone walls of All Hallows Church, Honey Lane, for the last few days was not lost on Joan. Not in any way. Warin had been recognised by the Smythfeld tanner man, as she had rechristened him, meaning that whatever reasons he had been pursuing the man had to be halted...for now. Not that any of this was explained to her, nor why the tanner man had been pursued in the first instance. All this Joan had deduced for herself.

Yet, this was not a complaint. In fact, she was inordinately pleased that Warin had chosen to be ensconced here, with her, since she enjoyed his company very well.

He was different to the gruff, surly man she had believed him to be two years ago. Indeed, beneath the sardonic masculine sinew was a complicated, interesting man—one who intrigued her more than she had imagined possible. And Joan knew, she felt deep in her bones, that the feeling was mutual. She could deduce that too. The man liked her, and mayhap possibly admired her. It would be the little looks, the compliments and the small smiles that he directed her way. Not to mention that he was easy to converse with. And when Joan thought back to that horseback ride in Smythfeld when she was sitting practically on his lap...

Well...

What Joan did not understand was what his interest in her meant. Was it friendship or more? Had he organised that glorious ride out of pity or something else entirely? God, she hoped it was not out of pity—since that would be far too humiliating to contemplate. Even so, was he beginning to care for her? Was he courting her? Without first consulting her brother? No, that could not be.

These questions whirled around her head, making her wish she could be a little braver, a little bolder, and consult her sister by marriage. Brida might be able to shed light on all of this...as Joan understood so little about her growing feelings for this man. But she felt uncomfortable discussing her friendship with Warin to anyone.

In any case, Joan was not a woman to have any such interest bestowed on her. She was not, nor had she ever been desirable to any man or had ever been a suitable prospect for marriage, despite her brother's rise in stature. It had been yet another fact that she had bitterly reconciled herself to, with all that hope and desire all but dashed. It was her dwindling sight that men found so objectionable. The belief that she might somehow pass the affliction on to any of their future progeny.

This was all hopeless conjecture anyway. Warin de Talmont might very well be directing his interest in her because of the unfailing sense of duty he felt towards her—protecting her, as the sister of his long-standing friend. Nothing more than that. Humouring her by agreeing to take her to Smythfeld on Market Friday and procuring wonderful horseback rides for her pleasure.

Yes… She exhaled, scanning the outside courtyard of the church and settling on the man himself as he played with the children. Yes…that had to be the reason.

Joan found herself moving slowly towards him with only the help of a new walking staff that Warin had apparently come by. She noted that he was attempting, yet failing, to engage the little fair-haired orphan maid, who never spoke to anyone, least of all a knight as imposing as Warin. The little girl was sat a distance away on a raised stone seat, trying to ignore the man who had got on his knee as he presented her with a single-stem dandelion, topped with a cloud of velutinous seed ball.

The scene made her heart trip over itself. It was so achingly tender, so utterly compelling, and yet Joan knew emphatically that he would not succeed with the girl. No one had.

'If you close your eyes tightly like this and blow the white fluffy seeds of the flower away, and make a wish at the same time, it is said that your wish shall float away until an angel hears of it and grants it true,' Joan could hear him say as he held the flower out. 'Would you care to try?' But the girl just shuffled along the seat until she had her back to him.

Oh, dear…

'It is good of you to engage the child, Warin.'

He got to his feet and expelled a sigh, turning towards her. 'Not successfully.'

'Sadly, that is the truth for me, too. For all of us, I dare say.' She shook her head and smiled faintly. 'But I am glad to find that you're still lurking here among us still.'

'Well, let me inform you, mistress...' he leant towards her '...that I am known by many as a prodigiously good lurker.'

'I am sure you have very much pinned the art of lurking down. I witnessed for myself how you lurked around the street corners of London.'

'Only because you were liable to get yourself into mischief.' He tilted his head to one side and raised a brow.

'Oh, yes, a very prodigious lurker.'

'If you continually mention that word, I fear I might be compelled to lurk elsewhere.'

She laughed softly. 'I do have a liking for it, but I shall refrain from using it again, since it distresses you so.'

They smiled at one another at the absurdity of their conversation, but in truth she wanted to make his situation lighter.

He sighed, dragging his hands through his hair. 'In all seriousness, I wish I had *lurked* with more purpose in Smythfeld. I might then have avoided being recognised.'

Joan knew this was a sore subject and that the man was doing his best to be resolute in the face of that particular failure, but surely there would be another time, another day.

She matched his sigh with one of her own. 'Don't lose heart, Warin. I have every faith that you shall find the man.'

'Do you? I am not entirely certain how that could possibly be.'

'Ah, since you are confined here?'

He stiffened immediately. It was obvious that Warin de Talmont was not happy about being here, making Joan consider who had made the decision, since it had clearly not been him.

'Not that I know precisely why you pursue him.' Joan bit her lip as she tried to gently coax more information out of him, knowing that it was futile.

'As I said before, there is really no need for you to know any details.' His answer was short and pithy, but he must have realised this as he quickly added, 'Although, I hope you are aware I am exceedingly grateful for your help, in Smythfeld. You made some excellent observations.'

The corners of her lips curled upwards, since that very *excellent observation* had depended on her sense of smell rather than relying on her poor sight.

Joan had initially had no choice but to adapt and allow this side of her to flourish. However, in time it had become something that she had taught herself to master, becoming more and more proficient—the need to use her other senses.

'I am glad to have been of some help.'

'It was certainly more than that. Thanks to you, we now know far more than we did before.'

It was a testament to the extent that the man trusted her and felt at ease in her company by divulging the *'we'*.

She pondered whom that might include, but refrained from asking, knowing she would just expose his mistake.

'And does that knowledge now open other lines of enquiry?'

Joan wagered that those lines of enquiry would, no doubt, include tanners and merchants of animal hide and pelt who were involved in the production of leather.

'You know emphatically that they do.' He was smiling at her in that way again. The one that made her skin tingle and feel far too warm.

She swallowed uncomfortably. 'I can only surmise.'

'Ah, but I am certain you could do more than that, Joan. And you should know that this new information will be used to track and catch him.'

'Then I am curious as to the reason why you spend your days here. After all, should you not be the one using that information to track and catch the tanner man yourself?'

Joan leant towards him and closed her eyes, blowing the cluster of seed ball from the dandelion Warin was still holding, and wondered whether it was prudent to even make a wish. Possibly not as they never came true—none of hers ever had.

She opened her eyes and found his eyes fixed on her, his jaw tense and pulled tight. Ah, mayhap she had goaded him a little too much and yet she still knew very little regarding the tanner man. Not that she should know anything at all as this did not concern her.

Ah, Warin did not seem at all happy with her keen and excellent observations now.

'I was recognised, Joan, and cannot put myself in that position again.'

She nodded. 'I assume it would be too perilous?'

'Indeed, and it would make the task of tracking and catching far too onerous.'

A silence stretched between them as they both mused the predicament that Warin had found himself in. There must be something that could be done.

Just then a few of the children who were playing in the middle of the grassy quad in the centre of the courtyard approached them, one shuffling his boots on the ground, the other holding a long strip of material and hood.

'We were wondrin' whether you'd play with us, mistress. And you, too, sir, if you would be kind enough to oblige us.' The boy continued to scuff his foot on the grass as he mumbled, his head bent low.

'I am not sure, Adam.'

'Please, mistress.' His voice brought through the other voices, pleading in unison.

Their enthusiasm made her smile inwardly. Besides, Joan enjoyed these games with the children.

'Very well, children. Very well. Saints' above, you are all so boisterous today. Sir Warin, if you would be so kind?' She held out her hand, which he took with a small, bemused smile.

Children's games were clearly the very last thing that Warin de Talmont wished to participate in, but he did not complain, nor did he refuse. And that made Joan like the man better for it. He had entered into the fray and with small lively children, when he had clearly had other matters to address. Joan mused on how she had once thought him irascible and dour.

'So what is the game you all wish to play?'

'Hoodman's Blind.'

'Ah.' Her lips twisted into a wry smile. 'My favourite.'

Joan insisted that she would be the eponymous hood-man first and was fashioned with a cloth tied around her eyes, followed with a dark hood that fitted over her entire head, ensuring that she was indeed blinded. She was then spun around on the spot a handful of times, with the game beginning in earnest. Joan had to grope around the area, her ears filling with the excited giggles of the children as she tried to catch hold of anyone, grasping them in her clutches and using her hands and nose to determine the identity of her prey. For many, this might be easier in theory than in practice, but not for Joan. This was a game that she excelled at.

Using her nose to smell the various scents and her ears to pick up the smallest sounds and movements of the children, not to mention the handsome knight in their midst, she moved lithely and with more tenacity than when her eyes were open and covered by material and a hood. Strange how Joan never considered why that may be.

It was, in truth, disconcerting how she had adapted to being shrouded in darkness. Mayhap it was the knowledge that this was what awaited her one day, when her whole world would finally be plunged into bleak darkness, that she had no choice but to accept it. Joan had attempted to prepare herself for the inevitability of it all, with this being the main reason why she had sharpened her other senses as much as she had. It was a necessity. As much as breathing air.

And although she was lucky to have the support of her brother and his family, she had to maintain her autonomy. Without that she had nothing. Without that, life would suffocate her and be too unbearable. It was this that kept her clinging on, and pushing forward. She had little choice but to forge a new path for herself, one that would nevertheless be mired in difficulty and frustration.

Banishing these morose musings that had wormed their way into her head, Joan turned her mind to the task at hand. She attempted to catch her victim, any victim, and reminded herself that this was just a game. Yes, only a child's game and nothing more. She could hear the delighted squeals as she dashed in one direction and then another, waving her arms in the air. Turning, Joan grasped a child in mid-run.

'I have you,' she exclaimed and was met by applause.

Joan took off the hood and material tied around her head and squinted, pinching the bridge of her nose. She felt the sudden strain around her eyes exposed to the burst of sunlight and when she finally opened them, she settled on Warin, who had been watching her intently. From this short distance, Joan could only actually see the hazy outline of the man—the rest she pieced together from memory. That was all, no detail—just assumption. As ever.

And just like that an unwelcome spark of despair and anger snaked through her momentarily. Joan was accustomed to her condition. But in the small recess of her mind, she sometimes grappled with the unfairness of her situation. For no matter how much her feelings for Warin de Talmont grew, her limitations and deficiencies would always stand in the way. They would always make her somehow lacking. It made her feel unworthy.

God, but enough! she remonstrated with herself and pulled her mind back to the game.

'It is your turn to be the hoodman, Adam.' She gulped, snapping her attention to the child stood beside her. Expelling a deep sigh, she helped the child don the material and hood.

Thank goodness that the game commenced again.

And just as soon, it halted again. This time it was Warin's turn to get caught. With an exaggerated spin he managed to trip himself up, landing on the grass with a thud, much to everyone's whoops, cheers and laughter. The most unexpected of which had come from the little orphan girl, who was watching from her appointed stone seat on the periphery of the courtyard.

Joan raised a brow and exchanged a surprised glance with Warin, who gave her a quick shake of his head. No, they should not register the girl's burst of giggles, as it was unconsciously done. But it was a sign of progress nevertheless, albeit a small one.

'Thank you,' she whispered as she helped tie the material around his eyes. Her fingers brushed against his face, sending a ripple of awareness through her. 'Although I cannot believe the lengths you would go to elicit a smile and a laugh. And at your own expense. You are more than you first appear to be, sir.'

His mouth quirked up. 'I aim to please.'

'Indeed.' She covered his head with the hood and stood back. 'And now behold the hoodman knight.'

'Besides, I must do something, if I am to tarry here.' Warin started to prowl the area, in an attempt to catch his prey.

Joan nodded and considered again his predicament and the restrictions he seemed to have imposed on him.

'You know I do understand, Sir Knight, that it might be perilous if the tanner man actually recognised you.'

'Indeed, Joan.' He turned abruptly, following the sound of her voice, waving his arms and trying to catch her, as she deftly moved out of his way. 'I'm glad you appreciate my circumstance.'

'Hence the reason why you tarry here, bestow your person on us and play our childish games.'

Warin stopped for a moment and dropped his arms. 'I can remove my person from these hallowed walls, mistress, if it is unwanted.'

She smiled. 'No, that is not what I am implying. All I am saying is…what if he no longer recognises you?'

Warin began the game again, stepping in one direction and then another, trying to catch any one of them as they all circled around him, 'What is it that you are saying, Joan?'

'Well, you could always think to dissemble.'

'Dissemble?' His hand shot out and caught hold of Joan's apron tie. Giving it a firm tug, she spun around, losing her footing and falling straight into his arms. 'What would you have me dissemble as?'

He removed the hood and the material tied around his head, with one hand dropping them to the ground, and gazed at her with such intensity that she suddenly felt breathless and unable to think. And she was still wrapped in his arms, pressed close to him. So close she could just about detect the warmth glittering in his eyes. She pulled out of his arms and took a step back as heat flooded her cheeks.

She swallowed uncomfortably. 'I cannot say, but mayhap a disguise that would conceal whom you actually are.'

'Not bad, Joan.' He crossed his arms across his chest and grinned, making him look so much younger. 'Not a bad gambit at all.'

Yes, she might be lacking, but at least Joan could help him with his endeavours, whether he wanted it or not.

Chapter Eight

'A priest?'

That had been Joan Lovent's idea for him to dissemble as.

A sombre-looking, coif-wearing priest, hiding a mass of his dark hair and carrying the ubiquitous length of rosary beads and a wooden cross worn around his neck. The innocuous disguise was completed with a hay-filled sack tied around his belly beneath his tunic to give that rotund appearance so common among Christ's clergy.

Warin had naturally not divulged the truth to Joan that, in the course of his work, he had resorted to dissembling many times. And on occasion, even a priest. He knew it was prudent to allow her to believe that it was all her idea and even gave her the impression that dressing as one filled him with abject horror.

It bemused Warin when Joan had informed him, sardonically, that he could hardly dress as a woman. Little did she know that her own brother had been forced to do just that a couple of years ago when he had been accused of treason. But whereas Tom Lovent was fair and had just managed to get away with donning the attire of a woman, there was no possibility of Warin doing the same—not with his dark stubble! And nor would he consider such a scheme.

'Stop fidgeting, Warin,' she mumbled from the side of her mouth. She was perversely dressed once again as a young squire, and was using a walking staff as they slowly made their way east. They would eventually leave the city gates, cross the river and make their way to the marshy settlement of Bermondsye, which was rapidly building a reputation as housing the best tanneries in all of London. Here he would use the excuse of visiting the Cluniac Priory of St Saviour—a popular site for pilgrimage—as a way to possibly discover more. All in the hope that he might acquire further information.

Especially as his fellow Knights Fortitude had already surveyed the area and come up with naught.

'This robe is excessively damn itchy. How could anyone endure it without fidgeting?'

'Priests are men of God and have no need of such earthly comforts.'

He threw her a crooked smile. 'Oh, I rather doubt that. I think it more likely that this was the only material they could spare to be made up for a man as tall as me.'

'Well, I suppose you do not have the usual physique of a priest, hence the necessity in adding the bulk around your...er...middle.'

'Which, alas, is also exceedingly uncomfortable, but I suppose it cannot be helped.' He sighed. 'At least this guise allows me some anonymity, so that I can con-

tinue my investigation. Although I still should not have
agreed for you to come with me, Joan.'

No, he should not have. He should not have allowed
the woman to accompany him through the dirty, smelly,
crowded streets of London. It was dangerous, even
dressed as she was. But she was relentless, stubborn
and infuriating once she had decided upon a course of
action. Joan Lovent had been nothing but belligerent
in getting her way. And get it, she did.

'Nonsense, this gives your disguise far more cre-
dence. Besides, you provided escort for me and now I
am merely returning the favour.'

God's breath!

'Well, I am still uneasy about this and the only reason I acquiesced was because I know that you would
have come anyway, even if I had disallowed it.'

'Ah…' She nodded, clearly amused. 'You know me
well enough to know that I would do just that.'

'Quite.' His lips twitched in the corners. 'At least
this way I can keep my eye on you.'

Which was true. And soon, very soon, he would re-
linquish that responsibility back to her brother, Tom, as
the man had sent a missive informing their group that
he would soon be returning from Salisbury with their
liege lord Hubert de Burgh. In more ways than one, that
moment could not come soon enough.

For, in spite of his reservations, Warin enjoyed Joan's
company far more than he should. Far more than he
cared to ponder on. She was intelligent, spirited, kind,
witty and beautiful. And courageous—it did not escape his notice how her condition made her desolate at
times, even when she tried to ignore her circumstance

and continue forth. She was a remarkable woman and, despite his best efforts to keep her at bay, she had managed to somehow get beneath his skin. Indeed, everything about her fired heat through his veins. But this attraction was futile as it could never be acted on. Not in any manner. He simply had nothing to give. Least of all, to a woman.

Warin had vowed after the brutal murder of his wife and child that he would never love another and would remain a widower for the rest of his days. He did not deserve or expect happiness—not when he had been unable to assure theirs as was his duty—his duty to protect and keep them safe, which he had failed miserably when he had been away in the Holy Land.

The dreadful twist of fate was that, while he had done everything he could to rise through the ranks as a warrior knight and reap the rewards of his endeavours, Warin had lost the two people who had given his life meaning and purpose. He had been unable to do the one thing that he had sworn to do with his marriage vows. And the truth of that failure cut and tormented him to his core. He pushed these musings away, knowing that it did not serve him to dwell on the past.

'Is the tannery in Bermondsye very far from here?'

'Ah, I take it that you have not been there either?' He raised a brow, reminding her of their visit to Smythfeld on Market Friday before it all went terribly wrong. Before he had once again blundered and allowed the man with the scar—or the tanner man, as Joan had called him—to slip through his fingers.

'No, as it happens, I have not.'

'Well, it is really not too late if you wish to change

your mind. I can escort you back to All Hallows, or even back to your home.'

'Oh, no, I find that my curiosity for the marshes of Bermondsye is much aroused.'

Did the woman have to use such provoking language? It played such havoc with his senses and made a sudden surge of heat course through his veins. 'The offer is there, in any case,' he muttered gruffly.

'I appreciate your concern, Warin, but that is out of the way now that we have ventured this far east of the city and I would never dream of abandoning you,' she teased. 'I do believe you need me.'

Hell's teeth…

No, he did not, he could not need or want this woman. Not ever. She was a distraction he could ill afford and, however much he was drawn to her, he had to resist her. He had to cease wanting to be in her company. Which begged the question of why he had agreed to her being here. Now. With him on a mission that could prove dangerous. God, but mayhap he had gone mad.

The men who were possibly mad, if not disappointed with him, were his Knights Fortitude brethren, Nicholas d'Amberly and Savaric Fitz Leonard. Not that either man had betrayed any such emotions. Yet that did not stop Warin enduring the guilt in failing to apprehend the tanner man once again. And, to his shame, being recognised by the bastard as well. Hence the reason why he'd had no choice other than to remove himself from his work, lest he was recognised further, putting their whole mission and even their Order in peril.

It had all been damn frustrating. During the time he had been stuck within the walls of All Hallows, with the constant temptation of Joan Lovent, a handful of spurious, false threats had been made against the Crown, each designed to confuse and bewilder, thereby placing more pressure on his Knights Fortitude brethren.

They turned the corner of the infamous Watling Street, which teemed as always on this stretch with the hustle of trade. Cattle were manhandled and manoeuvred along, as merchants packed up their wares for another day. A small group of young children in ragged clothing played with sticks in the dirt. Filthy refuse was dumped from a dwelling, mixing with the existing dirt and sludge on the pathway. The stench of the Thames filled his nostrils, cloying and foul. And at the far end of the street, drunks spilled out of the tavern hanging on to one another for support and, if they were very lucky, a woman who might promise them far more than that.

God, but this was not the best route to have come with Joan, but it was too late to turn back now as they would be hemmed in by a herd of bovine. He grasped her arm, quickening their pace, when a young beggar woman clutching her infant child practically collided into them.

They jolted as the woman bowed her head reverently over her child. 'A blessin' for me and my chillen, Father.'

He flicked his gaze to Joan, who looked just as stunned and horrified as he.

'I… I cannot.' He could not think of what to say. 'I am afraid I have not taken my vows yet.'

'It don't matter as yerra man o' God. Could yer oblige me…please?'

The young woman lifted her head then, sending a shock of recognition through him. Warin inhaled sharply and took a step back, dropping his arms to his sides, his hands shaking and clammy.

The same large brown eyes, same heart-shaped face, same dark tendrils tucked beneath a short veil, carrying a young infant on her hip.

Only the woman standing in front of him was not *her*—the veil was filthy, her face streaked and smudged with dirt and the clothes she wore were torn and mismatched. No…no, it was not his Ada and this was not their child.

He swallowed several times, dislodging a damn lump in his throat, and finally remembered to breathe. In and out. In and out. He blinked, breaking the strange spell, and reached inside his cloak to untie his leather pouch.

'Here, take it,' he grunted, holding out a few silver coins. 'Take it. This will help you and your child far more than any blessing might.'

'Thank ye.' The woman beamed. 'Oh, thank ye, Father.' She skipped away, leaving Warin wondering what the hell had just happened to him. He adjusted his breathing and calmed his thumping heart, standing there unable to move a muscle.

'Warin?' Joan's voice flooded his senses. 'Warin, are you unwell?'

He blinked and shook his head, dispelling the strange madness that had gripped him suddenly. 'I am perfectly well, I thank you.'

'But that woman…you looked as though you had seen a ghost.'

'I thought I had, but, no.' He rubbed his forehead on

a sigh, looking into the distance from a different time and place. 'The young woman looked like someone I once knew, that is all.'

'I see.' Those two words uttered from the lips of Joan Lovent carried so much perceptiveness.

'Come, let us not tarry. We need to make haste before the new bridge becomes even busier than usual.'

They ambled down a quiet road off Watling Street, which was thankfully a little cleaner.

'Was this woman you once knew someone that you once, mayhap, cared for?'

He nodded, knowing it was pointless to deny it. 'Very much,' he murmured. 'A woman I cared for and whom I loved deeply. My wife, Ada.'

Joan felt as stunned as Warin had only moments ago, with this revelation. Not in all the time she had known the man had she ever been aware that he was married or once had been and been in love...*deeply.*

'I did not know that you were married.'

He grimaced. 'Why should that matter?'

'I did not say that it did.'

'It is not important,' he muttered bitterly.

Joan wanted to tell him that it was important. That *he* was important.

'Of course it is.' Had she whispered that?

'Why?' He turned to face her. His face, cold and steely. 'She is dead. Our child is dead. I was once a husband and a father—and now I no longer am. That is all there is to know on the matter.'

Joan felt as though her heart had broken into a thousand tiny pieces for this man who stood in front of her.

Without thinking, she reached out and cupped his jaw with her hand.

'I am sorry, Warin.' She brushed his jaw with her fingertips, feeling the sharp edges and planes of his face, the rough, prickly dark stubble. 'I am so sorry for your loss.'

'There is no need to be and no need to worry your tender heart, Joan. It happened a long time ago.'

She sighed. 'Even so, it is not my tender heart but yours that concerns me.'

'I have none, mistress.' He gently removed her hand from his face and guided it down to her side. 'I thank you for your concerns, but they are wasted on me. Come, we shall continue forth.'

She frowned, but held her tongue as they continued to walk in silence, making their way through the narrow, cobbled roads and pathways.

'If I may, can I ask how they perished?' Her unruly tongue eventually got away from her.

Which naturally made Warin tense instantly beside her.

Oh, dear.

'You may ask, but I might also decline to answer.'

Oh, heavens, she really should not push him further. It was clear that it was an unwelcome topic of conversation.

'I do not wish to intrude, truly I don't.' She looked up, biting her lip before taking a deep breath. 'It is so that I might understand a little better.'

'Leave it alone, Joan,' he snapped.

'Yes, of course. I only thought that I could be of help, somehow.'

He shook his head, scowling. 'Not every soul you meet can be saved. Not everyone can be redeemed. Some are beyond even your help, mistress.'

'I… I do not comprehend you.' Her brows furrowed in the middle in confusion.

'Damn it, Joan, they died because I was not there to protect them.' Revulsion was etched on his face, his anger kept in check. 'I was not there. And they died because of me—my failure, my shortcoming, my inability to do my duty by them. Believe me, nothing…nothing on this earth could ever help in that.'

For once, Joan was at a loss for words, unable to comprehend what this man was saying. Her breath froze as the shocking words he had spoken sunk in. Yet she could not believe a word of it. It seemed wholly incomprehensible that Warin would blame himself for the deaths of his wife and child, but that was what he seemingly did. He obviously still did for his emotions to remain this raw, this hurt, a constant reminder. If only she could do or say something that might ease his pain. If only she could bring some comfort to him. But Warin was right, not everyone could be saved. Not everyone could be redeemed.

Joan felt helpless to do much about something she had no knowledge of and could not understand.

'I am sorry,' she said again, knowing how inadequate those words were. But he remained silent, evidently wanting an end to the conversation. Which she obliged, even as more and more questions piled in her head. But for once Joan held her tongue, knowing it was prudent to do so. She did not want to cause him further pain, reminding him of a past he had no wish to visit.

The silence stretched as neither of them spoke for a long time.

'I apologise, too, Joan,' he said finally on an exhale, his dark despair seemingly a little abated. 'I find that I am unable to discuss that part of my life. Not with anyone.'

She leant on her walking staff, feeling a little weary. 'I do understand. There are many incidents in my life that I also find difficult to converse about.' She stopped walking. 'But please know that if you ever change your mind, I am at your disposal.'

'I thank you,' he said softly, stopping again and taking her hand in his. 'You are uncommonly kind, Joan.'

She felt her face grow warm. 'Well, I do have two rather good ears that I should put to use.'

'Yes.' He smiled. 'It seems that you do.'

She felt the sudden spark of heat, an unfathomable intensity emanating from him that made her look away. Taking a deep breath, she snapped her gaze back and returned his smile, feeling her cheeks grow even warmer.

'I do mean it, Warin. My ears will always be here for you, whenever the occasion might arise. Should you ever need me.'

He nodded his thanks, dropping her hand, and continued to escort her along the way.

Chapter Nine

Joan had to admit that by the time they had reached the newly built London Bridge, she was excessively fatigued after much travail on foot. Yet she could barely contain her excitement as they passed through the impressive stone gatehouse of the bridge and paid the toll to cross it. The magnificent structure might be, as Warin predicted, extremely busy at this time of the day, but it had a vigour and an energy about it that was rather infectious.

Both sides of the bridge had timber-beamed buildings of various sizes, with gabled thatched roofs. Some were evidently used privately as dwellings and others had the ground-floor chamber used by merchants and guilded craftsmen selling their wares, with living chambers on the upper floors. Some she could just about see or detect the scent of—others were pointed out by Warin.

There was a booth occupied by a mercer and next to that a haberdasher. On the other side, a cutler was selling his polished swords, daggers and shields glinting as they caught the sun. They continued strolling past the fletcher beside the bowyer, both working tirelessly to produce and sell their intricately carved bows and arrows and greeted Warin with a nod as they passed, evidently familiar with him.

How strange.

They meandered past a beautiful stone-bricked chapel, with concentric arches, a decorative doorway and light streaming through the coloured glass of the windows topped with a rib-vaulted roof. It seemed so incongruous for the bridge to include a chapel, when there were places of worship nearby on either side of the bridge. Yet somehow the grand structure in the centre somehow made the bridge balanced and well proportioned.

'I think we can stop for a repast here.' He gripped her elbow and tugged her gently towards a timber dwelling with a large wooden door a little further along from the chapel.

She smiled up at him, nodding. 'That would be most welcome.'

Warin guided her inside the Three Choughs tavern and made their way around to the back of the busy space where he somehow secured a table, with an arched window overlooking the river. It seemed that this was a favourite haunt of his, as many of the patrons, just as the merchants before, nodded or greeted him as they made their way to the table. Either his disguise was not good enough since he was easily recognisable or he had done this before—which could not be right, could it? Joan made a mental point to address this with Warin once it was opportune to do so.

'It seems that you have been here before.'

He shrugged. 'It seems that I have. I pass through here many times during the course of my work and the faces who frequent here naturally become familiar ones.'

Joan had little time to think about the matter as two men stealthily approached their small table. One drew up a stool, scraping it across the floor, pushing the strewn rushes beneath it, while the other sank into the seat beside Warin. Joan instantly felt that she had met him before.

'What the devil are you doing here, de Talmont?'

Warin did not answer, but she could feel the atmosphere was strained, if not a little tense.

'Well, from his appearance and his chosen travelling companion—Mistress Lovent, I assume?—' the man muttered wryly, 'I can hazard a guess.'

Ah, yes, Joan had recognised the man—it was the friend of Warin's whom she had been introduced to previously. She looked up to find him smiling at her.

'Greetings, mistress. Fancy finding you and my friend here, in this tavern, of all places.' He raised a brow. 'And dressed once again as a young squire, I see.'

There was something in his tone that made Joan wonder whether if it had been these men who had imposed upon Warin the restrictions of his recent movements.

'Yes, fancy,' she muttered from beneath her hood.

'Well, are you going to do the introductions, de Talmont?' the other man drawled.

'If I must. This…' Warin motioned to the man opposite

'…is Savaric Fitz Leonard, Joan, an associate of mine, and Nicolas d'Amberly, whom you have met before.'

'Enchanted, Mistress Lovent.' Savaric Fitz Leonard flicked his gaze in her direction and even with her poor sight, she almost gasped. His eyes were so unusual— a vivid hue of yellow and honeyed brown set within smoky dark eyes, giving them an almost cat-like appearance. And the exposed skin of his face and hands was dark olive, making Joan wonder whether he was from faraway, sun-kissed shores.

'I am happy to make your acquaintance, sir.' She looked to the man beside him. 'And how nice to meet you again, Messer d'Amberly.'

'Oh, the pleasure is all mine, mistress,' the man murmured as he clasped her hand and pressed a kiss on the back of it.

'For goodness sake, she is dressed as a squire,' hissed Warin, grabbing her hand back and returning it to her lap. 'Someone might deduce that she is not a boy.'

'Cease your worry. I rather doubt that anyone would notice such thing, from where we are sitting. Although, I wonder, if I should ever see you in a kirtle, mistress?'

'And I wonder how that might be relevant, sir?'

His lips curved into a wide grin as he addressed his two friends. 'I like her,' he muttered, indicating with his thumb in her direction. 'She's got spirit.'

'Why are you both here?' Warin scowled.

'Alas, we could ask the same of you.'

'God's breath, leave it, Nick.' He exhaled through his teeth.

'Tut, tut, we are testy. And did you hear that earlier, d'Amberly? I have been reduced to being just an *associate*.'

'And if you continue to sneer in that fashion, de Talmont, it would set permanently on that brooding face of yours.'

Warin crossed his arms across his chest, his nostrils flared, looking as though he might be contemplating murder. And yet Joan could not help but think that these men were connected by a deep bond. Far more than mere *associates*.

A tavern maid came by, placing a jug of ale and mugs on the table, making a few pleasantries since she, too, seemed to know these men as regulars before leaving to tend to another table.

'Well?' Nicholas d'Amberly sat back and raised a mocking brow. 'Are you going to explain?'

No, he damn well was not. Warin glared from one man to the other, hoping they would get the message to drop this topic of conversation, otherwise they were liable to rouse the suspicion of the woman sat opposite him. Besides, he did not answer to these two. Despite everything that had happened, and the failure thus far in capturing the men involved with the Duo Dracones, Warin was not going to actively jeopardise their mission, whatever Savaric Fitz Leonard and Nicholas d'Amberly might believe.

And he could no longer hide in a damn church while his fellow Knights of Fortitude did all the work in trying to gain more information about the traitorous group who were creating havoc and dissent in the city. They must capture them and capture them soon.

Only in the past week, the group had spread rumours about a huge rise in scutage among the merchants, which soon escalated to such an extent that a mob descended on Westminster, demanding to know the reasons for this. This was, mercifully, dispersed quickly, but it could have turned particularly nasty had the mob not been appeased and been convinced that there were, indeed, no such new taxes.

Warin grabbed one of the hot rolls of bread that the maid placed in the middle of the wooden table, along with a round of cheese, cold meats and a pot of apple, gooseberry and ale chutney, took a bite out of it and shrugged. 'I was merely showing Joan the new bridge, since she had declared a want to see it.'

'Merely, he says.' Nicholas d'Amberly shook his head. ''Tis such gallantry that you take it upon yourself to escort the fair and lovely Mistress Joan on outings from Smythfeld to the bridge.'

Warin ground his teeth together at the impudence of the man, referring to Joan in such terms—even if they were true.

'Just so,' Savaric Fitz Leonard muttered as he watched Warin over the rim of his mug. 'Although I wonder whether the fair mistress's own brother would sanction these *mere* outings, had he knowledge of them.'

Damn, but Warin wanted to drag the man by the scruff of his hood and wipe that smirk off his face. Who in heaven's name had want of foes with friends such as these two?

'You are acquainted with my brother, sir?'

'Only a little.' Savaric Fitz Leonard kept his eyes

focused on Warin as he answered. 'We have only met but a handful of times.'

So, what was this new warning? Were his brethren ready to inform Thomas Lovent that, rather than protecting his sister and making sure she was as far away from this mission, Warin had woefully embroiled Joan by bringing her along with him? Not only that, but he had blatantly disregarded their directive to keep away from venturing around the city for now. Is that what they were implying? What this was all about?

Hell's teeth, but how could Warin convey to them that he could no longer sit idly by? That he needed to do his part as a member of their Order, be useful, and contribute in the only way he knew how.

And as for Joan Lovent? Well, neither of these men knew her or had any idea what the woman was like. How perceptive and wilful she was and how much of a nuisance she posed to be, had he not brought her along with him. He dreaded to think how she would have attempted to follow him and, when that failed, the possible danger she might needlessly have put herself through. She could certainly be a menace if she chose to be and yet...

Yet Joan was unlike any other woman he had ever met. And she had him in knots. He felt drawn to her in a manner that confounded him. He wanted to have her close and at the same time he resolutely needed to have her as far away from his person as possible. It was disconcerting that he could not help but want to spend time with her, converse and laugh with her.

Not that any of it mattered. Soon, very soon, he would entrust Joan's safety and protection back to her own brother and would no longer have that responsibility. He would also no longer need to spend time with her, converse or laugh with her, as asinine as that reflection happened to be. And, no, Warin would not dwell on why that notion filled him with an emptiness he could hardly fathom. But no matter, until then, he would do as he saw fit—without reference to either of these men.

He rose. 'Come, Joan. I think it time to leave.'

'Sit, de Talmont,' Savaric hissed under his breath. 'Besides, you have not finished your repast and, more importantly, neither has Mistress Joan.'

'I find I grow tired of the present company.'

'Harsh, but I shall ignore it. Come now, sit before you cause a scene.' Warin slowly sat back down, glaring at his friend. 'Good, now let me pour you another mug of ale.'

Warin noticed the exchange of a surprised look between his two friends and let out a deep sigh. He knew that he was not himself. He knew his reaction was not the usual one he would normally deploy—but the mounting tension, from his failure at Smythfeld that resulted in being cooped up in All Hallows, to his unwanted attraction to Joan, when he was only supposed to ensure her safety, was making him increasingly agitated and uneasy. Yet it was also something else that had twisted his gut so tightly that he felt he could hardly breathe. Even now he felt raw and unsettled after he'd seen the beggar woman with the child who had resembled his late wife, Ada, and his daughter. And God, how disturbing the whole incident had been.

It remined him of the failures of his past and brought everything that had come to pass to the fore. It made him aware, once again, of how unworthy he was as a husband and a father—a man who was unable to protect the woman he was bound to—the woman he loved along with their only child.

Their deaths had torn and ripped his soul apart and he had never been the same man since. It had changed him irrevocably and Warin had carried their deaths as a talisman, never forgetting the dishonour he brought on himself—the loneliness and grief his only constancy. It was the reason why he lived for the work he did for the Crown—as a way to prove himself. As a way that he could absolve himself of the stain of their deaths and restore some semblance of peace.

In truth, he had been grateful to have been chosen, recruited into this murky world—a knight without any familial ties or allegiance to any overlord. It had suited Warin to live within the shadows and engage with the work he did without any other obligation, just as the men who sat with him around this table had. It was what bound them together. It was what they shared as one—fealty to each other and the Order of the Sword.

'Very well, we shall remain here a little while longer.'

'Good.' Savaric Fitz Leonard nodded, popping a morsel of food into his mouth. 'Now eat. This chicken is particularly flavourful.'

'Indeed it is,' Nicholas d'Amberly added, brushing the crumbs off his gambeson. 'And I know with all certainty that this chicken is butchered from this side of the bridge—from within the city walls itself.'

'In truth, it might be prudent for you to turn back and remain there until we can ascertain that the poultry and other livestock from the other side of the bridge...'

'Indeed, all foodstuff.'

'Yes, thank you, d'Amberly. So that we might check that all food supplies are adequate and safe for consumption on both sides of the bridge.'

Warin felt his jaw drop and was stunned that his friends had thought to resort to this prattle in front of Joan Lovent. As if she would be taken in by this absurdity. She would know it instantly for the ruse it was.

'I had no idea,' she said, sinking her teeth into her chicken. 'Is there a big problem then in the foodstuff brought from Bermondsye and beyond, only we were going—?'

'To buy fruit pickles from there,' he interjected. 'Since it is the best that one can hope to procure, or so I have heard.'

God's breath, now he was at it.

'I never knew that you were so appreciative of fruit pickles, de Talmont.'

'Oh, didn't you know?' He leant forward and spooned a dollop of the apple and raisin pickle in to his mouth. 'It is my particular favourite, Fitz Leonard, and I was rhapsodising so much about how delicious it was to Mistress Joan that we decided to venture here to purchase some from the local source.'

'I comprehend entirely. You came all the way to view this busy, stinking bridge and then to buy some fruit pickle that you might easily find within the city?'

'Nothing like Bermondsye pickle, d'Amberly.'

'Of course. Fruit that is grown on the marshy terrain of Bermondsye that is then made into pickle is very fine indeed.'

Savaric Fitz Leonard nodded in bemusement. 'Some might say that it is almost rare.'

'Shounds rather special…' Joan muttered happily, as though this discourse was not in any way as absurd and ridiculous as it was. 'And I, for one, cannot wait to sample it.'

The three of them turned and stared at her in unison.

'And you are dressed like a monk, I see, de Talmont,' d'Amberly remarked with a smirk. 'Just the sort of garb one needs when buying pickle from Bermondsye.'

'No, you have that wrong.' She tapped her nose and swayed slightly. 'Warin is dressed as a priesht, not a monk. A vera, vera handshome priesht.'

Oh, God, was Joan…drunk?

'Not that one should notice prieshts as anything other than holy men, serving God.'

Fitz Leonard raised a brow. 'How much has she had to drink?'

'I am not particularly sure.' D'Amberly shrugged. 'Although I must admit that I did keep topping up her mug.'

'You did what?' Warin hissed, his hands clenched into fists on the table.

'He just informed you, Warin, did you not hear? Messher d'Amberly kept topping up my mug.' Joan smiled inanely. 'Again and again. So I kept drinking and drinking.'

God give him strength.

'Did he now?'

She nodded. 'Yes, I was parched and he is an obliging sort. Besides, I am not in any way drunk. Not even remotely—although I can see double of you, Warin, which is rather splendid as I have difficulty seeing even *one* of you.'

Hell's teeth!

'You need a good thrashing, d'Amberly.'

'Why? Because I am an obliging sort?'

'As well as a toe-curling miscreant of a scoundrel.'

'You besmirch my good name, de Talmont.' The man had the gall of feigning being upset. 'Alas, you hurt my feelings.'

'I shall hurt a lot more than your damn feelings.'

D'Amberly rolled his shoulders and sighed. 'How could I possibly know that Mistress Joan would become inebriated after just a few mugfuls of ale?'

'Since she is not the usual woman that you consort with,' he spat.

'Very true.' A slow knowing smile spread on his lips. 'And all the more reason now to escort the fair lady back to her abode, de Talmont. We can manage without you.'

'No, no, no. I tell you that I am not befuddled,' she protested quietly, giving her head a little wobble.

'And we get to the heart of why you purposefully encouraged Joan to drink more and more ale.'

'It's for your own good. Go back to the city. Better still, take her back home.'

'Yes,' Fitz Leonard agreed. 'We shall manage to capture the...er, the reptiles by setting a trap.'

'I do not like reptiles,' Joan mumbled. 'Shlimy, shlippery vipers, with the look of the devil.'

'Very true, mistress. One should take care not to get bitten by one.'

'Indeed, the bite can be lethal.'

'Damn you.' Warin stood up. 'Damn both of you.'

'I promish I am not drunk.' She stood swaying, as Warin stepped towards her, wrapping his arm around her. 'My head spins a little—but I am only a tiny little bit addled. Oh, and you, Warin, are still vera, vera handshome, even if you are cross. Do not be cross,' she said, pinching his chin.

'No, Warin, do not be cross,' d'Amberly retorted, mirth lacing his words.

He clenched his teeth, and with a withering glare Warin turned on his heel, without saying another word, escorting Joan outside the tavern. He pulled his hood down, running his hand through his hair, knowing that the day was now lost no thanks to his associates. Warin had no option other than to take Joan back home, hoping that, by the time they arrived, the effects of the ale might have worn off.

Of all the devious, unscrupulous, underhanded tricks his friends had resorted to, this had to be the worst—to purposefully pursue a goal of getting Joan Lovent inebriated so that it would force Warin's hand to take her back home was shameful. The awful truth was that he had actually failed to notice d'Amberly continually topping up her mug, since he had been so engrossed in his own damn woes. What the hell was wrong with him?

Feeling every drop of frustration, Warin had the sudden urge to hit something hard and painful. They walked back in the direction they had come, past the Chapel of St Thomas à Becket, a chapel used by pilgrims on their way to Canterbury, and a place of significance to the Knights of Fortitude.

'Come, Joan, I shall take you back home.'

'And why, pray, should you do that?' She pulled out

of his grasp and turned to face him, giving him a slow mischievous smile, her manner changing almost immediately from the one she had presented only moments ago. 'I told you I am not drunk. Nor am I addled in any way.'

Warin's jaw dropped a fraction as he realised what she was saying, what she had done, in truth. It was Joan Lovent who had managed to deceive and mislead them all. And how well she had pulled it off.

'I can see clearly that you are not.' Warin shook his head, crossing his arms across his chest and returning her smile. 'You, mistress, are trouble.'

Why, she even had him fooled.

'Thank you.' Her smile widened to a grin. 'And I believe we can now continue to Bermondsye without any further interference?'

An unexpected bark of laughter escaped from his lips. 'Yes, I believe you're right. Shall we?'

'Lead on, good sir.' She grasped his arm with one hand and used her walking staff with the other. 'But tell me, what or who are these reptiles you all spoke of?'

Damn, but Joan Lovent was most definitely trouble—in every sense of the word.

Chapter Ten

Joan had enjoyed this expedition through the city of London, as well as the excitement of experiencing the new bustling London Bridge, immensely. But what had been the best part of the day by far was venturing inside the tavern on the bridge itself and being able to deceive not just Warin but his friends, into believing that she was so inebriated from the amount of ale Nicholas d'Amberly kept sloshing into her mug that she needed to be taken home.

In truth, she had surprised herself with her own daring and it was a wonder that she had not given herself away by succumbing to peals of laughter, as she almost had. As she had wanted to. But instead, she kept on with the ruse.

Joan knew what the man was about, from the moment he, along with the intense and brooding Savaric Fitz Leonard, began questioning the reasons why Warin was there and why he had brought her to this part of London.

As they continued to berate him, more and more

questions mounted in her head regarding the three men sat around the table and how they were connected to one another as well as to her own brother. It was all so perplexing. All of it.

Joan was certain that she would never get answers from Warin just by asking him. No, she had to somehow coax it out of him or unravel the pieces bit by bit, hoping it might make sense.

Warin, along with the other men, seemed to be shrouded in mystery and intrigue and, despite herself, she was drawn to uncover more.

Besides, there was something about him—something inexplicable that pulled Joan towards Warin de Talmont. He alone stirred very different conflicting emotions in her. Every time he caught her eyes, or his lips curled with a faint reluctant smile, she felt as though her insides were melting. Joan found that she became a little breathless, a little unnerved and far too aware of him. His size, his height, broad shoulders, his long lean legs, and that face…oh, not to mention that dark hair, which she longed to thread her fingers through. God but she had the most ridiculous notion to reach out and touch him. Trace all the little details that her eyes failed to.

And when they had stumbled upon the woman and child who had mistaken him for a priest earlier, his visceral reaction—the shock, confusion and sadness that emanated from him—made her heart go out to him. She had had the sudden need to soothe him.

'Are you well, Joan?' he drawled, throwing her a quizzical sideways glance. 'Only I would not want you to swoon, especially after you have just convinced me of your little performance back there.'

'No, do not fear. I shall not swoon, even though the day grows a little warm and the air is a little fetid.' *And you, Warin de Talmont, are becoming far too enticing*, she thankfully refrained from adding.

'Come.' He held her hand firmly in his as he guided her through the throngs of people on the bridge. His hand felt warm, strong, capable and entirely protective. 'I would not want you to swoon because of the air either. Tell me, though, however did you manage to drink that much ale without succumbing to the usual effects?'

'Well, I am not entirely sure, but I can tell you that it's a recent discovery. Even my brother had been begrudgingly impressed with my, er…talent of drinking copious amounts of ale, without it going to my head. Although he warned against displaying it in public. You won't tell him, will you?'

'God, no. That among many things, Joan.' He raised a brow.

They reached the other side of the bridge, where people waited to pay the toll to cross and walked through the stone gateway that led to the parish of Southwark, which Bermondsye was part of. They continued along the main street, passing the open, slightly marshy pastures and arable land with ploughmen working the land and small timber dwellings on either side. They made their way along a narrow pathway that led to the causeway towards Bermondsye, which ran parallel to the River Thames.

'The closer we get to the tanneries, Joan, the more putrid the air will become, so you will need to cover your nose and mouth.'

'Hark!' she muttered in mock outrage. 'And now you tell me.'

'And you believe that would have changed your decision to accompany me?' He laughed, his shoulders gently lifting up and down. 'Because, Joan, if it were down to me, I would never have brought you here.'

'You make it sound as though you had little choice in the matter.'

'That is because I had none,' he retorted ruefully.

'Hardly fair. Your description of me might be construed as rather unflattering, sir.'

'Never that, mistress.' The man winked and she caught it. He actually winked at her, unless he was squinting because of the sun. 'But you know as well as I that your curiosity would have got the better of you and I could not have risked you following me and getting into mischief.'

'I? Get into mischief?' She huffed in mock indignation. 'And there I believed you enjoyed my company, sir. It seems I was wrong.' She chuckled.

He stopped walking and tilted his head to the side. 'Oh, you are not wrong, Joan. I enjoy your company. Far more than I should,' he murmured softly.

She frowned, looking away. What did he mean? That he enjoyed her company despite himself? Mayhap she should not have been so insistent that she accompany him. After all, Warin de Talmont was only supposed to provide her protection while her brother was away. And even then, she had managed to gain his escort to and from All Hallows against his expressed wishes.

'I have arranged for us to travel the remainder of the journey on horseback, if you are amenable to that.'

Oh, God, that would mean that she would once again have to sit on a saddle with her back nestled against

Warin de Talmont's chest. His huge arms wrapped around her. Her breath shuddered as she exhaled.

'Yes, of course.' Joan smiled weakly at him. Mayhap she was feeling the effects of all the ale she had drunk earlier after all.

They walked to the stables where Warin had arranged a horse for their perusal and before long they were positioned just as the last time she had ridden with him. And just as then she felt the growing tension in her body, being this close to the man.

'Are you unwell, Joan?' Warin was closer than she had anticipated as his jaw grazed her skin, making her heart quicken.

'No, I am perfectly well.'

'I am glad.' His voice was laced with something akin to amusement, making Joan wonder if he knew that she had trouble breathing being enfolded in his arms. 'Then let us be away.'

They continued to ride in silence along the pathway that opened out to a dirt track where they were met with the awful stench of the tannery even before they had approached it.

'Remember what I said, Joan, cover your nose and mouth. I would not like you to be exposed to these fetid humours and you may wait by the horse until I return, once we get there.'

'Oh, I am afraid that will not be agreeable.'

'Not agreeable,' he repeated. 'Naturally it won't.' His breath grazed the exposed skin of her neck.

'No, I think I shall come with you, Warin. I have no patience to wait and in any case you might need me.'

'True, I might.' He chuckled softly.

'Are you humouring me, sir?'

'For shame, mistress. As if I would do such a thing.'
He pulled the reins a little tighter to the left, making the
horse trot in that direction. 'But you might wish you'd
heeded my warning regarding the tannery. I do not want
to spend longer than I must there myself.'

The row upon row of industrious timber shacks and
buildings came into view as did the foul stench that enveloped the tannery in Bermondsye.

Warin pulled the reins to a halt, jumped down and
helped Joan dismount. Her eyes could just make out
the intensity of his gaze before he glanced down at his
hands still holding her around her waist and removed
them quickly, as though his fingers had been scorched.

'Shall we?' he said on a choke as they stepped into
the tannery yard.

'From the little I can see, and from the noises here,
not to mention the noxious smells that you were good
enough to mention, I can well believe that this is a hive
of industry. But I would be obliged if you could describe what you see in a little more detail. I do not wish
to miss a thing.'

'Certainly.' He nodded. 'I can observe, at the far
end of the yard, the pits where they prepare hides by
removing hooves, horns and such. Not that I see, but
somewhere, mayhap inside the timber buildings, they
would be soaked in unmentionable liquid to loosen the
hair and fat which would be scraped off, readying the
hides for the tanning process itself. It would also house
a pit where the hides would be soaked in the oak bark
and other unmentionables for a long period of time.

And over here in the yard is where the leather skins are stretched and even dyed.'

'But everything seems so still, Warin. I would have thought this place to be much busier than it seems to be.'

'Yes.' He frowned as he scanned the whole area. 'So would I.'

Just then a few tanners stepped out of the yard and approached them. 'May we 'elp you?'

Warin pulled down the material he had tied to cover his nose and mouth. 'Yes, we are here to enquire whether there have been any strange goings-on at your tanneries?'

'Ah, thank the lord.' One of the men pulled back his deep hood and stepped forward. 'You must be from the Palace of the Bishop of Winchester?'

A good assumption, since Warin was dressed as a priest. And rather than deny this proclamation Warin inclined his head a little, which seemed to pacify the man. 'And a good job, too, as a few of the city men had come here putting their noses where they weren't wanted,' the man carried on. 'But we don't answer to them.'

Joan had a suspicion that Warin was trying to damp down his excitement at what he might discover here. It was, after all, the reason why they were here in Bermondsye.

'Would you care to enlighten me regarding everything that has happened?' Warin probed.

'I certainly can, Father.' The man nodded grimly. 'The hides have been tampered with, in the pits yonder.'

Warin's brows knitted. 'With what?'

'No one 'ere knows, sir, but we 'ave no choice but throw them to rot. They're already 'alf putrefied.'

'But we need compensatin', Father,' another man piped up. 'Our 'ole liveli'ood has been marred by this an' it'll take much time to recoup our losses.'

The handful of men who had gathered round them agreed noisily with the man.

'I can offer a little remittance for now, but if you will, I would like to see these putrid hides for myself.' Warin turned around to face Joan. 'And you, *boy*, you shall stay here and keep hold of the horse, until my return.'

Joan had little choice but to acquiesce and waited beside the horse until a short time later when Warin returned from the timber outbuildings with the tanners in tow. The men seemed to have been subdued and appeased, judging by the manner in which they walked back, the tension seemingly seeped from their limbs. Joan wagered that Warin had paid them silver for their losses with the promise of more for their help and information.

'Thank you for your time. But before we go, have any of you seen a tall thin man with a long scar across his face running from his forehead down to his chin?' Warin muttered. 'Either here at the tanneries or at the cattle farms you use?'

'No, Father. No one of tha' description,' one tanner replied as the others shrugged or shook their heads. It seemed that the Smythfeld tanner had not been here or had not been recognised unless someone here was lying to protect him.

'Thank you all, you have been most useful. Now we really must be away.'

He nodded at her.

'Wait! Before you go, there is something that I forgot

to show you.' An older tanner retrieved a basket that he'd set aside on a stone wall and made his way back to their gathered group. 'This hay…' he pointed at the contents of his basket '…is what the farmers supplyin' the hides use. And they 'ave been complainin' that their cattle have been tampered wiv. An' many of their bovine are getting vera sick. They say it might be the hay, since it seems different.'

'Tis witchcraft, it is!' one of the men from the back of the gathered group bellowed.

'I shall be the judge of that. May I?' Warin grabbed the proffered basket and smelt the contents, passing the basket to Joan. 'Do not touch anything,' he warned her before addressing the tanners again, as he put on his mittens. 'Thank you for your assistance. If you don't mind, I should like to take some of this hay for further investigation. And, no, it most certainly is not witchcraft but something far worse. An opprobrious villain who means you ill—all of you. And until I get some answers you must take action to guard your tannery.'

'We will, Father, we will. Thank you kindly.'

Warin collected some of the hay and placed it inside a leather drawstring pouch and tied it to the saddlebags before they took their leave of them.

They made their way back to the stables in silence and returned the borrowed horse before walking back to the bridge.

'Well, that was quite fruitful, do you not think?' Joan glanced at him, pulling down the face covering and wondering what, if anything, he had made of it all.

'Mmm? A thousand pardons, I was lost in reflecting all that we have learnt.'

Joan liked that he had used the word *'we'*. It made her feel included somehow.

'I take it that there has been much that you have learnt?' She raised a brow, knowing that he would not answer her directly. 'May I see the sample of hay that you took?'

'Very well, but be careful, Joan. I suspect it might have been despoiled with something noxious.'

They stopped a moment while Warin opened the leather pouch and held it out to her. She breathed in the scent of the hay and frowned.

'What is it?' Warin tied the pouch and strapped it to his belt buckle this time.

'I cannot say precisely, only…' She tapped her chin absently. 'Only there's something in that sample that seems incongruous.'

'Incongruous?'

'Yes, I can detect a note of something that would not ordinarily be associated with hay.'

'Interesting. And do you know what that might be?'

'No, but it does seem familiar—something strangely common and everyday.'

Warin seemed to puzzle over her words, his brows knitted. 'That could be anything.'

'No.' She looked up at him. 'No, Warin, whatever it is, the scent carries a herbaceous note.'

'Herbaceous?' His brows shot up. 'Are you certain?'

'Yes, but I am afraid that is all I can distinguish.'

'I thank you for it. Your discernment is most helpful. Come, let's be away.'

They continued to walk back in the direction they came and crossed London Bridge, paying the toll once more. But this time they engaged a wherryman, and yet another acquaintance of Warin's, on the quay to bypass the city and take them by skiff down the river and let them down near the jetty by Fleet Street.

In that time, Warin had divested his attire of a priest and had swapped it with clothing that he brought with him, while Joan sat rigidly on the skiff with her back to him. She had a shameful inclination to peek at the half-naked man behind her, but resisted the temptation. How mortifying to be this wanton. This scandalous. It was all she could do to continue to stare out ahead and turn her mind to the puzzling scent in the hay.

Joan knew with certainty that she had breathed in that faintly acrid yet herbaceous scent before. But where? When?

'May I examine the sample of the hay again, please?' she said without turning around. 'And do not worry, I have not forgotten not to touch it.'

The answer came as the leather drawstring pouch flew over her head and landed at her feet. 'Be careful, Joan.'

'I shall.' She untied it and, without touching any part of it, inhaled deeply and shut her eyes, trying to place where she had last come across it. Could it be at All Hallows? En route to get to the church? Or possibly somewhere else? And then she remembered. *But of course...*

Orchards, summer breeze and the warmth of the sun on her face. That was what this evoked in her—yet it was also something that was also extremely deadly, one that she remembered of long-ago fables to warn children of its potency. Indeed, the scent she remembered was far closer than she had initially believed!

'I think I know what it might be.' She was so excited in this new discovery that she turned around only to find that Warin was tying the laces of his tunic, making her cheeks flood with warmth. The man was fully dressed, but something about what he was doing was so intimate that she could not help but gawp at him.

'You were saying?' he drawled as he put his arm through the sleeves of his padded gambeson. And even with her poor sight she knew instinctively how well he looked. How very, very attractive he was. Everything about him was raw, potent and alive. Her skin prickled as she turned her head back around.

'Oh, yes, I was, was I not?' She swallowed uncomfortably, shaking her head a little in the hope that it might clear. 'I believe I might know where I have detected that scent before.'

'You have? Where?'

She smiled. 'I shall show you, Warin. Once we reach my brother's manor.'

They disembarked and walked in silence as they reached her brother's large stone house on the edge of the Strand. Entering the arched doorway, they went inside the small courtyard and bypassed the entrance to the chambers of the house, veering around the side of the building where the kitchen was housed. Joan greeted some of the household servants and retainers as they made their way through and ambled out in the pretty kitchen garden.

'Where exactly are you taking me, Joan?'

'You shall see, but it is somewhere small and secluded.'

'Are you? I thought you were showing me a discovery of great import.' Warin grinned, producing a dimple near the left corner of his lips. Naturally she had never noticed this anomaly, but in that moment, in that light, her eyes managed to pick it up. 'I must say that it seems that you are taking me for an assignation, instead.'

'For shame, Warin,' she said in mock outrage. 'I would never think of doing such a thing.'

'No?' He raised a brow. 'My mistake then. Lead on, Joan, lead on. I find that my curiosity is roused.'

Oh, must the vexing man use such words?

Dusk had settled over the horizon, but there was just enough light for Joan to show Warin her findings. He followed her through the rose garden and walked to the furthest part of the garden, opening the gate to the apple orchard.

'There, in the hedgerow by the stonewall, you can see the flowers that must have been added to the hay once they had been dried and had the petals removed.' She smiled up at him. 'And as I said—very common and everyday flowers.'

'Dead man's bells?' he muttered absently, following the direction she had pointed to.

'Precisely.' Joan nodded. 'The foxglove.'

Warin turned to face her. 'Are you certain? Absolutely certain?'

'Yes. Sometimes when I sit beneath my favourite apple tree, yonder, the wind whips through, carrying the subtle but distinctive putrid waft. So different to, say, lavender—which happens to be my favourite flower.'

'Lavender is your favourite? That is a surprise.'

'Oh, it might be quite unremarkable to look at, but it has a gorgeous, exquisite scent and that to me is far more potent then appearances—unlike the foxglove.' She blinked, looking away. 'Besides, I would wager anyone to say that it's different to the notes in that hay. You can compare for yourself.'

'I'm sure that you are correct.' He gave her a weak smile. 'Either way it is as I feared. The cattle that the tanneries used must have been poisoned. And by a flower—an ordinary flower.'

Chapter Eleven

Warin and Joan continued to stare at the border of the last blooms of the dozen or so foxgloves that grew in the hedgerow before they wilted and died for another season.

'I find that once again I have you to thank, Joan, in my endeavours,' he muttered softly beside her. 'You, mistress, are a marvel.'

His words brought about the inevitable rush of heat, as her cheeks and face flooded with so much warmth that she thought she might well expire. Thank goodness that the fading light from the sun was now casting shadowy darkness, providing her with some measure of concealment. And thank God for these secluded corners.

'I am happy to be of help.' She shrugged. 'But do you know why someone would do such a thing? Could it be the man you pursued in Smythfeld, or that it could be something perchance related to…?'

He held up his hand. 'While these are all excellent questions, Joan, mayhap they can wait for another day?'

Ah, so Warin had no intention of further discussion

or perhaps he was intent on keeping some of his findings to himself.

'Yes, of course.' She sighed. 'But I told you that it was a common and everyday scent in the sample hay.'

'You did.' He smiled. Or rather she believed he did, since it was even harder than usual to detect such a thing, in the fading light. 'I am grateful for all your help, Joan. In truth, you never cease to amaze me.'

'Do I not?' She smoothed down the tunic, trying to damp down the beat of her raging heart. 'Mayhap I am not the usual type of woman *you* encounter either.' Joan hoped that her teasing reference to what Warin had said to his friend, Nicholas d'Amberly, earlier that day might gain her a chuckle or even a smile, however small, but no—Joan could sense that the man was brooding and had turned to look at her with such intensity that her breath caught in her throat. The tension fairly hummed between them.

'No one could ever say that you were a usual woman—whatever that might be,' he said softly.

Well, now… What had the man implied? 'I really cannot say whether you are bestowing a compliment or an insult, sir.' Again, she tried for a little mirth, a little humour.

Yet once more, Warin de Talmont watched her so intently that the fine hairs on the back of her neck stood to attention.

'You know that I would never do that,' he murmured. His voice was so low and dripping with something that Joan could not quite comprehend, but whatever it was made her toes curl in her boots. 'It would be churlish, especially after all your help.'

It was so quiet and so still in this part of the orchard that Joan could only hear the quickening of her breath.

'Yes…yes, I suppose it would.' She moistened her lips and laughed nervously. 'And it would spoil the attempts at gallantry, which you mentioned before.'

She hoped that this time the humour laced in her voice might break through the intensity, but no. And was it her imagination that he had stepped a little closer?

'Then allow me to attempt it once more.' He gently turned her by her shoulders to face him. 'And say that there is nothing ordinary, common or everyday about you, Joan Lovent.'

'Oh, then what could I be, if not ordinary?' She had meant it in jest. And as soon as the words had left her lips, she regretted uttering them, wishing that she could claim them back.

'Something infinitely more,' he said on a whisper.

How had this conversation come about? One moment she had been showing him the foxgloves that related to the nefarious substance in the sample of hay, the next…this. Not that she knew what *this* was. She was not worldly enough to understand this subtle interplay, but she understood the attraction. And oh, yes, she was certainly attracted to this man.

Indeed, the whole day Joan had felt restless, their companiable discourse fraught by the undercurrent of desire—yes, that was what it was—*desire*—which thrummed between them, punctuating every moment they spent together. And how was it possible that the very thought of Warin de Talmont now made her want to swoon? Lord only knew how she had ever thought him to be sullen and forbidding before.

'I thank you,' she murmured, tilting her head up and blinking several times. 'Although it cannot have helped that I have distracted you and imposed myself as I have done since the very first day I saw you again.'

'Yes,' he drawled softly. 'You have been very distracting.'

With that, he bent his head and kissed her. His lips were surprisingly soft against hers, slanted over them, gliding and achingly tender. Yet this kiss was her very first and Joan did not know what to do. She stood as stiff as a lance, unable to move, unable to breathe. And as if he sensed a doubt, realisation must have caught up with Warin as he stilled. He had shocked not only Joan, but seemingly himself and slowly, ever so slowly, he pulled away from her.

It was then that she knew. She knew instinctively that she couldn't end her first kiss with Warin de Talmont as if it were a mistake.

Joan wound her arms around his neck and pulled him back towards her, rising up on her tiptoes, crushing her mouth against his, so inelegantly she almost stopped to ask for instruction. Warin smiled against her lips before gentling the kiss, his mouth caressing her seductively that it brokered a pleasure so acute, it fairly sucked the breath from her body.

Joan matched him, holding on to him, following his lead and slanting her lips over his, allowing him to cover and shape them languidly. Then he did something entirely unexpected. He touched the seam of her lips with his tongue, making her gasp in surprise, and it was then that his tongue entered her mouth and slid against hers in the most sensual, most carnal way imaginable.

That was when the kiss changed altogether and became so fierce, so heated. And so deep. It sent a jolt through her as he tightened his hold around her waist, pulling her closer still. Closer so that she was pressed against the wall of his hard, sinewy body. She went willingly into the embrace, needing to be enveloped by this man, needing to be held by him, else her knees might buckle beneath her. But it was not close enough—a need grew inside her, a need that she had never known existed, to touch and slide her body against his. A need to divest them of all their clothing. Skin to skin. As one.

Heavens, but what wickedness was this? And yet at that moment Joan simply refused to care as she greedily wanted more. So much more. It seemed that she was indeed wicked and wanton.

Warin ran his fingers up and down her spine, making her shiver. He had ignited something wondrous that had caught and blazed in her veins. And she did not want it to end. This…this moment was one that made her heart sing—with a kiss so passionate and filled with so much splendour and longing.

A brilliant spark of light burst behind her closed eyes as he devoured her mouth. God, but Joan might swoon after all. Or mayhap she was drunk despite what she had claimed outside the tavern earlier. Drunk—with the intoxicating desire that threatened to claim every part of her body.

'Oh, God, Joan,' he whispered against her lips.

She opened her eyes as Warin gentled the kiss, nipping the corners of her lips, once, twice and once more, lingering before pulling away. He dropped his arms to his sides and blinked as though he were waking from a slumber before fixing his gaze on her. He stared, seemingly stunned by what had just transpired between them.

Joan perceived that his hands were shaking and he seemed to have difficulty retaining his control. She glanced away and noted the blurred fading light in the orchard, with everything around them in that moment exactly as it was before the kiss. From the pathway to the house, the orchard, the trees and thickets and even the breeze rustling through the leaves. But she knew that everything had changed irrevocably, with a kiss that was far from being ordinary and certainly not everyday. Oh, yes, her world had shifted and changed and seemed suddenly more vibrant and vital.

'God, Joan,' he said again, taking a small step back. 'I should not have done that.'

'No, I dare say *we* should not have.'

'Your brother entrusted me with your safety, Joan.'

'I know.'

'And your protection.'

'Yes, I know that, too.'

'And I have failed him. I have betrayed his trust.'

Why did she have the sudden urge to scream her frustration? 'Have you? How unfortunate.'

He ran his fingers through his hair and sighed. 'You must comprehend that this is something that I should have prevented. I had not meant to kiss you in that manner.'

'And what manner was that, pray?'

'This is no jesting matter. I lost control with...with desire.' It was somehow a relief to learn that he had felt something akin to her. 'I am afraid I forgot myself and for that I can only apologise.'

'Then so should I, Warin, because I, too, forgot myself. And how good of you to remind me of it,' she added sardonically.

Joan did not know why she was taking out her frustrations on him and yet she had not wanted to hear an apology on the back of what had ignited so quickly between them. It made the whole thing seem quite sordid.

They heard footsteps crunching on the pathway coming towards them from the main hall, stealthily. And then suddenly, whoever it was had reached them.

'Good evening, Joan, and what are you doing in the orchard by yourself?'

'Tom?' It took a moment before she realised that her brother had returned and only a moment later when she threw herself into his arms. 'It is wonderful to have you home!'

'I am pleased to see you, too, Sister.' He kissed her forehead. 'And I see that you are not alone here. Good evening, de Talmont,' he said without looking in the man's direction.

'Tom.' Warin gave him a curt nod. 'I hope your travails have proven…worthwhile.'

'They have.' Tom glanced from Warin to his sister. 'Come, I think you and I need to talk.'

Warin knew. He knew the moment that his lips touched Joan Lovent that he was doomed. He could not regret kissing her but, by God, he had been reckless. Reckless and foolish to kiss the woman in her own gardens, when anyone might have happened upon them. And they did—her damn brother of all people.

He felt extremely annoyed with himself for even allowing it to happen. It had only meant to be a chaste kiss—one that would convey his gratitude for everything that Joan had done in helping him. But then she had pulled Warin closer, kissed him back. All his senses had come alive then and he had revelled in her wild abandon. The restraint and control that he had been keeping in check since he had started escorting Joan had given way and Warin had been lost in that moment of need and desire. Now, however, he felt like an ass. A prized ass, who was about to get reprimanded by the master of the house for his very poor conduct.

Warin noted Joan's stiff spine as she walked with her head held high alongside her brother and knew that, before he spoke to Tom, he had to reassure her. She was, in all likelihood, feeling just as he. He waited behind, allowing Tom to pass through the wooden doorway, and as Joan passed through he caught her hand and squeezed it gently before releasing it as they entered Tom's private chamber adjacent to the back of the main hall. Warin had visited the chamber countless of times and usually in secret when discussing Crown work. But never with Joan.

'I believe that Brida is expecting you presently in the solar, Sister.' Tom smiled.

She hovered for a moment, opening her mouth to say something before slamming it shut. Joan then nodded curtly at her brother, ignored Warin altogether and turned on her heel to leave the room.

'Welcome back.' Warin stared at the door which Joan had just left before turning around to face Thomas Lovent, who had fetched two silver goblets and a flagon from the wooden coffer set to the side of the stone wall, beneath a large tapestry.

'My thanks. The trip with our liege lord Hubert de Burgh was, to answer you from earlier, successful—but only for now. Would you care for some wine, de Talmont?'

'Thank you, yes.' Warin took the proffered goblet from his friend, taking a huge gulp. 'What do you mean, "for now"?'

'I meant that the accusation against de Burgh for poisoning the Earl of Salisbury has all been quashed, thank the Lord. The man might have died in strange circumstances, which is still being investigated, but not by de Burgh's hands. How long this reprieve is to last—I do not know. One thing is for certain—de Burgh is gaining more and more faceless enemies hiding in the shadows.'

'It would seem so. After all, Hubert de Burgh is still the most powerful man England, so naturally many would love to see him fall from grace.'

'Indeed, and since King Henry will come of age to rule in his own right within the next few years, many are beginning to anticipate a shift in power and are conspiring against de Burgh to bring that about sooner.' Tom sipped his wine, watching Warin over the rim of the goblet. 'Speaking of which, would you like to tell me what has been going on here in London, in my absence?'

'As I said in the missive, it has been exceedingly slow gathering information. However, today, we might have made a gain.'

'I'm glad to hear it, de Talmont. What are these findings?'

'We ventured to Bermondsye earlier today and visited the main tannery there. And although they did not remember anyone fitting the description of the man with the scar involved with the Duo Dracones, they did impart some valuable information there.' Warin warmed his hands near the hearth, the fire adding some mellow light and warmth to the chamber. 'Both the hides in the tanneries and the livestock from the farmers they use have been tampered with, Tom. In the case of the bovine—they have been getting sick due to the hay being laced with a noxious substance.'

'I take it that you know what that might be?'

'We do now—it's laced with dried stems and leaves of the foxglove flora.'

'Foxglove? Are you certain?' Tom frowned as he leant forward. 'And you believe this might have something to do with the Duo Dracones?'

'I do. There are too many coincidences with the man we sought, his association with cordwainers, who are familiar with tanneries and suppliers of leather. I also saw him at Smythfeld cattle market of all places—seeking someone—an associate perhaps.'

'I see.' Tom nodded, frowning. 'It seems that there are some very dark forces at play.'

'There's more, Tom. The tanners in Bermondsye had made their complaints to the Palace of the Bishop of Winchester, which is less than an hour's journey away in Southwark, over a week ago. However, they had heard nothing until we went there, assuming we had been sent by the Bishop's palace.'

Tom sat forward. 'Now, that is interesting information.'

'Precisely—and furthermore, no one from the Palace of the Bishop has yet to visit and address their complaints.'

'We might be looking too much into this, but the enmity between the Bishop, Peter des Roches, and our lord, Hubert de Burgh, is nothing new. Yet it might also be the reason for the man's involvement in bringing down de Burgh. So it cannot be discounted either.'

'That is exactly what I thought.'

'And yet—the Bishop of Winchester being involved with the Duo Dracones? It seems so fantastical, so unfathomable. In any case, I cannot see at this time, from what you have told me about the tanners and the contamination of the supplies in the tanners' chain of produce, how any of this might be related to the Duo Dracones. None of this links together—yet.'

'We shall find out one way or another.'

'If so, then it needs to be investigated in more detail and with utmost care. The Bishop of Winchester is a powerful man, as you well know, and also has King Henry's ear.'

'You can be assured of that discretion, Tom.' Warin nodded, staring into the man's eyes. 'As always.'

'Good. And have you discussed all of this with the other members of the Order?'

'Not yet. We came here directly.'

'I see.' The man got up and poured more wine into his goblet and topped up Warin's as well. 'This leads me to the topic of my sister.' He did not take his eyes off Warin. 'Would you care to explain why you have used the word "we" so often in relation to Joan?' What was Warin supposed to say to that? However he explained this, it would still reflect poorly on him. 'Do not say that you involved my young sister in any of this?' Tom's voice was low and steely, laced with warning.

'No, not by design.'

'Not by design?' he repeated, raising a brow sardonically. 'Well, I am certain I shall sleep soundly tonight knowing that!' Tom clenched his jaw and shook his head. 'What have you done, de Talmont? Joan has never known anything about the nature of my work... our work.'

'Damn it, Tom, she is still unaware of that.'

'Is that supposed to appease me?'

'That is for you to judge.' Warin knew well and understood better where his friend's anger stemmed from, but still he refused to be cowered by it.

'For God's sake, de Talmont, I asked you to look out for my sister, not to take her on jaunts to Smythfeld and Bermondsye, involving her in the work we do!'

How in God's name had the man found out about Joan accompanying him to Smythfeld? Possibly in the usual way—from Nicholas d'Amberly and Savaric Fitz Leonard.

'Joan is willful, determined and tenacious. Short of locking her in a chamber, I had no choice but have her with me—so I could look out for her more effectively.'

'Compared to the danger she might have been exposed to, because of you, it would have been better had you locked her in a chamber. Anything but this.'

'You do not mean that, Tom. And besides, Joan would probably have found a way out anyway.'

'And what the hell were you doing in the furthest part of my garden, alone with my sister at twilight?'

'That,' Warin said, bristling at the implication, 'is none of your business.'

'Oh, on the contrary, de Talmont. It is very much my

business. I am Joan's guardian and I take that responsibility very serious.'

'That is good to know, but Joan is a woman grown.'

'You are talking about my young innocent sister, de Talmont,' he growled.

'Who is no longer a child, Lovent.'

The men stared at each other, neither blinking, before Tom shook his head and looked away.

'Joan is a remarkable, beautiful woman. Intuitive and exceedingly clever.' Warin had to stop himself there. God knew he could heap far more superlatives to describe Joan Lovent.

'True, but she is also impressionable and tender-hearted.' He sighed deeply. 'You should not have involved her, Warin.'

No, he knew implacably that he should not have. From the first time when he had encountered Joan Lovent in the dirt and filth of the city's streets to their journey to Bermondsye today, he had known that truth. And yet… Warin also knew how much he had wanted to spend time in her company despite knowing it was wrong to. This attraction between them could lead nowhere. Nevertheless, he wanted to talk to her, smile with her. God knew how much she eased the loneliness, a heady balm in his damn miserable life. He was drawn to Joan in a way that knocked the breath out of him.

'I know, Tom, but it was unintentional. It is also worth noting that, without her, we would not have made any progress. It was because of Joan that we now have the intelligence relating to the hay and the foxglove. It was because of her that we made the connection to the tanneries in the first place.'

'I see, so you have used her for more mercenary reasons.'

'Damn you, no!' Warin clenched his hands into fists, dropping them to his sides. 'What do you think of me?'

'Someone who has taken liberties with my sister.' Tom's lips twisted into an unfamiliar grimace. 'You are lucky that I consider you a friend, Warin, otherwise you would be facing the end of my sword.'

He knew that Tom was justified in his reaction and he knew that if he had a sister, he would be just as upset having found them together as Tom had.

'Then I am thankful for small mercies.' Warin smiled faintly. 'Although I would certainly give you a good fight.'

'I am certain you would.' He raised his goblet to him. 'But you must understand that I would always protect my sister's honour.'

'And I would expect nothing less, Tom, but there is really no need.' Warin sighed deeply, running his hand through his hair in frustration. 'I care about Joan.'

There was a punctuated silence permeating in the chamber before Thomas Lovent spoke after a long moment.

'Is that so?' Tom said quietly, taking another sip of wine. 'And do you mean to court her, then?' That stunned Warin into silence. He simply had no answer. As much as he longed to spend time with Joan and as much as he could not deny the strength of his attraction to her—even though it shocked him to his core—it was not enough. Warin would never marry again. And Thomas Lovent knew that for certainty. He nodded at him. 'Just as I thought.'

Warin opened his mouth to say more, to defend himself, but really there was nothing more he could do or say that might restore some semblance of equanimity here. He had to leave and cease this connection with Joan Lovent.

'If that is all, then I think I shall take my leave.'

'We shall talk again, Warin, but mayhap not here.'

'No.' Thomas Lovent evidently knew it was best to sever all ties with his sister as well. At least they both knew where they stood. 'Until the morrow.'

Warin left the chamber, feeling wretched with a visceral need to smash his fists into a jagged wall of stone—God, but he would gladly welcome the pain.

He exhaled through his teeth, as his eyes caught a movement in the shadows outside Tom's private chamber and knew instantly who would be there.

Chapter Twelve

Warin crossed his arms across his chest. 'I suppose you heard all of that?'

Joan Lovent stepped out from the darkness and tipped her head up. 'How could you tell it was me?'

That made him smile. 'Because it is you and I know *you*, Joan. I know the way you move and even the very scent of you,' he murmured, stepping closer. Was it his imagination or had she flushed? It was difficult to say since the only light provided was flickering in the sconce. 'It is what you have taught me, after all, to comprehend more than just what I see before me—even in this poor light.'

'If that is so, then I am glad that I have provided a parting gift.'

'Ah, Joan.' He brushed the back of his hand against her cheek, revelling in the softness. 'If only...if only I had more to offer.'

*Someone as wonderful as you...*he stopped himself from adding.

She licked her lips absently, making them glisten in the light. His eyes dropped to them—to that small movement. Warin only needed to bend his head a little and their lips would meet, they would catch and ignite with that slow burning need once more, taking them to a place where they could not go. He wanted to feel her again in his arms—to feel her lush body pressed against his. Joan might be slowly breaking through his defences, thawing the wall of ice that encased his heart, but he had to resist everything about her. There was simply no other alternative.

'But I... I...'

'No, do not say anything,' he whispered, placing a finger against her lips.

He shut his eyes and breathed deeply, breathing her in.

For as long as he could remember he had wrapped his heart with guilt and bitterness, not allowing anyone to get close in case they, too, were taken from him—just like his wife and child. God, he could not think about them without feeling the shame of his failures wash over him.

There was nothing for it other than to retreat because even the possibility of losing another was unconscionable. He had always been so careful, so impenetrable, and yet this perceptive, beautiful woman with long, untamed strawberry-blonde hair who kissed with a wild fervour had somehow forced her way through his defences and made him forget the vows he had made. That after Ada and their child had been found with slits through their throats, he would never be found so utterly wanting. By the time he had rushed back to England, all those years ago, they had long been buried. They had long been gone. And although Warin had eventually caught the perpetrators it had not been enough. He could not bring them back.

And it was this very reason why he had decided to make it his life's pursuit in finding adversaries and bringing them to justice and it was why he wanted to give his life in service to the Crown. And everything that had happened earlier had been a timely reminder of what he owed the very people he had loved and lost. No, he could not lose sight of that. Not again.

He opened his eyes and took her hand and bowed over it. 'It has been an honour, mistress.'

And with that he turned and strode away. It was for the best—indeed, to be without any dependents, without forming any attachments. That was the only way for him to live.

Joan stood there for a moment in the hallway outside her brother's private chamber, unable to move. Unable to breathe. What had just happened on this night? In fact, this day and night had gone from the thrill and excitement of venturing to areas of London unfamiliar to her—from London Bridge, the tavern and meeting Warin's friends, playing drunk, and then to the tanneries in Bermondsye, where she had been an integral part of uncovering pieces of a puzzle...*for him.*

'Without her, we would not have made any progress. It was because of Joan that we now have the intelligence relating to the hay and the foxglove. It was because of her that we made the connection to the tanneries in the first place.'

She had done it, all of it, because she had wanted to be of use to Warin and spend time in his company. Outside of her brother and his family, along with the clergy and children at All Hallows, she had never had anyone else to call a friend—even if she felt far more for him than she would a friend. In truth, Joan had never known anyone who had paid any addresses to her or even wanted to get to know and understand who she was—except for Warin de Talmont.

He had been the one bright light in her dull, drab life and she had wanted to hold on to that ray of hope, however brief it might have been. Not that she had considered that it would be this brief, this transient.

Joan's eyes filled with tears as she pondered whether the man had just bid her a farewell—for good? Is that what he had meant with his parting words? She felt sick to the stomach at the thought that she might never see Warin again. Or if she did, that it would be fleeting and formal.

Yet mayhap everything that had transpired between them, every passing smile, glance, thrill of attraction and desire had been in her own head. Mayhap he had been resolute to be only just a friend, looking out for and protecting her, doing her brother's bidding while he had been away. And now that Tom had arrived back in London, it would no longer be necessary to spend time together or even for Warin to escort her to All Hallows, as he had done.

God, but she felt empty.

Even that incredible kiss earlier had been initially given in thanks, had it not, since she had managed to help him with his investigations? And it was she who had pressed her body to his. It was she who had pressed her lips to his once he had pulled away, hoping in vain that it would not end. It was Joan who had been wanton, enticing him, and he had reacted exactly how she had expected. Heavens, but he had even been the one who had the foresight to end the kiss before they fell into something far deeper.

Oh, God, how mortifying. And yet Warin's words to her brother confirmed that he did indeed care for her.

'Joan is a remarkable, beautiful woman. Intuitive and exceedingly clever.'

And he had also admitted to the same desire that had run through her veins and had plagued her.

The door of Tom's chamber opened and her brother walked into the hallway.

'Joan? Are you still here?'

'Evidently, Brother.' Her eyes stung then.

'Why have you not gone to Brida? Why have you remained in the darkness?'

She felt a chill run down her spine. 'Because I am always in the darkness, Tom. It is where I belong, after all.' Even to her own ears, her voice was flat and impassive.

'Hell's teeth, Joan, are your eyes hurting you? Have you exerted yourself too much? Where is your walking staff? Come, take my hand and I shall escort you to your solar.'

'Stop it, Tom. Stop!' She sunk her teeth into her bottom lip to prevent the sudden need to weep. 'Can you not comprehend that I feel so stifled? Can you not understand that sometimes I feel so…*smothered*? I am going blind, Tom—blind! And I have had no choice but to reconcile myself to that certainty many years ago. I have gone through the tears, the pain and the heartache of knowing all that I would come to one day lose, but that does not mean that I need to be cosseted as though I am invalid. I could not bear *that*.'

She knew that she had shocked her brother with this

outburst that he did not deserve and for a moment he seemed too stunned to say anything.

'Have I done that to you, Joan? Have I made you feel as such? Because all I have ever wanted is your well-being and happiness.'

'And I am grateful for it. I know that there are many, many people in my situation, Tom, who do not have the support and love of a brother as generous as you. I am indeed fortunate. However, Warin is right, I am a woman—grown.'

'I do know, Sister.'

'I am glad, because I also have the same hopes that other women have and while I am eternally grateful to have a home with you and Brida—this is your family and your home.'

'Oh, Joan.' He cradled her cheek. 'It will always be yours as well. You must know that you are part of this household.'

'And I thank you for it, but that does not stop me, sometimes, from wanting my own. Even if it is hopeless and futile for a woman with my condition.'

'If it is Warin de Talmont who has inspired such reflections, you must know that he will never marry again.'

'I know.'

'Although it seems that he does care for you.'

'I know that, too.'

'God's breath, Joan, I am sorry.' Tom reached for her and she went to him and did not care that she was crying, something she had not done in years. 'I cannot countenance anything happening to you. Neither can I stand by and watch you get hurt. I made a vow a long time ago that that would never happen again, not…not like before. And I always keep my promises.'

Joan knew how her brother had suffered and had been so consumed with guilt because he had not been there when their family had perished in the fire that started in their small manor, when Joan was the sole survivor. He had made an oath on everything that was holy that that would never happen again—and he would always be there to protect and safeguard her.

'I should not have allowed myself to get close to him.'

Joan felt foolish now for allowing her heart to be open—it had made her far too exposed and vulnerable.

Tom sighed. 'Warin is one of the most honourable and steadfast men I know—I would trust him with my life. He would have had my blessing in a heartbeat if he were to court you, Joan. But he has been resolute that he will never marry again.'

'I know,' she whispered.

'Then it would be best if you forgot him.'

Yes, mayhap it would. It would be best if she did not see or think of the man again and then, in time, forget him in earnest.

Joan discovered, however, that it was not as easy as she had envisaged it might be to forget Warin de Talmont. Her journeys to All Hallows in the following week, on which she was now accompanied by her brother, were far more solitary affairs even though she tried to paste a smile on her face and behave as though all was well with her. Yet her insides were in knots and she could barely eat or concentrate on any given task properly. At least her brother had now reluctantly accepted her patronage to All Hallows and even supported her, although he still had reservations about her choice of church being so far from home and within the city gates.

Joan had believed that if she ceased seeing Warin that it might help her forget him more easily, but discovered, instead, that she missed him all the more. Her head was heavy, her eyes felt somewhat sore and her heart ached terribly. Yet she could not understand her own reaction to any of it.

She felt bereft and restless, without any real notion of why she was so affected. It was not as though Warin had made her any promises and it was not as though they had formed any real lasting attachments. She had not even spent a length of time in his company, so why did she feel so befuddled and confused? Even if Tom had not found her alone with Warin deep in the orchard and having just kissed one another senseless, it was always inevitable that *this* would be the outcome.

She lifted her head in the courtyard of the All Hallows Church and ushered the last few remaining children into the small chamber in the timber outbuilding at the back that doubled as a small teaching room, where the children could sit and listen to the gospels.

Joan turned at the sound of footsteps behind her and recognised that her brother, Tom, had arrived far earlier than he usually did.

'What an unexpected surprise!' Joan exclaimed, her lips curling upwards. 'What are you doing here?'

'I thought to provide you with yet another surprise, if you would care for it.' He bent his head and kissed her on her forehead.

'Oh? What do have in mind?'

'Well, since Brida is close to her confinement and unable to leave the house, I wondered whether you would accompany me to the Tower? The Royal Court is in residence and it might offer a little amusement, a little diversion, do you not think? That is if you can be spared from here for the remainder of the day?'

Diversion indeed! This could be just the thing for Joan to occupy her mind elsewhere—in the pomp and splendour of the Royal Court. Tom had never taken her to any such occasion, fearing that it might overwhelm her with so many people, sounds and distractions. And yet ever since her outburst outside his private chamber over a week ago, he was trying to be far more accommodating, far more understanding and patient. He never spoke of Warin or the nature of their work, which Joan now knew dwelt with unsavoury secrets, not to mention dangerous work for the Crown. Not that she spoke to him about that.

'I am certain I can be spared and would happily accompany you to the Tower. However, I do not think I am correctly attired for such an occasion, Tom.'

'Never fear, Sister.' He winked, grinning and dropping the large sack at her feet. 'I come duly prepared.'

'Oh…oh…' She shook her head in disbelief. 'In that case, I'd be delighted. This is indeed a very welcome surprise, thank you.'

Joan dressed in haste and wore a simple linen veil with a simple silver circlet on top, holding the sheer material in place, and rushed to meet Tom outside. From there he, along with a few of the household servants, escorted her through the narrow streets east of the city, making their way to the White Tower set within a moat near the edge of the River Thames.

They meandered across the drawbridge and the imposing Cold Harbour Gatehouse, which was heavily guarded as would be expected with the Royal party in residence. From there they strolled into the innermost wall and into the inner bailey of the Great Tower, with such stark whitewashed masonry that it was commonly known as the 'White Tower'. They walked in silence along the narrow, cobbled pathway that led to the tall, majestic tower with four turrets above the battlements.

'He will not be there, Joan, if you are concerned that he might.' She almost stumbled at the mere mention of Warin de Talmont for the first time in over a week.

'Who can you mean?' Joan knew it was petty to act as though she had not thought of the man every hour of the day. Yet she did have her dignity to think of. And she would rather have her brother believe that she had been far more successful at forgetting him than was actually true.

'Warin de Talmont. He has work outside of London to attend to, so you do not have to be concerned that you might encounter him here.'

'Oh, Tom, I had not given him a thought.' She smiled, hoping that she had convinced him of the lie. 'But I hope that Sir Warin is not in any danger?'

'No, he is a very experienced soldier, Joan. There's no need to worry.' Her brother returned a smile so similar to her own that she wondered whether he, too, had been bending the truth. Mayhap she might glean a little more regarding his situation later.

'Very well,' she muttered, tilting her head to the side. 'Shall we?'

She placed her hand in the crook of her brother's arm as they continued towards the Tower.

Warin glanced around the banqueting hall above the state apartments in the White Tower, wondering when he might be afforded an audience with both Hubert de Burgh and Thomas Lovent. Both men were due to arrive at the Tower imminently and the sooner he could confer with them the easier he might feel. He had arrived back in London much sooner than expected and, after a quick wash and change of clothes at his own lodgings, he had made his way to the White Tower so that he could impart the important information that he had discovered. And it could not wait as it usually did. No, it was imperative that they were notified urgently, so as to consider their next move.

He caught the eye of a courtier or two he recognised and bowed his head in greeting as more and more people gathered, awaiting the arrival of the young King Henry in this exalted chamber with the imposing, high-vaulted ornate ceilings and large arched windows running along the length of the room. Huge pillars of painted wooden columns soared to the ceiling on either side of the central entrance with the standard of King Henry draped between every archway.

Warin inhaled deeply and exhaled slowly, as though he were catching his breath properly for the first time that week. The mad rush to acquire any information about the tanners in relation to the Duo Dracones along with the other members of the Knights Fortitude meant that they had left, venturing far and wide to many vicinities outside of London to look for evidence that could tie their findings together. He hoped that they, too, would arrive back soon, so that they could assemble at their usual meeting place. And with all the excessive amount of work that had engaged much of Warin's time recently, he had had little time to think of anything else. Thank the saints.

It had been over a week since Warin had been caught with Joan Lovent in her brother's orchard. And it had been over a week since he had thought of her. In truth, every time his mind strayed to all that had transpired both that day and, more importantly, that eventide, Warin had stopped himself. He had to, else he would go mad. He knew that he could go through the same experience again and again, but still come against the same difficulties. Of wanting her but knowing it could never come to anything. In truth, it would be best to keep from seeing Joan and hope that in time he would leave the memory of her behind.

He stepped to the side and smoothed his blue woollen gambeson down with one hand before running his fingers through his hair, hoping that his rushed appearance might pass muster.

A troupe of musicians stood in the small gallery above, heralding the arrival of the Royal Court in the Tower, making the hum of the assembled courtiers gradually quieten. Warin darted his eyes in every direction, hoping that Tom would also soon arrive. And just then the man did appear—he walked through the arched doorway accompanied by a young woman. A young woman who would, naturally, be no other but—Joan Lovent.

Chapter Thirteen

Warin had not been prepared to see Joan Lovent again so soon and here at the White Tower of all the unexpected places. The sight of her knocked the breath out of him—in truth, he felt as though someone had punched him hard in the stomach. But by God, what a welcome sight she was. She looked a little shy, a little unsure stood beside her brother, clutching his arm with a tentative smile playing at her lips. And she wore an expensive purple velvet kirtle tied over a long-sleeved tunic, with her long, silky hair drawn beneath a sheer cream veil, topped with a silver circlet.

Joan's appearance was no less than any of the other courtiers present here. If anything, she was the most beautiful woman he had encountered within this chamber and God knew he had never seen her looking so exquisite and captivating. Warin smiled inwardly, realising that he had not been the only man who had taken notice of the alluring woman.

'Ah, I can see just where you are looking, my friend,' a voice said from behind his shoulder. A voice Warin knew instantly belonged to Nicholas d'Amberly.

'So, you have returned from your…errand as well then, d'Amberly?' Warin muttered without taking his eyes off Joan in the distance. She was, it seemed, being introduced by Tom to many of the people in attendance.

'I have and just in time to make merry here.'

'Quite.'

'Here, take this.' D'Amberly sidled up beside Warin, passing him a mug of ale. 'To your good health.'

'And to yours.' Their mugs clanged before they each took a sip of their ale. 'Did you have much luck with your endeavours?'

'I believe so. Some interesting information has come to light.'

Warin nodded. 'Good. Once Fitz Leonard has also returned to London, we must all compare our findings. But before that, I must seek an audience with Tom and Hubert de Burgh.'

Nicholas flicked his eyes from Warin to Joan and then back again, shaking his head. 'Are you certain that there are no others whom you wish to seek an audience with?'

'I cannot know what you mean, d'Amberly.'

'Can you not?' The man beside him sighed as they drank their ale. 'I would leave well alone there, my friend. Tom Lovent would not appreciate your pursuit of his sister, knowing that you would never seriously court her.'

A muscle leapt in his jaw. 'You are mistaken, I assure you.'

'If that is the case, then you have my unreserved apology. But, Warin, take heed of my warning.'

'There is no need, I promise you.' There was every

need and for Warin it was another reminder that while he might appreciate and delight in seeing Joan again from afar, that was all it could ever be between them. Besides, he had more important business to attend to, which he had to accomplish as soon as might be. 'Come, d'Amberly, we need to make Tom Lovent aware of our arrival.'

They made their way across the magnificent, long banqueting hall and approached Tom, who stood beside Joan.

'Good day to you, Tom, and to you, Mistress Joan.' Warin bowed, keeping his eyes fixed on Joan, whom he noticed had stiffened on hearing his voice. She quickly looked away and chatted with someone beside her.

'Ah, so you have managed to get back to London earlier then I had anticipated, de Talmont. And I see that you are also here, d'Amberly.'

Was it his imagination or was Thomas Lovent somewhat irked by their presence there? It was certainly true that Warin had not expected to be back in London, but circumstances made it possible for him to return sooner. 'Indeed, and there lies the very reason why I rode back so expediently.' He leant forward and whispered, 'I need to confer with both you and our liege lord, Hubert de Burgh.'

'Can it not wait until the morrow?'

'No, Tom.' He flicked his gaze briefly at Joan, who now had her eyes pinned to the ground, and shook his head. 'It cannot.'

'Very well,' Tom hissed. 'We shall speak soon.'

The high-pitched sound of the buisine trumpets heralded the arrival of King Henry and his entourage. He walked ahead, with Hubert de Burgh following a step behind, in regal splendour from the entrance of the long chamber to the ornately carved wooden king's seat set on a raised dais at the far end of the room, which was not so dissimilar to the one at Westminster Hall.

They stood in a line and Warin found himself standing awkwardly between Joan on one side and her brother on the other. He shifted across as someone jostled against him, which naturally meant that he was now standing far too close to Joan. Her shoulder and arm touched his, as they stood side by side, sending a frisson of awareness through him. The back of his hand brushed against Joan's, inadvertently, and he left his hand there, touching the back of hers. God, but her skin was so delicate, so soft compared with his, but that was not what surprised Warin. What made his pulse hitch and then quicken was that she did not remove her hand as he had expected. It seemed that she, too, craved this small contact.

He closed his eyes, allowing the moment to stretch while he savoured the small pleasure of this touch. Feeling emboldened, he hooked her little finger with his, and opened his eyes staring out ahead. Again, she allowed the touch, allowed this intimacy of the caress. Warin let out a shaky breath and realised just in time that the King had made his way down to their assembled line. Just as quickly, Warin let go of her finger, untangling himself from her touch.

King Henry acknowledged his subjects as they bowed and curtsied as he passed by. He reached their assembled group and paused, helping Joan rise up from a deep curtsy.

'This must be your sister, Sir Thomas?' he asked.

'It is, Sire.' Tom dipped his head. 'May I present Mistress Joan Lovent?'

'Indeed, and it is my pleasure, mistress,' the King murmured, tilting his head. 'I am happy to make your acquaintance.'

'I am honoured, Sire.' Joan kept her head bent low, demurely earning a small smile from King Henry, who nodded his appreciation before turning and continuing to walk to the King's bench and seat. He climbed the steps of the dais before turning around with a flourish and sat down with the Royal party following suit, filling the seats around their young sovereign.

The silence that had filled the chamber was broken with a sudden hum and chatter of noise. Joan seemed abashed and stunned that the King had taken the time to speak to her. And yet that did not surprise Warin— she did not see herself the way others did, nor did she have any comprehension of how alluring, how utterly captivating she was. It was one of the many aspects that he liked most about her—how unaware and unassuming she was about her unique charm.

Tom stepped away to have a brief word with Hubert de Burgh, who was on the King's right side, and returned back with a frown etched across his face.

'I have been summoned for a parley with de Burgh before we can all convene with him together,' he muttered from the side of his mouth.

Warin made a single nod. 'Very well, I await your request for my presence.'

'Good.' Tom seemed reticent about leaving his sister with Warin and d'Amberly. What the devil did Tom Lovent think he would do? Drag Joan somewhere dark and inconspicuous, so that he could make an assignation with her? Ravish her?

He glanced from Warin to Joan, eventually making a decision. 'I hope I can rely on you to tend to my sister?'

'As always,' Warin hissed. His jaw was so unyielding and brittle that he felt it might break.

Tom scowled at him, a small warning hidden in the depths of his eyes as he passed Joan her walking staff before leaving to meet de Burgh. 'Come and meet us shortly, de Talmont.'

Warin made a single nod and glanced at Joan, who looked away.

'Well, is this not pleasant?' D'Amberly beamed. 'To be together again, in such convivial surroundings?'

'I shall have to take your word for it, Sir Nicholas,' came her rejoinder.

'Then allow me to say more, Mistress Joan.'

'Must you?' Warin groaned as his friend continued to seemingly ignore him.

'Oh, yes.' He caught Joan's hand and bowed over it. 'I must convey what a real delight it is to finally see you in such feminine attire.'

'You really are such a tease, Sir Nicholas.' Had Joan just giggled at that nonsense? 'You should, in truth, not notice such things.'

'No, d'Amberly should not,' Warin ground out, wanting to add that only *he* should.

'That might be so, mistress, but you look so charming—in fact, I would wager that there is no one here who is equal to your beauty.' He flashed a grin. 'Do you not agree, Warin?'

One day, mayhap sooner that he'd expect, Nicholas

d'Amberly might find himself murdered, very slowly at his hands.

'Yes…yes, I do.' Warin's eyes grazed her from head to toe. 'You look very fine indeed, Joan.'

Her face flooded with colour. 'Thank you,' she mumbled, lifting her head and looking in his direction. Warin wondered, not for the first time, whether she could discern the depth of his feelings. The very same emotions he had difficulty tempering.

'Would you care for some wine, mistress?' Nicholas said, breaking the quietness of that moment. 'If memory serves, ale might not…er, quite agree with you.'

'Yes, I thank you. I find that I am in need of light refreshment.'

'Then allow me to fetch you a mug, Joan.' Warin started to move, wanting a moment to gather himself together and still his beating heart. He returned a little later, bearing Joan's wine and feeling a little more composed.

'Here, Joan.' As he passed the mug of wine, his fingers grazed hers—his hand wrapped over hers and once again he felt powerless with the strength of yearning that soared through his blood. That simple, sudden need for her touch. Whatever composure he had mustered flickered away in that moment and he felt just as disconcerted as before.

He removed his hand and let it drop to his side. 'I shall take my leave for now. I must see Tom,' he said gruffly and, with that, he walked away.

Warin found Tom Lovent and Hubert de Burgh in a small private chamber, manned by a couple of their liege's own household guards.

'Ah, good to have your company, de Talmont. What news?' De Burgh nodded over the rim of his goblet. 'Thomas, here, informs that you and the rest of the Order might possibly have made some progress?'

'Yes, my lord, I believe we might. Although Fitz Leonard has yet to arrive back and I do not know what d'Amberly has uncovered yet, I doubt, however, that it would be too dissimilar to what I have discovered.' He glanced over at Tom and frowned before continuing. 'Unfortunately, the pattern of disturbances at tanneries and contamination of cattle fodder that we found in Bermondsye is being repeated everywhere from the information that is being gathered.'

'How far-reaching is this?' Tom asked.

'From the inventories of every tannery and cattle farm that we have approached—from the workers to the lords, stewards and bailiffs, whom we have managed to gather information from, and based on their concerns and complaints—I would wager it is as far-reaching as it can be.'

'But to what end?' de Burgh said in frustration. 'I do not comprehend why this is happening.'

'There are many reasons. For one thing it undermines the Barons and lords, their ploughmen and farmers as well as tanneries and merchants and their livelihood to produce the vital commodity of leather.'

Tom grimaced. 'Which will eventually affect the City of London itself. A highly effective way to use merchants to attack the heart of the Crown and diminish its revenue—through trade.'

'Yes, and it would drive the cost of leather up, meaning that many trade guilds will have no choice but to resort to importing leather from France and elsewhere.'

De Burgh scratched his head. 'But I cannot recall from my bailiffs that this has been a problem on any of my lands.'

Warin and Tom exchanged an uneasy look. 'That is what the Order has been speculating, my lord.'

'And it might also be the point of all of this,' Tom added.

'I do not understand. Do you believe that I might somehow be the intended target for whatever nefarious reason?'

'Yes, my lord,' Warin muttered. 'I think this might be another way to implicate you as the person responsible for all their recent misfortune. Only recently you were suspected of poisoning the Earl of Salisbury and had to rush to that part of the county and quash the rumours.' Warin sighed, shaking his head. 'It seems that this might be yet another attack on your person. And this time, the finger of blame will point directly at you.'

'God's blood! But how and why?'

'It could be that whoever is behind the Duo Dracones wants to diminish your absolute power and authority.'

'As well as the close affinity you have with the young King.'

'Think about it, my lord—what do you believe would happen when more and more noblemen realise that while their lands are affected with this serious problem, yours still prospers?'

'They would blame me.'

'As would the merchants. They would believe that

you instigated this situation for your own gain and for profit while weakening them.'

Hubert de Burgh muttered an oath under his breath and threw his hands in the air. 'Then what in the saint's name are we to do?'

'For one thing, we do not reveal what we know—not to anyone.'

'And for another, we secretly approach every affected ploughman and farmer and make them aware that they have to throw out everything that is contaminated and start again with fresh hay for their cattle and recompense them for their losses. As for the tanners—they must be vigilant and limit access and have guards posted around their sites—which we can help implement, as well.'

Tom nodded in agreement. 'It will take time and resources, but it should eventually work effectively, my lord.'

Hubert de Burgh looked from one to the other. 'Very well, but in that time I want the bastards responsible for all of this.'

'Yes, my lord.'

Warin returned back to the chamber and darted his gaze, finding Joan chatting happily with Nicholas d'Amberly. His chest clenched tightly and he took a deep breath as he made his way back towards them.

'Ah, there you are.' D'Amberly smiled inanely at him. 'Now I will leave you, mistress, in the care of de Talmont for a moment or so. Try not to pine for me too much.'

'I'm not sure how I shall survive the loss of your company, Sir Nicholas.'

'Never fear, mistress, I shall be back in no time.' He winked at Joan, damn him. 'In the meantime, de Talmont here, who is known for his courtly charm, will tend to you.'

Warin exhaled and moved to stand beside Joan, looking around the great chamber. The silence that stretched between them was inexorably painful, thanks to the ridiculous situation they now found themselves. How could he have been so reckless? How had he allowed matters to get away from him as much as this? It all seemed so inconceivable for someone as steadfast and single-minded as him to be this overwhelmed by *feelings*, for the love of God! Feelings for Joan Lovent that he had to suppress and discard. Still, he could hardly ignore her or remain quiet in her presence.

'I hope you have been keeping well, mistress,' he muttered eventually.

'Yes, thank you. I hope you have as well, sir.' Her voice was quietly reserved. 'My brother tells me that you were out of the city.'

'Indeed. And now I am back.'

Well, this was awkward.

'Yes, so you are.'

A man accidentally pushed into Joan, for which he stopped to apologise, but it did make her stumble and slip. Warin reached out to assist her, but she did not need him—she did not want his assistance. Using her walking staff, Joan felt her way around, grappling to right herself with as much dignity as she could muster.

He dropped his outstretched hand and stepped towards her. 'Here, lean on my arm.'

'No, I can manage, thank you.'

'Very well.' He moved around her to act as shield should any other fool think to get too raucous and clumsy and shove into her again.

Warin scanned the room and this time he noticed a nuanced change with the gathered courtiers, who openly stared at Joan. They had been inquisitive to know more about the woman on whom the young King had bestowed his admiration only a short while ago. But now with the realisation that not all was as it seemed with Joan, their curiosity bordered on macabre fascination. He had a sudden urge to protect her from these people. They posed far more of a danger than any persons who might make her stumble and fall accidentally. Warin could not help but get angry on her behalf with this change—this sudden intrusive interest in her. It was repugnant.

Could she not sense it—their censure? Their pity wrapped in something that felt far more akin to scorn. God, but Warin wanted to grab the hilt of his sword and take up arms against anyone who meant her harm and he would do it, too, in a heartbeat. Instead, Warin dropped his arm to his side and clenched and unclenched his hand. Tom should not have brought her here. He should not have allowed her to be exposed to these people's ridicule.

'Why are you here, Joan?'

'I beg your pardon?' She blinked in surprise.

'I asked why you had come to court?'

'And why should I not?'

'For many reasons.'

She exhaled through her teeth, irritably. 'Tell me, Sir

Warin, are you asking or accusing me of something? Either way I believe that you forget yourself.'

He raised a brow. 'Do I, now?'

'Yes. I did not come here in a vain hope that I might encounter you, if that is where your anger stems from.'

'That is not the reason. I know that you could not have known I would be here, Joan.'

'I am glad because I do not answer to you, Sir Warin, and it is not your concern why I have come to court for the first time,' she hissed. 'Mayhap I wanted to be among more enlightened people who are not so afraid of living.'

He narrowed his eyes. 'I suppose that is your assessment of me?'

'If it is, then it will have no effect on you. After all, I am only someone to escort, watch over and make sure doesn't fall over into the rushes.'

'And you find fault in that?'

'No, but mayhap I want to be among those who would not be ashamed to be seen in my presence.'

He was stunned for a moment into silence before he spoke again. 'You would believe that of me? That I would be ashamed to be seen with you?'

Joan worried her lips before eventually answering, 'No...no, I don't.' She rubbed her forehead. 'But then why should I not have the privilege of being here? Am I not worthy to be here among the Royal Court?'

He caught her wrist. 'You are worthy of far more, Joan Lovent.'

She shook her head and pulled her wrist from his grasp. 'Then why should my presence here be an issue? I do not comprehend you.'

What could he say that would not insult her further? Mayhap something that would pull her quick intelligence away from the truth. 'Your presence here poses a risk when your brother and I have other matters to attend to.'

'As I said, neither Tom nor I knew that you would be present here, otherwise…otherwise I might have declined my brother's invitation. But do not worry, Sir Warin, Tom shall return shortly and, once he does, I doubt that I shall pose any further risk to you, or anyone else for that matter.'

God, but was it possible that he had given more offence to this woman then he already had? 'That is not what I meant, Joan. Only that it would be prudent for you to be vigilant and not expose yourself to any danger.'

'Here?' Her brows furrowed in the middle in confusion. 'At court? You jest.'

'I wish that I was,' he muttered under his breath.

Joan's countenance changed all at once, her eyes filled with confusion that gave way to surprise and then settled on amazement.

Hell's teeth, not again.

Warin groaned, knowing that he had once again piqued her interest into his affairs. Her brother would want his head for this and mayhap he would be right to do so.

'That is very interesting.'

Oh, God help him…

'I believe I misunderstood your concerns, but never mind that now.' She leant in a little closer. 'I have made a finding myself, but did not have the opportunity to mention it to my brother.' She lifted her head, her eyes filled with concern, but also with excitement. 'Although, had I revealed it to Tom, I fear he might have taken me back home.'

'What is it, Joan?'

'At some point after I was made many introductions, I believe…in truth, I know that I smelled a familiar scent. The same notes as the hay in the Bermondsye tannery—the slightly sweet, yet decaying scent of the foxglove flora.'

'Are you certain that it was here? Within this chamber?'

She nodded. 'I am.'

'Yes.' He nodded slowly. 'That is very interesting.'

Chapter Fourteen

Joan might not be able to see Warin's face clearly as it gradually became animated and alert with the news that she had just imparted, but she could certainly sense it. All at once they could fall back on being comfortable in one another's presence with the familiar comradery they had shared as they unravelled this mystery. As long as Joan did not forget that this was all it could ever be between them. In any case, she would rather have this then the uncomfortable silence that prevailed earlier. God, but that had been excruciatingly awkward and unnerving. One moment Warin had been touching her hand, with the astonishing intimacy it evoked in the hall, the next he was hostile and cold, behaving in a manner unbefitting a man of his standing.

'When did you encounter the scent again, Joan?'

She frowned, trying to recall when it had been. Oh, yes, they had just arrived and she had pondered on the glorious smells wafting from the kitchens and then…

She snapped her head up. 'It was when we first entered this chamber. I had not thought of it at the time, as I was a little nervous since this was my first visit at Court. And then I saw you, which made me far more apprehensive, but for good reason because frankly you were not pleased to be in my company...'

'Not true, Joan.' His voice seemed a little bemused. 'But please proceed—you were saying that something took your notice when you first entered?'

'Precisely.' She nodded. 'It was only when I was still a little annoyed that you believed I should not have come to Court because I seemed out of place to you that I suddenly remembered something that really was... out of place.'

'The scent of the foxglove flora?'

'Yes.'

'And do you remember the person or persons that might have carried the scent?'

'I am afraid not.' She shook her head in resignation. 'It was the scent that was left in their wake, so, no, I cannot recall the person.'

'I understand.' Warin rubbed his chin. 'This is really important, Joan, but do you think you might be able to detect it again, if we hunted for the scent?'

A slow smile spread on her lips, as the court musicians began to play. 'What do you have in mind, sir?'

It had been truly incredible to Joan how this day was panning out. One moment she had been so nervous, so apprehensive about being at Court, but before she knew what had happened, she had suddenly come face to face with Warin again, with the subsequent feelings of anger that he inspired. And now unexpectedly the man had his arms around her, leading her to a dance. *A dance*…of all things!

Joan could not remember the last time she had danced, but mayhap not since she had been a child. But to dance and move in time to music especially here at court while being held by a man—and not just any man, but Warin de Talmont—well, no, *that* she had never done.

A bubbling mixture of trepidation and excitement rushed through her. She told herself that it wasn't because she harboured this closeness with Warin—no, she had to put those feelings to rest, once and for all.

'Concentrate, Joan,' Warin muttered in her ear from behind as he wrapped one arm around her waist and the other outstretched, with his hand clasping hers gracefully in the air. 'Listen to the music, listen to the beat and allow me to lead you along the floor that has been cleared for this very purpose.' They moved effortlessly, slowly, two steps forward and three steps back, a twirl with their arms entwined in a circle and around once more.

'You're being far too rigid, Joan,' he said in the low voice that sent a shiver through her. 'Soften your shoulders and limbs and make your movements appear a little more fluid. A little smoother. Close your eyes and glide with me.'

'Like this?'

'Just so. And incidentally, I never believed you to be out of place here.' She felt his breath tickle the curve of her neck. 'I want you to know that.'

'Well, that is a comfort.'

'Good.' He clasped her close. 'Now I shall sweep you

around and across every part of this chamber and as we move you shall have the opportunity to assess whether you can once again detect the scent you did earlier.'

'Very well and I shall try not to fall over.'

'You will not fall, Joan. Not when I have you in my arms.'

Joan ignored the way her heart hammered in her chest with those words uttered so softly. Instead, she turned her mind on counting each step, trying to remember the sequence of the dance as Warin darted his gaze around the room.

'Allow me to describe the room at this precise moment. On the dais at the end of the chamber, as you might well know, sits King Henry, clapping exuberantly. In fact, I would wager that this impromptu music and dance has been hastily put together at his behest.'

She smiled inwardly. 'I am sure you have the right of it.'

'Around the King, members of his family, noblemen and courtiers are seated, with servants bringing large silver trenchers of meats, cheeses, bread and fruits for the top table. Down the side of the chamber, where we stood earlier, long tables have been pulled out and these, too, have trenchers of food and jugs of ale and wine being piled on to them. On either side men and women are stood or sat in clusters, chatting, making merry or clapping to the music.'

'Thank you for that very detailed description.' She blinked over her shoulder in surprise. 'And I cannot believe that you remembered my sight is worse in this flickering low light of the candles and burning torches.'

'Of course I do. I remember everything about you,

Joan. Every small yet significant detail,' he murmured in her ear, sending a rush of heat through her veins.

She opened her mouth to say that she, too, would never forget Warin de Talmont from everything he had said to her, to the time they spent together—but an inconvenient lump had lodged itself in her throat, so she said nothing instead. Yet it was true. Joan would never forget this, the time she had spent with Warin— from horseback riding in Smythfeld, to playing games with the children in the garden at All Hallows Church, to drinking in a tavern with his friends, confiding in one another about their pasts and working together in Bermondsye. Above all—that glorious passionate kiss that she had thought about constantly and relived time and again in the long nights since. And now this— being held in his arms and dancing to a step she had no knowledge of. Joan felt as though she were treading with trepidation, once again, into the unknown and not knowing how this dance would end.

'We have yet to move along the whole length of the chamber. But tell me—has anything yet stirred your memory from earlier?'

She swallowed, uncomfortably remembering the reason for this dance. 'I am afraid nothing has.'

'No matter, Joan. This is perfectly pleasant and, if you will, you'll allow me to continue to lead you along on our merry dance.'

'I shall, since this perfectly pleasant dance is another first for me.'

She felt his hold of her tighten, as he led her in a flourish, around the wooden columns, spinning until they were now at the far corner of the hall in the assembly line of dancers. 'Is it wrong that I feel far too gratified to be the one sharing this rare experience with you?'

'I would not dream to suppose what you should feel, Warin.'

He chuckled softly against her ear. 'Yet you do seem to delight in telling me at every opportunity.'

'I believe you are mistaken.'

'I believe I am not.' Joan sensed that he was smiling as he led her slowly around the room. 'Now concentrate, Joan, tell me anything that you can detect. Anything that is of note, or unusual.'

'Very well, I shall try.'

They continued to move around the chamber in unison with the other couples dancing the same steps as them. A thrill of anticipation chased along her skin, making Joan wish that she was dancing for the same reason as the others, rather than attempting to detect some nefarious assailant, who might or might not even be present here.

'Would it be too early to enquire whether you have been able to distinguish the scent from earlier?'

'Patience, Warin.' She tilted her head up, taking in a deep breath and closing her eyes again. 'Although this is proving far more difficult than I originally imagined.'

'Undoubtably. But I have faith in you, mistress.'

She chuckled, shaking her head. 'I am glad that one of us has. But in truth, there are far too many different aromas wafting in this chamber. Trying to pinpoint one—which, incidentally, is far more subtle than, say, the enticing smell of the trenchers of cooked meats— is not easy.'

'Then we shall impose ourselves in these groups of

courtiers until you are satisfied that the lingering scent is no longer in this hall,' he said before leaning in and whispering, 'And it might be best that we ascertain this before your brother returns.'

'I regarded you to be one of Tom's closest friends and allies?'

'Oh, I am, Joan, but even he knows that it would not be prudent to leave me alone with you. Not that I blame him.'

She laughed as a lick of shiver went down her spine. 'Should I be worried? Am I in danger with you now?'

'You would never be in danger. Not with me, Joan,' he said softly. 'But, alas, I cannot help what others might believe.'

'Then I care nought for anyone's opinions but yours and mine. That should be all that matters.'

'Sadly that cannot be and it is not the way in which the world works.'

Warin was right, of course. Her brother was not just her guardian, but someone who had her best interests at heart. To that end, he would see her continued association with Warin as nothing good, with all the possible hurt that it could possibly inflict. And because Tom loved her, he would do everything in his power to protect her from that.

And yet, she could not help herself—Joan was drawn to Warin de Talmont in a way that was both alarming and confusing. It took her breath away and left her restless and longing for more.

'Yes, I suppose you must be right.' She exhaled deeply as they turned around one another. 'But, much as I love my brother, I cannot live my life seeking his approval for every decision I might make—be they good or bad.'

'I believe you do just the opposite of that. And may-hap that is why Tom is as protective of you as he is.' He leant forward and whispered in her ear, 'Since I have remarked many times—you are trouble, Joan Lovent.'

She gasped in mock outrage. 'I believe you might want to reconsider that remark, Warin de Talmont.'

'Oh, and why is that?'

'Because I might otherwise just walk off and refuse to help you. And let's be honest with one another, you *need me.*' Did she imagine it or had Warin just taken a small shaky intake of breath as he tightened his hold of her?

'What I need is neither here, nor there. But I am grateful for your help, Joan.'

'As I am of this dance.' Her heart sank, knowing that it was soon to come to an end. 'It has been the most splendid experience.'

Warin wrapped his hands around hers and twirled her around so that she spun and stopped in front of him, the hem of her kirtle swishing at her feet. 'My pleasure, mistress,' he said softly, bowing as she curtsied, signal-ling the end of the dance.

'Come, Joan.' He held out his hand. 'Allow me to take you on a jaunt around this magnificent hall, as I point out particular interests such as artifacts and tap-estries of note.' He leant close and whispered, 'And to allow you the opportunity to do more of your uniquely famous detecting.'

'Famous, am I?' She pressed her lips together, sup-pressing a bubble of laughter.

'Mayhap your infamy extends to just one or two persons—well, namely me.'

'Then in that case, lead on, Warin. You know how I enjoy a good jaunt.'

Warin took her by the hand and guided her around the hall, pointing out the Angevin Coat of Arms, the standard of King Henry.

'Above you, Joan, is the vaulted ceiling, carved in great oak beams and decorated along its length, and down the wooden columns it is sculpted with heraldic emblems and mythical beasts. Here, give me your hand and you can feel all the rich detail of it for yourself.' Warin guided her fingers over the sculpted column, tracing the intricate shapes and patterns carved delicately into the timber.

'Such fine craftsmanship.'

'I would wager it is the very best.' His fingers hovered over hers as they touched the cold wooden surface together. And even though she had been dancing in Warin's arms only moments ago, there was something so unexpectantly intimate about this, something so beguiling in this caress that chased across her skin, making her blood soar. How could every little touch, every graze of his hand, affect her so?

'And it is painted in gold, red and blue with such extraordinary care.'

'It is a thing of beauty.'

'Yes,' he murmured, 'it is.' But Warin was not looking at the intricately carved and painted column, but directly at *her*. His look carried so much heat and so much longing that Joan felt she might actually burn from its intensity, melting at his feet.

Warin let out a shaky breath and dropped his hands to his sides. Once he had gathered himself he spoke once more, but his voice carried a husky tremor. 'Come, let's keep moving.'

Joan, too, had to catch her breath once more. She reminded herself again why Warin had danced with her in the first place. And why he offered to take her on this jaunt about the chamber—it was to find any further information about the foxglove flora scent she had detected earlier, preferably matching it with the person who had carried the scent. That was all—nothing more.

Warin darted his head in every direction, searching as he guided her away from the carved column. 'Anything, Joan? Or is it still for nought?'

'Still nought, I am afraid.'

'Mayhap if we once again go through the sequence of happenstance, it might alert you to something you might otherwise have forgotten.'

'Very well.' She nodded, glad of the change in discourse. 'As I mentioned earlier, Tom and I arrived through the main doorway. And before long I was being introduced to an array of people.'

'Can you remember anything about them? Anything at all that might be of help?'

'Let me see.' She closed her eyes and tried to recall the mundane and uneventful moments from earlier when she had first arrived at the Tower. 'I remember the feeling of being nervous and apprehensive, as I explained earlier. Then…oh, yes, there was a young woman whom I was introduced to, and also her husband, who did not look familiar, before you ask.'

He smirked. 'Glad you are able to guess what my questions might be. It saves much time.'

'You are welcome.' Her lips twitched in the corners. 'As I was saying, there were also a couple of much younger men, who had requested an introduction, which I have to admit I was quite flattered by.'

'Just so.' He shook his head. 'But it is hardly difficult to understand why they should they seek an introduction to the most beautiful maiden in the chamber.'

'Oh, stop your nonsense'. She swatted his arm. 'I shall pretend that you did not say such ridiculous things.'

'It is not ridiculous, Joan. I speak only the truth.'

'Thank you, but I shall ignore it all the same and continue with what I was saying.'

He crossed his arms across his huge chest which fitted so snugly inside an expensive-looking padded woollen gambeson. Joan realised that Warin had never looked so fine. So incredibly handsome in his gruff, rugged way. She had been trying so hard to ignore him, pretending he was anywhere but there in the same chamber as her, that she had not acknowledged him in any way. Well, she was certainly noticing him now. Joan looked away and closed her eyes in the hope that she might also put a halt to this regard of him.

'I cannot remember anyone else that I might have been introduced to, as I said I was a little apprehensive about being there. And apart from them, there were servants, musicians and such milling around.'

'No matter,' Warin muttered, in a voice that tried to conceal disappointment. 'We shall continue to circulate around this chamber, if that is agreeable? Mayhap you might recall something more or even pick up more of the foxglove flora.'

'Of course. Besides, you're doing a splendid job of highlighting the particulars of this chamber. Tell me, Warin, what is that above us protruding out from the wall?'

'It's the musicians' gallery. They played from up there while we danced.'

'I had wondered whether the music was coming from some higher celestial plane.'

'No, just the minstrels' gallery where the... Wait one moment.' His eyed widened, suddenly alert. 'Did you just say that you had seen servants and musicians when introductions were being made?'

'With my eyesight, such as it is, I can never be too certain, but I believe so.' She frowned, trying to recall the sounds, the smells and even a change of movement. Joan might not be able to see with exacting clarity, but the nuances in a person's movements, as well as the expressions and intonation in speech, gave her the missing pieces she needed where her sight failed to give her more information. And this she had learned to use effectively.

'Yes, yes, I believe I did. I noticed a man carrying a long wooden flute. And he seemed a little out of place.'

'Mayhap because he should have been with the other musicians up in the gallery rather than milling down here with the guests.'

'Possibly, but it was the instrument that struck me being out of place. The man held on to it as though it were something infinitely more precious than a mere instrument.'

Warin flashed her a quick smile before rubbing his chin. 'I wonder if you would care to take a little stroll to the gallery, mistress? The view up there is one not to be missed.'

'Then I would like it above all else.' She nodded in excitement. 'I am rather fond of these jaunts after all.'

Joan held on to Warin's hand as they walked out of the hall and climbed the narrow spiral staircase that led to the wooden gallery, overlooking the side of the hall. There were a few people, that she could just about make out, whom Joan assumed to be musicians, especially since they all wore the same chestnut-coloured surcoat as one another.

One of them turned and spoke out. 'Can we 'elp you with anything?'

'Actually, we were of the mind that you might be able to help us.'

'Oh, with what exactly?' the man uttered irritably. 'We are busy, as you can see.'

'Of course,' Joan muttered, pasting a smile on her face. 'We wanted to extend our thanks to the wonderful music that you have entertained us with. You are all so immensely talented.'

'Our pleasure, my lady,' the musician said, his voice a great deal softer.

'And we would particularly want to extend our gratitude to the flute player, if he is here?'

'Not wanting to be rude in front of a lady like yerself, but you won't want to extend anything to that cur,' the man scoffed. 'He never played a single note on his flute. He just upped and left before we were about to start playing.'

'Did he say where he was going?' Warin demanded.

'No, sir—only that he 'ad to see someone urgently. Next thing we knew the fella was mingling downstairs in the hall with such fine people as yourselves.'

'Interesting. Did you notice anything else of note?'

Another of the musicians scratched his head, frowning. 'Fact is, I saw the fella approachin' His Excellence the Bishop of Winchester himself. As if someone of 'is standin' would want to stop and chat with 'im.' He shook his head in apparent disgust. 'The Bishop was none too pleased, I can tell you. He seemed angry and next thing I know, he stormed off, not wanting to have anything to do wiv the man. Most entertainin', it was, and we seldom gets entertainment ourselves.'

'That is most illuminating—are you certain about this?' Warin leant towards the man. 'Can you describe the man?'

'He was tall, thin with a bald head and a long scar across his face. Now, if yer don't mind, we 'ave to get back to our performance.'

'Of course.' Joan smiled, nodding. 'And thank you again.'

They climbed back down the stairs and made their way back into the hall, hovering at the entrance.

'So to summarise...' Warin frowned, rubbing his forehead. 'The flute player—or rather the Smythfeld tanner, based on the musician's description—managed to gain access to the Tower because he sought to speak with Peter des Roches, the Bishop of Winchester, for whatever reason.'

'But why here? Would they not be exposed in such

a place as this? Especially since this man has been in hiding for so long.'

'That might be precisely the point, Joan,' Warin muttered. 'What if he had been made a promise—such as the payment of a lot of silver. But this promise was broken and reneged upon. The only choice left would then be to force the situation by being present here at the heart of the Royal Court. Not only would he expose himself, but also the one who made that promise in the first instance.'

'But would that mean that the Bishop of Winchester is somehow involved with all of this?' she said on a short gasp.

'Hush, not here.' Warin scanned the hall, darting his gaze in every direction. 'I simply do not know at this time.'

'One thing we do know is that the flute player, or rather the tanner man, must have been the one who had carried the scent of the foxglove flora, as it was present in the gallery.'

'That is a possibility.' Warin smiled down at her. 'Come, let me take you inside, while you wait for Tom to return.'

Chapter Fifteen

'I beg your pardon?' Joan Lovent's voice was suddenly a little cooler. 'You believe I should wait here for Tom, while you go where precisely?'

'That is none of your concern.'

'Ah, I comprehend you,' she said, her lips twisting wryly. 'Now that you have managed to use me to gather the information you sought, you think to abandon me here, while you pursue this unknown assailant—and on your own.'

'No, I am attempting to keep you safe. There is a need for expediency. I simply do not have time to wait for anyone else.'

'I am coming with you.'

He dragged her back by the arm, pulling her around to face him. 'Listen to me, Joan, this is dangerous. You must stay here for your own safety.'

'Which I can only be if you would allow me to come with you. I feel safe when I am in your company.'

'Is that so?' He raised a brow and crossed his arms across his chest.

'Indeed. Besides, the main assailant—the one who

you believe to be the Smythfeld tanner—might still be here—in this very chamber. So it would be far too dangerous for me to stay here, and on my own until my brother returns.'

'God's breath, woman—you are as wilful as you are obstinate.' He huffed in annoyance. 'I do not have time for this.'

'Then allow me to come. I might even be of some assistance.'

Warin knew the truth of that. Joan had helped him tremendously and he was not a man to deny her that.

Hell's teeth!

'Very well,' he muttered in resignation. 'Even though Tom is going to kill me for taking you with me.'

'Yes, but he might equally kill you if you leave me here on my own. So it might be best to be on the side of caution.'

'Just as I remarked earlier, you are trouble, Joan Lovent.' He shook his head, grabbing her hand. 'Come on then, let's be away.'

They made their way out of the hall and along the narrow anteroom that led to a large arched doorway. God, but his head was still reeling from their dance earlier.

'You need me...'

Joan evidently had no inkling how those words that she had so easily tossed his way while they danced had shaken him to his very core. Indeed, how they continued to tease and torture him. It made him feel like a half-witted dolt, at a time when he needed his wits, sense and quick perceptive judgement. It was not true, he kept repeating to himself—he didn't need anyone.

He bit back an oath and pushed these errant musings to the back of his mind and focused on the task ahead.

Warin noted the unbolted wooden door and whispered to Joan that they must be vigilant as well as quiet. Stepping inside, they found themselves in the majestic Chapel of St John. And apart from the two of them, it was seemingly empty.

The Norman stone chapel was stark in the simplicity of its design, with the tunnel-vaulted nave, aisles and east-facing apse that held an impressive arched gallery that curved, rising high above. Thick, round, unmoulded columns supported the main arches and, with high vaulted ceilings, the chapel was eerily silent except for their tentative footsteps on the stone slab flooring.

'What exactly are we searching for?' she whispered.

'Anything that looks out of place.'

'Very well. You can be the eyes while I shall be the nose and even ears.'

'Come then, "nose and ears". Let us search between these hallowed arches before moving elsewhere,' he hissed, as their footfalls echoed around the cavernous chapel around them.

'I do not think there is anyone here, Warin.'

No. Neither did he and yet…yet there was something not quite as it should be. For one thing, it was one of the few places within the fortified tower that was not heavily guarded presently, which would mean that it could also be an ideal place to hide.

'Let's climb the stairwell,' he muttered, pointing at the stone spiral staircase to the side of the nave. They ascended to the galleried floor above and ambled along down the narrow length that ran down the entire side of the chapel. Warin removed the torch from the metal sconce on the stone wall to gain more visibility as dusk settled and the light streaming through the glass windows was beginning to fade.

'I can hear something,' Joan muttered as Warin flashed the torch around.

They quickened their pace, turning the corner to the curved gallery that overlooked the altar and the hairs on the back of his neck rose. Instantly Warin was alert. He flashed the torch and noticed that there was a huddled heap on the ground, making him rush forth. He knelt beside the man who was lying on the floor and gently turned him over. The man was still alive but only just as his breathing was shallow and laboured. And judging from the dagger left beside him and the pool of blood emanating from his chest, the man had been stabbed.

'Can you tell me who did this to you?'

The man shook his head, as he continued to take small, stilted breaths. God, but the poor soul did not have long.

'Oh, Warin, is there anything we can do for him?'

'I am afraid not, but we can make his last moments as peaceful as possible.'

'Do you think this is the real flute player?' Joan said from beside him.

'Yes, I would believe so. And he's clutching a scrap of torn material—the same chestnut colour as the musician's surcoat.' Warin turned his attention back on the man sprawled on the ground. 'Did you see your assailant? Was he by any chance tall, thin and with a long scar across his face?'

The man nodded slowly and took one long, strained breath. It was, unfortunately, also his last. Warin closed the man's eyes and made the sign of the cross, as Joan stood up and whimpered softly. He took her in his arms and wished that he had not brought her along—not that she would have listened to his reasoning.

'I cannot believe it,' she whispered.

'I can,' replied Warin. 'It seems that the man we seek has many stains on his soul, including murder. And the bastard had no compulsion in ending a man's life to further his gains. But I wish that you had not witnessed this, Joan.'

'Mayhap my diminishing sight can be a blessing at times. Besides, I am no stranger to watching someone breathe their last breath, Warin.'

'No, neither am I. We both have been exposed to that, sadly.'

Just then retreating footsteps could be heard from below.

'Who goes there?' Warin bellowed and was met with silence. And after a short moment the footsteps were heard again, but this time at a much faster pace.

'Come, let's be away.' He grabbed Joan's hand and led her back down the stairs, just as whoever had been present stormed out of the chapel.

They pushed through the wooden doors, looking in every direction. A hurried footfall and a long surcoat or mayhap a cloak flapped behind him as the man turned a corner. He was running towards the main spiral staircase, making his way downstairs.

'Stop him!' Warin cried out to the startled guard standing by the main entrance to the stairwell leading up to the State Apartments. But they had dithered too long, letting the man from the chapel run past them.

'Damn it, man. I told you to stop the brigand.'

'I am sorry, sir, but I cannot leave my post.'

'Listen to me, this is a matter of emergency. You must alert Sir Tom Lovent and alert the Constable of the Tower to secure and fortify the castle, closing the gates. No one should be allowed in or out of the Tower's curtain walls. Do I make myself clear?'

'On whose authority, sir?'

'On the authority of my liege lord Hubert de Burgh, the Earl of Kent—now, move!'

He let go of Joan's hand and turned towards her. 'Stay here, Joan. I am going after him.'

'And I shall come with you.'

'I have not got time for this.'

'No, you do not, so let us not lose sight of him. Come on, let us not tarry.'

Hell's teeth, but the woman was stubborn and un-compromising. Still, he could only marvel at her tenacity. Indeed, when Joan Lovent wanted to do something, she did not allow anything or anyone to stand in her way. Warin had to make certain that no harm would be-fall her by allowing her this measure of indulgence. And he hoped that she was not going to be an impediment to his work or that he would not come to regret this.

They heard the footsteps running down the stairwell as they followed, giving chase. They followed him down as quickly as possible, but since Warin had Joan in tow, this was not fast as he would have preferred. They gained on the man as he went through the main kitch-ens, which was a hive of busy activity and graft where no one heeded Warin's request to detain the man they presumed to be the man with the scar across his face.

Instead, he continued to make his way down another corridor that led to a stairway going down into the undercroft, buttery and other storerooms as they continued their pursuit, trying desperately to gain on him.

Suddenly they were once again surrounded with a deafening silence in the dark, low-vaulted chambers, which held large containers of spices, dried fruits, herbs, dried meats and smoked fish. Warin gripped Joan's hand in his and with his other hand he waved the torch in different directions to offer a little visibility. They made their way through the rows of wooden shelves, which were stacked, holding presumably more stores of dried food stuff. Yet he could still not fathom where the assailant could be. He had to be there somewhere in the undercroft chamber, otherwise they would have heard his footsteps moving away. They continued to slowly make their way along, trying to ascertain where the man was hiding.

A chill chased down his spine and the fine hair on the back of his neck rose in anticipation of the unknown.

'It would be best if you came out.' Warin's voice echoed around the cavernous space. 'The Tower is now completely secured and there will be no way out of here. There is simply no other choice, other to give yourself up. And if you do give yourself up, my liege lord might be able to grant you clemency, especially if you provide us with the names of your associates.'

Just then a large container hurtled to the ground, spilling its contents of cloves to the ground.

'Be careful!' Warin lost his hold of Joan's hand as more and more large wooden containers came tumbling to the ground. 'Joan? Where are you?' All he heard was muffled noises and someone being dragged along the floor.

Damnation. He knew he should not have brought her along with him.

'Warin, I am here,' she screeched. 'Let go of me, you brute!'

Warin realised that the bastard must have made a grab for her. He raced towards the direction where Joan's voice had come from and suddenly came up short. Warin flashed the torch in the smaller storeroom off the main one and there on the ground was a figure huddled on the floor.

'Joan?' He strode inside. 'Are you well?'

'Yes, it's me,' she whimpered. 'Take care, Warin. He threw me in here, but I do not know where he is. He's hiding somewhere in the shadows.'

'Come, give me your hand and we'll be away from here.'

But before he had even reached Joan's outstretched hands, the wooden door was slammed shut, with a bolt dragged across it.

Hell's teeth!

They were locked in this small, dank space in the furthest corner of the undercroft, without very little hope of anyone possibly finding them, unless a search was made specifically to find them. God, what a terrible situation they now found themselves in. Once again the man with the scar had thwarted Warin and he had done it by using Joan. Again. It was as apparent as the end of his nose that Joan should have been left back in the hall and yet decisions had been made hastily—decisions that he had little choice other than to stand by now.

'We are locked in here, are we not?' she uttered in a small voice.

'I will try to get us out of here, Joan. Never fear.'

'I don't,' she muttered in a shaky voice, betraying what she had just said. 'I trust you implicitly, Warin.'

'That gladdens my heart.' He grappled with the door, yanking the metal pull on the door again and again, pulling and wrenching the damn thing harder each time, but the door remained locked. 'However, it seems that we might have to endure the ignominy of staying enclosed in here—which I am not certain will be of short duration.'

'I know it is frustrating, Warin, especially after making such a steady progress today. But please do not worry yourself on my account.'

'It is more than just frustrating. And this failure is yet another disaster.' He finally let go of the metal door handle with an exasperated flick of his hand and exhaled through his teeth. He turned towards Joan and took two long strides before reaching her.

'He did not hurt you, did he?' God, but he should have checked on her beforehand. What the hell was wrong with him? Every decision he had made had been wrong, as he continually made mistake after mistake. And it could not be accredited to the fact that he was unsettled by Joan in such a way that he felt perturbed by his own reaction. No, this was his fault entirely and he alone would shoulder the blame—they were certainly wide enough to absorb that.

'No, Warin, he only pushed me in here. I promise that I am well.'

'That is a blessing. But I can tell you that the day

cannot come soon enough for me to get my hands on that bastard.'

'Nor I. I do not appreciate being pushed around by anyone. However, presently I am more concerned with the predicament we find ourselves.'

As was he. Warin had to think of a plan—a way to get them out of this awful mess.

'Can anyone hear me out there?' he bellowed, hammering against the door using his fists. 'Anyone? Heed our plea—we need assistance as we are locked in here.' He alternated between beating his fists against the door and kicking it and trying to force it open using brute force. But he was met with silence. And despite the force he used, it was futile—the damn door was a solid immovable plank.

Warin noted that the torch that he had placed on the stone floor was now flickering and dwindling in this small, confined space and it would not be long before it went out completely, plunging them into absolute darkness. He filched out his dagger and went to work on the door, trying to gouge and stab through the timber so that he might reach the other side. But it would take time—time which he presently did not have.

'Do you need any help?'

'No, but try and find any supplies.' He stopped a moment, dragging his hand across his forehead. 'I fear we might need them, if we're stuck here overnight.'

'Overnight?' Joan gasped in horror. 'I cannot be trapped in here overnight. What would Tom think? What would Brida say? Oh, how everyone would worry.'

'I am truly sorry and I hope that your family will not

be too distressed by your absence. I hope you know that I am trying everything that I can to get us out of here.'

'I appreciate that but, dear lord, Warin, my brother will come back to the hall soon and find that I am no longer there. And realise that *you* are not either. Can you imagine what he would think?'

'Sadly, yes. I had warned you not to come, but you would not heed my advice, Joan. You are always far too impulsive—far too wilful.' He sighed. 'And knowing you, you would have followed me anyway, had I forbidden it.'

'I came because *you* needed me.'

'So you keep saying.'

'Because it is true, whatever you might believe, Warin de Talmont.'

Oh, God help him with this woman. He wanted to deny it, he wanted to suppress it, but knew that it was probably true. And he hated that. It made him feel far too exposed, far too vulnerable. No, it would not do, he was not a man who needed anyone.

'It seems that you blame me for this misadventure,' she continued to say, hurt lacing her words.

'No, I do not, and all of this finger-pointing is not particularly helpful at this moment.'

'I dare say it isn't, but you can imagine why I might be a little vexed. After all, you even questioned why I was here at Court earlier.'

His dagger stilled in his grip for a moment, as he pondered on whether Joan should know the truth or continue to believe the worst of him.

'It is not what you think,' he murmured.

'Then please excuse my ignorance, Warin, because

I am a little confused. I had thought that mayhap you believed me to be somehow unworthy and unfit to be presented to the King.'

'And you believed that of me?' He could not help feeling outraged that she would even consider something as asinine as that.

'No…no, but you were certainly provoked by my presence, so naturally I wondered at the possible reason.'

'And that was your estimation of me? God, Joan, I never thought your opinion of me could be this low.'

'It isn't. In truth, I was reflecting more on *your* opinion of *me*.'

'But surely you know that my opinion of you is everything that is good and admirable. I could never tolerate your company otherwise.'

'Then you might want to enlighten me as I do not comprehend your hostility earlier.'

'Oh, God, Joan, must we discuss this now, when we have far more pressing concerns to think about?'

'True, but even so…' she muttered as she searched the shelves, tentatively, with her fingertips. 'I would hope it was not because you were embarrassed to be seen with me?'

'Hell and damnation, no!' He dropped the dagger and turned towards her, grabbing her wrist and pulling her towards him. 'How can you think that? I have never been nor will I ever be embarrassed by you—never, do you hear! Only by *them*.'

'Them?' She frowned, blinking up at him. 'Who, for the love of God, is "them"?'

'Who?' He grabbed her by the shoulders, frowning into that beloved face. 'Those damned courtiers who had been so solicitous to you one moment and then full of scorn, ridicule and disdain the next, when they realised that you had an impediment. They all but pounced on that knowledge of you, unfurling their claws with their ready spite and venom. I was ashamed of those people and I will tell you, Joan Lovent, but in that moment I was so angry that I wanted to unsheathe my sword and roar at them. Thunder and blast at any-one—anyone who would dare to even think to dispar-age you.'

Warin had worked himself up so much with that display of anger and frustration at Joan's situation that he was now breathing heavily as he searched her face.

That *beloved face*? When had he started to consider Joan in terms of being that? What in heaven's name was happening to him?

Chapter Sixteen

Joan reached up, her fingers shaking, and touched Warin's clenched jaw with soothing, caresses. She felt those hard, rigid planes of his face gradually release the clenched knot of tension. When had anyone ever championed her and felt so incensed about her situation as Warin de Talmont? It left her breathless. It made her want to cheer and weep at the very same time.

'Thank you,' she said on a whisper. 'No one has ever been so indignant on my behalf and your words mean more to me than I can ever say. But it is all rather needless.'

'Needless?' He frowned. 'I do not understand.'

Joan took a moment to consider her answer, especially as it was not something that could be easily explained. 'I am and always have been aware of the reaction of those around me when they learn that I am not whole—that I am not fully able.' She sighed, shaking her head. 'I have to accept it, admittedly with difficulty. But I do not allow their prejudice to affect me—not any more.'

'Christ, Joan. How can you live with that?'

'Because I have little choice,' she muttered, dropping her hand to her side. 'I am used to it. I am used to people's derision, scorn and censure—I have even had some who refuse to acknowledge me, in case I might pass on my affliction merely by association. Either that or they believe that I am somehow less—less intelligent, less agreeable...less of a woman.'

Warin threw his arms up in indignation. 'God's breath, none of that is true.'

'No, but I cannot stop those whom I meet from believing that.' She shrugged. 'It is simply a truth every single day of my life and there is nothing I can do other than to ignore it. I am not saying that I tolerate this behaviour, only that it is sadly unavoidable.' She sighed, shaking her head in the growing darkness. 'It started when I was young with my own father, who resented me because of my condition and blamed me for his own failures. He made me feel ashamed for being flawed and I believed it, too. But gradually I realised that if I continued in that vein, then he would have triumphed over me. So I began to live again to spite him and refused to allow the opinions of others to affect me in the way they once did. Not that it has been easy, Warin. I am not always secure with my limitations—nor can I pretend to be.'

'I understand, but know this, Joan. You are more—far more than any limitations that have been placed on you. Your inner strength, your determination and your unwavering courage exceed beyond all else.'

'Thank you,' she whispered on a choke.

How had they come to be this close to one another? How had Joan once again allowed herself to be this drawn to this man? She could not help herself. She could not help being enveloped by his belief in her, his protectiveness, tenderness and willingness to slay every single one of her demons.

Mayhap it was *she* who needed *him*.

'And you are flesh and blood, Joan. Naturally, there will be times when things are more difficult than others. There is no shame in admitting that.'

'I suppose not. But what I find most challenging, Warin, is not the unkindness of others, but something far, far more tangible.' She took a deep breath, not knowing whether she should disclose something so private. Something she had not shared with another living soul. 'It is all the small things I know I shall miss, once I lose my sight for good. The colours of the different seasons as they shift from one to the other. The look of happiness, joy or even sadness in those whom I cherish, especially my young nephew as he grows and changes. The ebb and flow of life with all its constant changes. The enjoyment from something as simple as cutting a juicy red apple before sampling it… I shall miss it all. I shall be scrambling to pluck memories from a different time, when my eyes did as they should.' She paused a moment before continuing. 'And no matter how wonderful it has been to go horseback riding, or to assist you with your endeavours, or even dance in your arms— nothing, nothing will change the fact that one day I will not be able to do those things in the way I do them even now. One day my sight will be gone for good and so will this life that I have built. I will be wholly dependent on others— It is that which makes me feel uncertain and anxious above anything else.'

'I am so sorry, Joan.' Warin sighed, pressing his forehead against hers. 'I have said before and I shall say it again—you are a remarkable woman. I want you to know that I am now and always will be at your service, should you ever need me.'

Joan had not expected such a promissory oath, not that she had intended to disclose as much as she had. The words had just slipped from her lips and now she felt stripped, bare, naked in front of this man as the light of the torch slowly extinguished.

'Then kiss me, Warin,' she whispered, her breath coming in short bursts.

He seemed taken back by her request for a moment. But only a moment before he acquiesced to her wish, cupping her face, with the pad of his thumb caressing her cheek so softly it sent a shiver through her. He bent his head, pressing his lips to hers, shaping and gliding over them. Oh, heavens, this was what she needed to alleviate all the hurt from her past—the pleasure of being in Warin de Talmont's arms. The pleasure of his kisses.

She revelled in the yearning, the tenderness and even reverence, but also felt the tightly knotted coil of control, as though Warin were fighting an inner battle with himself. His fingers traced the back of her neck and down the curve of her spine and settled on her bottom, giving it a gentle squeeze. She opened her mouth on a gasp, allowing his tongue inside to explore and taste her as though she were an exotic forbidden fruit.

She was greedy, wanting, and needing to be closer to him. Desire racked her body, making her tremble, holding on to him in desperation, in case she fell. But she was falling anyway, deeper and deeper. She craved more, wanting to taste him just as he had her. So she did. She tentatively touched his tongue with hers and imitated everything that he had done. And that was when he lost whatever battle he had with himself, when passion, lust and a desperate need ignited and roared between them.

He growled, pulling her closer, her breasts pressed against the hard wall of his chest. He kissed, nipped and licked his way along the line of her jaw, moving down as he sucked the throbbing pulse on her neck.

'Oh, God, Joan, what the blazes are you doing to me?' his murmured huskily.

'Really?' She felt as though she might melt into a heap. 'I have no notion of what I am doing to you. Not a bit.' Her breathing was heavy and wanton as he continued to kiss from her neck down to the top of her chest. 'But I do know that you make me want more and more. Tell me why that should be?'

'You know far more than you think. And wanting more is a very dangerous thing,' he whispered against her skin. 'It leaves a hunger that can never quite be sated.'

'That would be quite uncomfortable, I would imagine.' How had her voice remained so calm when her whole body felt so hot that it might well catch fire and burn with so much need? And all because of what he was doing to her. It was wrong, it was sinful, but Joan did not care. She wrapped her hands around his neck, her fingers dipping into his thick, soft hair at the back of his neck, and tugged him closer.

'And a kiss can also be dangerous, too.' He groaned. 'Because of where it might take you—to a forbidden place where it emphatically should not, however much you might want to.'

'And what if I don't want to stop? What if we just cannot?'

'We must.' Warin kissed her mouth once and then again before slowly pulling away. 'It would be prudent to, Joan, even if you tempt me more than anyone I have ever met. But I must resist and so must you, until this desire that exists between us flickers and dies. There can be no other choice.'

'Oh, I disagree.' She took a step back and wrapped her arms around herself. 'There is always a choice in such matters. It is whether or not one reaches out and takes that leap and risks everything they hold dear.'

'You know that is something that cannot be, Joan. Not when it risks something pure and good. Not when I am as broken. It is I who am not whole. It is I who am less than a man. You asked earlier whether I considered you to be unworthy—the truth is that it is *I* who am unworthy of *you*.'

'That is not true.'

'Is it not?' His voice was bitter and also strangely filled with remorse. 'I am undeserving of love, of hope and wonderment—in fact, anything that is meaningful and is of value—*you*, Joan Lovent. All I am fit for is this life that I somehow scraped together, but nothing more.'

'You cannot believe that, Warin.'

'I do and far too easily.' He sighed deeply. 'I had a life—one that gave me great fulfilment. I had love—a love of a woman that enriched my very existence. Indeed, they were riches beyond any man's imagination, let alone mine. And do you know what I did, Joan? Do you know what I did with all that good fortune? I despoiled it, I ruined it—I did not cherish any of it as I should. Nor did I hold on tightly to it. I did not protect it. I did not shield or care for that precious gift. I became complacent and in a heartbeat I lost it all! I lost everything.'

Oh, God, how terribly sad. 'What happened, Warin? What happened to your wife? To your family?'

The silence stretched before them and Joan wondered whether he would divulge this seemingly difficult aspect from his past. She considered changing their conversation to something a little more palatable, when Warin spoke in a voice that was soft and far away.

'My wife had remained in a hamlet where she had grown and lived all her life in Surrey with our young daughter. She was to look after our interests while I went on an expedition to France and later to the Holy Land as part of my mesne with my liege lord. When we had married, a substantial portion of land came as part of Ada's dowry, but what I had never been aware of was that this piece of land was much disputed. And once I was away, trouble really reared its head—not that Ada informed me, otherwise I would have returned.'

'What happened?'

'I received word that Ada and my daughter were taken and held for the ransom for this damn piece of land—which I would have given away in a heartbeat. But I was too late—the missive for their ransom was delayed and by the time I returned to England both Ada and my young daughter had been slain,' he spat out bitterly.

God, how dreadful. 'I am so sorry.'

'The terrible thing was that I never understood why they had been taken and killed. It served no purpose, if the intention was to acquire this land. But nothing in life is quite as it seems—as it was in this case. The man at the helm of this scheme was one who had always coveted Ada and believed that she was to have been betrothed to him. Once he had captured her he pressed his suit, but Ada would not succumb to his advances. And so he killed her and then he killed our child. Brutal, but efficient.' He paused, taking a deep breath. 'So I granted him the same courtesy he afforded my wife and child once I eventually got my hands on him.'

No less brutal and efficient.

'From then on I dedicated my life to finding, catching and eradicating individuals who perpetrate such crimes. This is why I do what I do—to rid the kingdom of men like that. And yet, the huge extent of what I do, regardless of all the successes, is never enough. The guilt I feel for the loss of my family never leaves me, Joan. I can never rid myself of the stain of their deaths. It is a constant on my conscience—the blame that I feel.'

'I… I am very sorry for the tragic loss of your wife and daughter, but you must know that what happened to them cannot be your fault.'

'Can I not?' His laughter was hollow and brittle. 'Then whose fault was it, if not mine? If I had not gone away in search of fortune and glory. If I had stayed, if I had done my duty by them—protected them as I should, as I had vowed—none of it would have happened.'

'You cannot know that for certain.'

He was aghast. 'You doubt my ability to have done my duty by them?'

'No, of course not. That is not my meaning at all. Only that you cannot control and contain everything in life. Even if you had been in the country, the outcome of this tragedy might have sadly been the same, despite your best efforts. What I am saying is that you cannot claim that it would been avoided had you stayed in England.'

'Even so, that is of no consequence, Joan. I am still responsible for their deaths—and it is a blame I must shoulder in perpetuity.'

'Then I am sorry for you as well because you have pledged yourself to live a half-life and nothing more.'

'So be it.'

'How can you be content with that? How can you shoulder the blame for a crime you did not commit?'

'But I did,' he muttered softly. 'Because it was as much my blade that sank into their flesh as it was that bastard's.'

'I fear you have convinced yourself of your blame and thus committed to a life of purgatory.'

'What if I have?' He exhaled in frustration. 'It's mine to bear alone.'

'You may continue to believe that, Warin de Talmont, if you wish, but I tell you here and now, that that is not true. You deserve far, far more than you suppose and I would wager that if your wife were alive now, she would agree with me completely.'

How could Warin make this woman understand that it was his failings, his shortcomings that culminated in their deaths?

'Your faith in me is as commendable as it is humbling, but however much you would like it to be so, I cannot be redeemed.'

'I do understand, Warin.' She paused for a moment before continuing. 'In truth, your situation is not too dissimilar in the way I used to feel regarding the deaths of my family after the fire at my ancestral home—especially my young innocent sister who relied on me to get her out of the burning building. But, of course, my sight let me down. Somewhere on the route out I lost hold of her hand and we were then separated—God, I still remember feeling so frantic, so desperate when I could not find her again. It was harrowing, but I somehow managed to get out of the building. So, yes, I understand the blame, the guilt and heartbreak of loss—and for me it was also knowing that the burden of my limited sight led to losing my beloved sister.'

'So what did you do to change that belief?'

'Father Paul—the priest who helped me come to terms with my diminishing sight—also helped me realise that what happened was not necessarily within my control—however much I desired it. To that end, had my sight been normal, it would not inevitably mean that I could have saved my young sister or any other family member. He told me that I should forgive myself.' She smiled at the memory, shaking her head. 'Not that it was easy to. It was extremely difficult to accept and I did resist it. But eventually I began to see that he was right. I could not be responsible for what happened. In truth, I will have to live with her loss for the rest of my life, but I now know that I cannot carry the blame— that belongs to the person who had started the fire. Just as it happened to you—you are not responsible for the deaths of your wife and child—the man who committed the crime is.'

'I would love nothing better than to believe that.'

'I appreciate that it is difficult, Warin—we grieve, we're heartbroken and so we embrace the pain of that loss, blaming ourselves for it. Consider the young orphaned maid who I took to All Hallows—she is remarkably similar to you, you know, and blames herself for the loss of her young charge. She, too, punishes herself for what she considers to be her failing in protecting the person she loved most. She believes she let her down and that's why she refuses to partake in any joy—in life itself. Like you she believes that she doesn't deserve it. She is wrong, of course…as are you.'

Warin was momentarily speechless, unable to form meaningful words to respond. Instead a small lump formed in his throat at this woman and her generosity and care for others—and her extraordinary need to help those less fortunate then her.

'That is why you bestow your aid and are a benefactor to All Hallows.'

'Indeed, and I am glad that you finally understand the importance of that small church.'

'Oh, I understand,' he murmured, cupping her face. He had once again moved closer to her, wanting to be enveloped by her very essence. 'And the more I discover about you, the more surprised I am by everything that you do. Everything that you are, Joan Lovent.'

Warin wanted desperately to kiss her again—he wanted to taste, to savour and to find the inner peace, the sanctuary that Joan somehow gave him. But he could not risk it. God, but every time he was close to her, he always misstepped around her. And even a chaste kiss or lingering touch would quickly change and ignite into something far more dangerous between them. He knew implacably that it was wrong to give in to the heat of desire that hummed between them. It would, as Joan had so eloquently put it, make him want far, far more.

He pulled his mind away from Joan's mouth. 'The light of the torch has gone out.'

'Does it matter?' she muttered.

'Not especially, but we are now not only stuck in this small space, but descended into complete darkness as well.'

Even though Warin could no longer see Joan clearly, he sensed the stillness within her. Damn, that was not well done of him.

The silence filled the room until Joan spoke in a quiet murmur, 'It's inconsequential as I am not afraid of the dark.'

Somehow he managed to catch her wrist. 'Tell me, Joan, is there anything that you do fear?'

'You,' she said on a whisper. 'The way I feel about you, when I know it cannot be reciprocated, frightens me more than you can ever know.'

He pulled her gently towards him. 'You are wrong if you believe that I don't reciprocate those feelings, sweetheart. And God knows but it petrifies me as well.'

'Because it can never go beyond these four walls.'

'Exactly, it can never go beyond that, Joan.' He pressed his lips to hers and groaned. 'It can never be more than that. Much as I wish that were not the case.'

Warin brushed the pad of his thumb over her lower

lips and kissed her again—just the once, he promised himself, but found it difficult to contain it to just that. He covered her lips, slanting over them, and coaxed her mouth open. Just one taste—only one more to indulge his senses—to sate his wants. But once was never enough. He knew that now—he always wanted more—so much more that it was slowly killing him having to find a way to stop.

He continued to kiss her, he continued to taste, to devour her. God, he wanted her. Everything about Joan excited him, his body, his mind. The woman had bewitched him.

Warin was so very lost in that moment that he had realised too late that the bolt of the wooden door had been pulled apart. And he had also failed to realise that the door had now sprung open and there in the light stood Thomas Lovent—Joan's brother. He was frowning deeply.

'So,' he said icily, 'this is where you have both got to.'

Chapter Seventeen

Damn, damn, damn!

Warin felt as though he was fast losing control of everything around him. What a predicament he, along with Joan, were now in. And all of their own making. But it was *he* who should have known better—it was *he* who knew the risks with the mission—well enough to refuse Joan accompanying him throughout the White Tower. And it was *he* who should have taken responsibility for the situation in the first instance. He wanted to roar his frustration, but all he could do instead was to hang his head. Apart from the knowledge that the damn tanner man had once again slipped through their fingers and was probably gone, he had shamed Joan and he had also shamed his friend—something that he could not abide.

Not that any of it had been registered by Thomas Lovent and the Constable and guards of the Tower as they escorted them out of the undercroft. They made their way back up the building until they came out of the inner bailey and then the castle's curtain wall.

It was only after they boarded a skiff to travel back, when Warin spoke. 'Tom, I would like to say that...'

'Not now, if you please.'

'But there is a man, a flute player, lying dead in the chapel,' Joan chipped in.

'Whom we have already found, thanks to the information parted by the constable, de Talmont,' Tom muttered through clenched teeth. 'But if you don't mind, I believe it might be best if we all travel back in quiet contemplation.'

They waded through the Thames and made their way to Tom's abode through the middle of the night in complete silence, barely acknowledging each other, reflecting on all that had happened.

It was dawn by the time they reached the Strand and, by then, Warin knew he had to take control of this situation before it drifted away from him.

'I would like an audience with you, Tom,' he said firmly as they entered the man's courtyard.

'And I with you, Warin. Let us talk in my private chamber.' Tom looked over his shoulder at Joan. 'It has been a tiring night with all that has happened, Joan. You must go abed.'

'But I wish to stay. I believe that what you discuss shall also affect me.'

'No, Sister, what I have to say is for de Talmont's ears only. But I promise that we shall send for you, if you are needed.'

'Tom, I insist. I would like to...'

'Please escort Mistress Joan to her solar.' He spoke to the hearth knight as he soundly ignored his sister.

The knight held out his hand and passed the walking staff to her, but just as she turned to leave, Warin caught her hand and squeezed it gently in his, bringing it to his lips and bowing over it.

'Goodnight, Joan, or mayhap I should say good morrow.'

That earned him the faintest, smallest of smiles.

'Indeed.' She curtsied. 'Good morrow, Warin.'

'Shall we?' Tom muttered from behind and Warin turned and followed the man inside the chamber.

For a long moment neither said anything before Tom finally broke the silence.

'Well? Would you care to explain why you were ensconced within that damned small chamber with my sister in the undercroft of the White Tower of all places?'

'I sent a message through the guards to the Constable of the Tower and to you that the man with the scar, for whom we have been searching, was in the Tower. He was right there, Tom. I could have waited until you had concluded your meeting with Hubert de Burgh or I could go after him myself.'

'And you chose the latter, of course.'

'I did.'

'But you did not go alone, did you, de Talmont?' The man's voice raised a notch. 'No, once again you heedlessly embroiled my innocent sister into our perilous work, which, may I add, Joan had no notion of until recently—because of you and because of your…association with her. God's blood, man, first you take her to Smythfeld, then to Bermondsye and now this.'

Which was putting it quite mildly. 'I know that Joan should never have been with me, but it was never my intention to have her accompany me around the Tower and it all happened rather quickly, Tom. The man was leaving and we had to follow, else we would have lost him.'

'Which you did anyway. Again…'

'Damn it, I know my failures, but I will catch the bastard and any associates he might have. Now, Tom, you must listen to me. There is much I need to tell you.'

That piqued his interest, momentarily. 'Well?'

'The man with the scar had, I believe, come to meet specifically with the Bishop of Winchester, Peter des Roches, who was not too pleased to see him, according to the musicians who witnessed the meeting in the hall. The whole encounter did not seem particularly friendly, apparently. And the Bishop had met the man dissembling as a flute player, while we were parleying with Hubert de Burgh. In fact, we found the real flute player, whom he had dispatched, in St John's Chapel later.'

'That is interesting.' Tom rubbed his jaw.

'Precisely, when you consider the enmity between the Bishop of Winchester and our liege lord, Hubert de Burgh.'

'But an incredibly odd, not to mention risky, choice for a rendezvous, especially with the Royal Court and Hubert de Burgh himself in attendance.'

'That is what I thought. One reason that I can come up with is that mayhap the man with the scar had no choice but to force a meeting with the Bishop, who, for all we know, might be distancing himself from the Duo Dracones. As well owing the man silver for services rendered.'

Tom nodded. 'Yes, yes, that is one explanation. In fact, this could be the link that we have been searching for between the Duo Dracones and the Bishop.' He took a deep breath and glared at him. 'Not that any of this explains why I found you with my sister, de Talmont. Do you even consider the danger you put her through?'

'Hell's teeth, Tom, I would have rather died than allowed any harm to come to her.'

'Very commendable, Warin, but that does not excuse anything that happened.' He could tell that his friend was just about holding on to his temper. 'It does not excuse the fact that you dishonoured her. It does not excuse the fact I caught you kissing Joan, *again*, but this time in a damn store cupboard, with the Constable of the Tower in tow and King Henry in residence. For God's sake, man, this was her first presentation at Court! Were you aware that she had intimated to me that she would like to be courted? That she wished for the prospect of marriage and even possibly a family of her own? Tell me who will pay attendance on Joan, once rumours about last night begin to circulate, which, believe me, they will. Hell's teeth, de Talmont, what were you thinking?'

That was precisely the problem—he did not *think*. Not when it came to Joan. God, what a damn mess he had got himself entangled in. Yet Warin could not stand by and allow Joan to be exposed to more censure, more ridicule, more scorn. It was his responsibility to get Joan out of this and salvage the situation.

'Mayhap I was only attempting to get ahead of the competition.'

'What does that mean?'

'I thought that was evident.' He shrugged, crossing his arms across his chest. 'I would like to make an offer for Joan's hand in marriage.'

Tom's jaw seemed to drop a touch. 'You? You would like to marry my sister?'

'Yes. If she will have me.'

'I do not comprehend you, Warin.' He shook his head in confusion. 'I was always led to believe that you would never take a wife, after what happened to your family.'

'Yes, but I will not have Joan put in a difficult situation.'

Tom rubbed his forehead and expelled an irritated breath. 'I thank you, Warin, for your concerns, but you need not worry about that. Joan's own family can protect her from that.'

Warin knew that it was true, but he could not countenance Joan's reputation to be safeguarded by her brother when he had been the one at fault to tarnish it in the first instance.

The truth was that although they had done little more than kiss, it had been when the Royal Court had been in residence, as Tom had pointed out. And since many courtiers would have noticed the two of them leaving the hall together, whispers of their kiss could be embellished and become far more than it was, once rumours of being found ensconced together in the undercroft was known. And once that happened, Joan would never be received again.

God only knew that he never wanted to be caught in such a circumstance as this, but there was little choice in the matter. He would have to put his own personal wishes aside, think of Joan and the only conceivable way to remedy the situation. Whatever misgivings he had for marriage, he knew this was the right thing to do. The only thing he could do to shield her. 'Nevertheless, I would still like to offer for Joan.'

'Would you now?'

'Yes.' He nodded in sincerity. 'I would like to be the one who protects Joan if there is to be any consequences from this—if there are to be rumours spread about her. I would be the one who can guarantee that if it were known that we have secretly been betrothed, or some such. Your sister means a great deal to me, Tom, and I tell you, I shall not stand for it. I would not have Joan's good name besmirched.'

They stared at one another, neither backing down until Tom blinked and looked away. 'Very well, so be it. I can mayhap bring this to Hubert de Burgh's attention and get a special concession to avoid these new marriage banns. The Bishop of London owes both de Burgh and me a favour, so I might be able to arrange it so that this whole debacle is cleared up as soon as may be.'

'This whole debacle?' Joan's voice came from behind them. 'What an unusual term to attach to a supposedly happy event.'

'Ah, Joan… Apologies, Sister, but I believed you to be abed.'

'I'm sure you did, Brother, but I hope you do not mind that I am present while you discuss and arrange my future.'

'Joan…'

'I know that I have little to offer, but I would like to ask whether I get a say in these discussions?'

Warin strode towards her and grasped her hands in his. 'Of course you do, sweetheart. This discourse is all about you.'

'And you, it seems.' She moved closer and quietened her voice. 'What has changed, Warin? You have mentioned more times than I can recall how you would never remarry. I do not comprehend any of this.'

'I can understand that this has come about quickly, but think about it, Joan,' he said softly. 'We were bound to get caught in a compromising situation. Every time you and I spend even a short time together, we find it far too difficult to fight against the obvious attraction between us.'

'But to wed? Is this not what you have carefully avoided?'

Yes…

'That is by the by, Joan. It is of no consequence now.'

'I would dislike it above all things if you felt forced to offer for me, Warin.'

'Do you believe that anyone has ever been able to force me to do anything against my wishes?' He brushed the back of his fingers across her cheeks. 'Besides, did you not urge me earlier to reach out and take that leap? Did you not say that there is always a choice in such matters? Well, this is my choice and I would like to ask you whether I can also be yours.'

Joan looked astounded. 'I do not know what to say.'

'Say yes. Say that you'll be my wife.'

Joan lifted her head and said nothing for a moment before a slow smile played on her lips. 'Very well. Yes… I shall.'

Warin kissed her lips briefly to seal their pledge to one another as an overwhelming feeling of peace laced with panic coursed through him.

Joan's hasty marriage was brought about swiftly. And after just a few short days, without the necessary banns, the day of her marriage had finally arrived. A day she could never have truly envisaged would ever come. And yet here it was.

However, Joan could not ignore the truth that she was marrying Warin de Talmont after being found ensconced with him in a store cupboard by her own brother. How quickly had her embarrassment and shame at the situation changed after a surprising offer by Warin. But knowing him as she did now, Joan knew that deep down it was his deep sense of honour and his innate need to do his duty by her that had led to the unexpected proposal. And this somehow made Joan feel somewhat nervous and uneasy. Mayhap these twinges of nerves were common among new brides.

Joan took a deep breath and answered a knock on her door. It was her brother who stood in the doorway, smiling at her.

'May I come in, Sister?'

'Of course.' She returned his smile and went back to searching for her painted cross, the token gift from her beloved sister.

'You look beautiful, Joan.'

Her wedding attire was a simple leaf-green velvet kirtle over a cream linen tunic, embroidered with dark green thread-work around the square neckline and the edge of her fluted sleeves. She wore a sheer cream lace veil which had once belonged to her mother on her head and topped this with a silver circlet.

'I thank you.'

'Here, allow me.' Tom took the cross, set on another chain, and fastened it at the back. 'I wish that I could give you the gold-and-pearl cross that our mother had intended for you, Joan. She would have wanted you to have it on your wedding day.'

But that along with far more precious things had been destroyed in the fire. Namely their family, their mother, their sister.

'It is of no matter, Tom. I have this.' She held up the simple painted wooden cross. 'I have you.'

'Yes, you do.' He cleared his throat. 'I think about them often, Joan. Our mother…our sister.'

'As do I,' she muttered softly. 'I often wonder how life would have treated them.'

'By making their way in the world, just as you and I have.' His lips quirked. 'I do believe that they would have been very happy for you today, Joan…as I am.'

'I know,' she whispered, a sudden lump forming in her throat.

'Although I must admit that I shall selfishly miss having you close by. And I shall miss not having you reside here.'

Oh, dear. Joan felt as though she might resort to tears if she did not defuse the situation. 'But I cannot imagine that you would miss my impulsiveness, my impetuousness, as well as my wilful, troublesome behaviour.'

'Oh, yes, do not remind me.' He laughed softly. 'Even so, I believe I shall miss it all—after all, that is what makes you special.'

She lowered her eyes, lest he witness the tears that had collected there or, worse, notice the slight trepidation in them. 'You are the best of brothers, Tom.'

He pulled her into a hug. 'I am your only brother, Joan. Tell me, are you ready to be wed today?'

'I believe I am.'

'Are you certain? I would not want you to commit to this if you have any doubts.'

Joan did have misgivings that stemmed from a sense of guilt about how her marriage to Warin had come about. It had not escaped her attention that if she had not followed him out of the hall, if she had just listened to his reasoning about staying where she was, none of this would have happened. He would not feel the need to protect her by an unwanted marriage—which surely this must be.

But the emotions that had led to that very moment had taken over both of them before there was even time to reconsider their actions. That was the one thing Warin had been right about—the desire and attraction between them which had become increasingly difficult to contain. It would always have led them to ruin, re-criminations or to this.

So be it. She would marry Warin de Talmont and she would make certain that he would never regret it. Indeed, she would do all that she could to make him happy.

'Yes.' She nodded. 'I am certain.'

They journeyed to All Hallows Church on foot and, once their party reached Honey Lane, they were met by some of the children from the church, who were busy scattering dried thyme and lavender as they walked along, releasing the perfumed floral and herbaceous fragrance in the air. At the arched doorway that opened inside, Warin stood with his two friends, Nicholas d'Amberly and Savaric Fitz Leonard. Joan's eyesight might be poor, but she did not fail to notice how well he looked, how handsome he was and how he was smiling broadly at her, making her heart leap.

He bowed. 'Good morrow, Joan. What a fine day this is to wed.' He held out his arm, which she took. They made their way through the archway before he paused and presented her with a bunch of cut autumnal flowers and herbs.

'These are for you.' Warin held the flowers out to her and Joan took them with a small curtsy. There was something about his whole countenance that made her ponder whether he was as nervous as she.

'Thank you. I can tell that they're beautiful.' She pressed the posy to her nose. 'And what lovely fragrance, especially the dried lavender. You remembered?'

'I did and had them dried for that very reason. I am glad you like them.' He nodded to the church entrance. 'Shall we?'

'My friend, as you can tell, is very keen to wed you, Mistress Joan.' Nicholas d'Amberly laughed from behind. 'So much so that he has forgotten to mention how lovely you look on this felicitous occasion.'

'Either that or nerves have possibly set in, eh, de Talmont?' Savaric Fitz Leonard added sardonically.

'Yes, thank you both for your unwanted observations.' Warin shook his head and muttered, 'Who needs friends such as these? But by and by, you do look particularly lovely, Joan.'

'Thank you.' The butterflies in her stomach unfurled.

'Well then, mayhap we should enter this holy place now. Do you not think?'

'Yes.' She smiled. 'I do.'

Chapter Eighteen

In no time, Joan was wed—to a man who had always maintained that he would never marry again. And yet he had done it willingly. He had done it in order to shield her from any possible unpleasantness. He had done it... *for her*. And Joan would never forget his selflessness.

'Are you well?' Warin muttered from beside her as he took a sip of wine from a silver goblet.

'Oh, yes.' She took a deep breath. 'I was just reflecting how exceptionally quick all of this has happened.'

'By "this", I suppose you refer to our hastily arranged marriage?'

'Yes.' She shook her head. 'Not in my wildest imagination would I have believed that this would be the eventual outcome of our friendship.'

'Ah, but we did cross the boundaries of what might be considered an acceptable friendship.' He took a bite from the skewered pheasant in a rich wine and berry sauce that he had taken from their shared trencher.

'And now, unbelievable as it might seem, we are married.'

'We are. But let us not look to the past, but the future. Besides, I am hopeful that our union will build on our particular friendship.'

'As am I.' Joan damped down her apprehension, realising that Warin was at least attempting to reassure her.

He held out a morsel of food. 'Try this, it is delicious.'

She took the proffered food and began to chew, finding it difficult to swallow.

'You are right, it is delicious,' she muttered, trying to garner some enthusiasm, but her appetite had all but deserted her, with her stomach turning on itself, instead.

'This is quite a wedding feast that Tom's wife has arranged.'

'Indeed, Brida was very happy organising every detail of this wedding celebration.'

They had put together long trestle tables around the gardened quadrant in the walled churchyard, since the weather was unusually warm for that time of year. Joan had wanted to have All Hallows involved in some way and it made sense to have both the ceremony and the feast there. Especially as it meant that all the orphaned children could also partake in the festivities.

Even the young orphaned maid, whom Joan had rescued, had manged a small smile and allowed Warin a kiss on the cheek. Oh, yes, the children had certainly enjoyed this day enormously. Joan only wished she could as well, but nerves were beginning to seep into her bones, which was not helped by the constant reminder that soon she would leave All Hallows, as she had left her brother's home, and start her own with Warin. And far sooner than that would be the prospect of the wedding night itself and everything that would entail.

'You are unusually quiet, Joan.'

'Am I?' She turned towards him, giving him a winsome smile. 'I was just reflecting on this momentous day. After all, it is not every day that one gets wed.'

'No, and I hope it has been everything you hoped it would be?'

'Of course.' Heavens above, but her smile was beginning to feel a little brittle, a little forced.

Joan turned back towards the pretty quad where she could just about make out the hum of chatter and laughter generating from their small wedding party—her brother and his family, Warin, his friends and a handful of the clergy and the children from All Hallows. She could feel their merriment and hear the warmth and mirth, yet at that moment she suddenly felt a little despondent, a little distant and cut off from everyone around her— something Joan knew was a ridiculous notion, as they were all so familiar and dear to her.

It certainly did not help that Joan's eyes felt particularly strained today. And yet it was another timely reminder that this was precisely the reason why her affliction made her different and why she felt as she did. God, but it made her feel wretched. How could she have believed her life would possibly be this favourable? Nothing ever was—not for her.

What had she been thinking? That because she was attracted to this man, because she had gone horseback riding with him, danced with him, kissed him and confided and shared aspects of her life with him, imparting her deepest convictions and beliefs, she could somehow have a claim on him? That she knew how to be a wife to him—a man who carried scars from his previous marriage? She who barely functioned on her own without another's aid, who one day would come to rely completely on others—on her *husband*—on Warin de Talmont, whom she was now bound to. How on earth could she make him happy? How in heavens could she be the wife he deserved and, Lord knew, he deserved more. Far more than a woman such as she—flawed, lacking and afflicted with such an impediment.

One day soon when she ceased to see altogether— would he come to regret this marriage? Joan could only wonder how this difficulty, this problem, could determine their future, their very happiness together. It was disconcerting that their marriage now seemingly rested on these unstable, shaky foundations.

Why had she believed she had all the necessary attributes as a woman, as a wife, to make Warin happy and content? That he in time would not come to resent her for being less than she was? Lord, how dispiriting and on the day she had pledged herself to the man, yet she could not help these musings from tumbling into her head.

'Would you care for a dance, Joan?' Warin murmured from beside her, pulling her back to the present. 'I believe that Brida's renowned lute playing has just commenced.'

Indeed, her sister by marriage was not only a proficient musician, but highly sought after to play by the Royal Court, not that she always acquiesced to the many requests made by courtiers to play.

'I believe that might be true but, alas, my eyes are a little sore, so unfortunately I feel unable to partake in such an activity.'

'Even if I promise that I shall not let you go and hold on to you especially tightly?'

She gulped. 'Even then.'

'Ah, for shame, Joan.' He winked. 'For I must now seek another who might grant me that elusive wedding dance.'

Joan watched as Warin strode across the court and solicited the fair-haired orphaned maid. Although the little maid had still not uttered a single word in all the time she had been at All Hallows, she had recently managed to break a small smile. She had managed to enjoy these festivities. It warmed Joan's heart that they were slowly making progress and breaking through the little girl's defences. And just to prove the point, Joan could just about make out that the maid had all but accepted dancing with Warin.

He carried her against his hip and twirled her around to the music, earning him a chuckle from the young maid. It was sweet, charming and utterly childlike in its innocence, which made her heart melt, but also brought a lump to her throat. With a sudden awareness, she realised the reason behind all her recent emotions. The reason why she felt as she did.

Joan knew now, with stark certainty, the reason why Warin de Talmont's happiness seemingly mattered to her as much as it did. Why she had been plagued by doubt and insecurity when another's opinions of her never mattered before. Why she was as nervous as she was of what the future held for her—for the two of them. It was now as clear to her as day and night—oh, Lord above, she was in love with him. And the knowledge of this was both staggering and utterly overwhelming. For Joan to realise this on the day of her wedding should have filled her with joy, yet it made her feel as though she were on the edge of a precipice, without knowing how it would all inevitably end for her—or indeed the both of them.

Warin was a married man again despite all his best efforts to avoid that possibility. And he could not help but consider how everything in his life would change irrevocably after such a hasty whirlwind betrothal. It had barely allowed the two of them to become used to the idea of their impending marriage. Which brought about a strange impenetrable barrier between them— an awkwardness that he felt to his very bones. In truth, it had all happened far too quickly. He knew and understood the reasons well and wholeheartedly agreed why there could be no proper courtship, in an attempt to spare Joan any possible unpleasantness. Yet it did not lessen the discomfort, embarrassment and, yes, awkwardness they now felt around each other. Their easy comradery and discourse had seemingly dissipated and had been consigned to the past.

As well as this, he sensed that Joan was nervous, more than she had ever been in his presence, which in turn made him a little uneasy. He had to do something. He had to break through this impasse.

'It has been a most splendid day,' he muttered as he took his seat beside his new bride.

'Indeed, it has…most splendid.'

'With such convivial company, a wonderful setting and delicious food. What more could anyone be in want of?'

'Yes, I could not be in want of anything more,' she muttered. 'And this is a veritable feast.'

He tried again. 'It is a veritable feast. Would you care for more pheasant? It is incredibly tender. You must have the lamb with mint and mead sauce, it is most succulent.'

'No, I thank you.'

'Mayhap I can tempt you with some pork braised in buttermilk and honey?'

'Thank you, but I am quite full.'

'Ah, but I do not believe I have seen you indulging in any offerings of food.' He felt her stiffen and bristle beside him. 'Of course, if you do not have much of an appetite, then that would explain it.'

'Yes, just so.'

He raised a brow. 'Let me see, now…you would not dance, you have no appetite. Truly, are you well, Joan?'

'How can I not be on such a happy occasion?'

'Quite.'

A faint smile hovered on her lips. 'You must not feel that you must constantly be looking out for me, Warin.'

'On the contrary, that is precisely what I must do.'

'Oh.' She bit down on her bottom lip, in the way she did when she was particularly nervous. 'I would not wish to be an inconvenience.'

'You are not.' He covered her hand with his. 'You are my wife, Joan.'

He heard a small, shaky intake of breath before she replied, 'So I am. How incredibly fortuitous for me.'

Damn. He had to break through the awkwardness that had seemed to have developed between them. He had to coax and jolt her out of her solemnity.

'Indeed, and as you are now my wife, there are certain prerequisites…or shall we say expectations?… that I have.'

She sat up stiffly and lifted her head a notch. 'Oh, and what might that be?' He had half expected her to laugh at what he was saying or come back with her own demands but, no, Joan seemed far more wary. Far more serious.

He licked his lip and continued with a half-smile. 'Well, I must admit that I am very particular about what I eat, especially the time I require my mealtimes to be.'

'I am sure that can be arranged.'

'Ah…well, good.' He scratched his chin, pondering on more absurdities. 'My clothes must all be washed, dried and laid out for my inspection at midday every Tuesday.'

She raised a brow. 'Well, I must say, that is very particular, not to mention slightly peculiar.'

'It is, but there is more. I also require that my feet are washed, rubbed and kneaded gently every evening before we turn in and certainly before Vespers.' He flashed her his most dazzlingly inane smile before continuing. 'For who could possibly offer a prayer with unkempt feet?'

'Who indeed?' She sighed irritably. 'And I suppose that your stipulation would be for me, as your wife, to be the lucky person who would wash and rub those unkempt feet of yours?'

'Naturally.' He chuckled softly. 'I hope you are in agreement with all of this. And that you will be able to accommodate my expectations of you as my wife.'

Surely Joan could tell that he was not serious.

'If that is what you require from a wife, then very well.'

Indeed, this whole discourse had not gone the way he had believed it would. Not in any way. He had wanted to provoke a laugh or chuckle from her by making a funny quip, or parting with such silly nonsense but, no, she believed him. And she did not seem in any way amused. In truth, Warin was not particularly good at levity or diverting witty repartee.

'I was jesting, Joan. None of what I said is true.'

'Oh…' her brows furrowed in the middle in confusion '…how very droll.'

He laced his fingers through hers. 'It was just a ruse, Joan, to break through this odd tension that has developed between us ever since we agreed to be wed.'

'Oh…'

'But allow me to say that I have no such expectations or prerequisites.' He sighed, shaking his head. 'Other than your contentment and comfort within this marriage.'

'But I do not even know how to be a wife, Warin,' she hissed under her breath. 'I do not know what I should do.'

Oh, Lord. He smiled inwardly. Could this woman be any more endearing? Had this been what she had been apprehensive about all this time? Evidently so.

'Joan,' he murmured softly, pulling her a little closer by the hand. 'I cannot profess to know how to be a good husband to you either. This is all very new to me as well, despite the fact that I was married before. In truth, I am now a different man to the one I was before and, as such, I am also at a loss as to what to do.'

She looked a little relieved. 'Then we are both in the same situation.'

'Yes,' he drawled. 'We shall have to find out and discover it all…together.'

She nodded, looking away, taking in everything around her. 'I noticed that you danced with our young mute orphaned maid,' she said, changing the subject.

'Did you, now?' He cut up an apple with his dagger, offering her a slice. 'Since you rejected me as a partner, I had no choice but to find a substitute.'

'And I am glad you did. I can wholeheartedly say that it was a revelation to have the child enjoy herself as she did. Thank you, Warin.'

'It was my pleasure.' He watched her over the rim of his goblet. 'I found that she reminded me, in many ways, of *you*.'

Joan raised a brow, evidently surprised by what he had said. 'Oh, how so?'

'By the way in which she somehow understands and reads a situation that she finds herself in. The child is incredibly intuitive.'

'As am I, presumably?' He topped up her goblet with wine and pressed it back into her hands. 'I had no notion that you were making such observations, during just a dance.'

'In truth, it is something I have noted before. But as for the dance—the young maid was a delight and I am glad she enjoyed it.'

'How could she not when she was twirled and spun around by a handsome knight?'

'I might not be good at jesting or being witty, but it seems that my talents lie in twirling and spinning young maids until they're far too dizzy to contemplate much else.'

She chuckled lightly. 'Well, now I am sorry I resisted such delights.'

He turned around and leant closer, whispering so only she could hear, 'Ah, but my hope is that you would not want to resist anything now, Joan.'

'And if I do?'

He shrugged as he took a bite from a slice of apple. 'Then I would have to make certain that there are more delights than just twirling and spinning that I might tempt you with.'

Warin smiled inwardly as Joan flushed and looked away at his brashness. Still, it brought to mind something that Warin had been pondering on.

'I wonder to what you might be suggesting?' Was it his imagination, or had Joan's voice become a little huskier, a little more breathless?

He held out more slices of fruit. 'A juicy piece of red apple that I would wager comes from your brother's orchard.' He winked. 'What else could I possibly be suggesting?'

What, indeed?

Chapter Nineteen

It did not seem too long after that Warin and Joan had bid their guests farewell and left All Hallows Church on horseback, making the short journey out of the city gates to Warin's simple but comfortable lodgings. And with every slow trot bringing her closer to her new home, Joan felt her stomach plummet and her brow becoming clammy. Once again she was nervous all over, knowing where this night would inevitably lead.

Oh, heavens above.

Warin's lodgings was along a small pathway a few roads outside Newgate. It was comfortably appointed above another dwelling, taking in the whole of the upper two floors, with its large and airy bedchamber and adjoining antechamber that had a large welcoming hearth with a bench set in front and a comfortable table. Lots of crockery was stacked upon it, as well as more of the fresh and dried flowers that Warin had presented to Joan earlier, arranged artfully in a large jug. This room in turn led to another smaller chamber, that seemed to be used as a storage cupboard—a place that Joan need not be reminded of.

She returned back to the main bedchamber and noticed that her wooden coffer containing all her clothing and other belongings had already been accommodated in the corner of the room. The fire crackled and spat in the hearth and the dotted candles were lit around the bedchamber, providing a warm, hazy, soft glow that welcomed her to her new abode.

'I hope you like it here, Joan.' Warin dragged his fingers through his dark hair that curled at the nape. 'But fear not, as this is a temporary situation since I intend to look for larger, more appropriate lodgings soon.'

'Oh, but I like it very well. It is surprisingly homely for a bachelor dwelling.'

'Ah, but it is no longer as such.' He held out his hand. 'Come, allow me to fetch you a mug of ale or perchance more wine?'

She definitely needed more of the dark red fruity drink to give her the necessary fortification she needed later. 'Wine, I thank you.'

She stood perfectly still as Warin left the chamber and returned with two mugs of wine, one of which he pressed into her hands.

'To your health,' he made a toast, lifting his mug before taking a sip.

'And to yours,' she returned the salutation, taking far too much of a big gulp, which made her cough profusely.

'Here, allow me.' Warin took the mug from her and gently patted her back. 'Better?'

'Better,' she croaked, nodding.

He took her by her hands and led her to sit at the edge of the bed, as her heart tripped over itself. She took in a shaky breath and tried to smile as she raised her face to meet his.

'You look as though you are about to meet a fate worse than torture. In fact, worse than anything that has ever happened to you before.'

'I admit that I am particularly nervous,' she chuckled, shaking her head.

'There really is no need to be, Joan, I promise.' He sat beside her, taking her hand in his. 'All we are going to do is to enjoy being with one another tonight. Nothing more, nothing less. But I shall say that if you feel you are too uncomfortable, too tired, too weary, and wish to go to bed and sleep, then I do understand. We can take this as slowly as you like.'

Joan turned her hand around, so that they were hand to hand, palm to palm, and laced her fingers with his.

'I am not too tired, Warin,' she murmured softly. 'Nor am I too weary.'

His other hand moved around the back of her neck and tugged her a little closer towards him. 'Good, because neither am I.'

He caught her lips and kissed her, moulding his mouth to hers before pulling away.

Warin stood in front of her and unfastened his gambeson, taking the garment off and throwing it on the wooden floor. He kicked off his boots and knelt at Joan's feet, taking her slippered foot into his hand and slowly peeling it off her foot before moving to the other. He then carefully placed each foot on his knee, rolling down her ungainly hose, slowly revealing her bare feet and ankles, and probably gained a glimpse of her calves. She gulped as he stood and lifted her to her feet to stand in front of him.

Warin took her hands in his and placed them on his chest. 'Will you help me undress?' he whispered.

She nodded, not trusting herself to speak, and did as he bid, her fingers fumbling as she untied the front ties of his tunic. Once that small task was completed, Warin gave her small smile before pulling the tunic over his head and dumping that also on the floor, his eyes never leaving hers. He was now naked from the waist up—his huge, magnificent chest on display.

Joan placed her shaking hands on his chest, feeling the hard planes and his wide shoulders, marvelling at the soft skin that covered the taut rock-hard muscles beneath. His chest rose and fell rapidly as she continued to explore and feel her way around him. Her fingers traced a long scar just under his ribcage. She ran her fingers up and down the length of it.

'I gained that one in combat a few years ago,' he murmured.

'And this?' She found another smaller, but more jagged scar to the side of his chest.

He chuckled softly. 'That was a particularly nasty blow that I received at a skirmish after the siege of Bedford Castle.'

She nodded, absently remembering that her brother had also been at the siege a few years back. Her fingers and hands continued to explore more scars and ragged unevenness dotted across the smooth planes of his chest, abdomen and large arms.

'This is all a testament to the hardened warrior you

are. That you have endured and survived the many conflicts you have been involved in.'

He shrugged. 'It is just the life of a seasoned soldier, Joan. Nothing more.'

She frowned, unable to grapple with Warin's dismissiveness of his own talents. 'Oh, I disagree. I believe it is a lot more.'

She wanted to add that *he* was so much more, but the heated look he gave her made her forget what she had wanted to say.

Warin reached down and removed her circlet from her head and then the sheer veil, turning to place the item atop the coffer, revealing her hair loosely tied up. She lifted her head and helped take out the ribbons that tied her hair. And then slowly she removed all the fasteners that held up her long hair, making it tumble all down around her shoulders and down her back.

She wondered whether she had heard the small gasp that escaped from Warin's lips. Taking a step back, she attempted to untie the ribbons at the front of her kirtle, but her fingers would not cease shaking.

'Allow me.' He pushed her hands aside and began to untie the ribbons, loosening the neckline of the kirtle, breathing heavily as the warmth of his fingertips seeped through the thin linen tunic. He then untied the sleeves that were attached to the slim shoulder strap and allowed them to drop down her arms.

Joan then lifted her head, giving him a shy smile, her cheeks flooding with heat as she took a deep breath and pulled the kirtle dress strap over one shoulder and then the other, then allowing the whole garment to slide down her body and fall to the ground. She felt his gaze on her as she stood in front of him with just a cream-coloured linen tunic, her heart beating a tattoo against her chest.

'Oh, God, Joan,' he murmured as he stepped forward and caught a tendril of her hair between his fingers. 'You are so beautiful.'

'As are you.'

He chuckled softly. 'Surely not. As we have established, I have far too many blemishes and scars that prove to the contrary.'

'But that only signifies that you are and have been a battle-weary knight, as you said. No scar can take away how powerful or how well you look. You are indeed a beautiful man, Warin.'

'I thank you, even though this is the first anyone has used such a word to me. You put me to the blush.' He grinned.

'I am glad because it draws attention away from my own flushed, crimson, blotchy face.'

Joan felt so self-aware, standing there wearing scarcely any clothing, wondering what in heavens she should do next. She felt excited, tense and apprehensive all at the same time.

'Is it really?' He shook his head, taking her hands. 'I cannot tell.'

Mayhap she should tease. It would certainly take the edge off. 'How very droll. Do you think that I believe such a blatant attempt to allay my embarrassment, when you can see perfectly well, sir?'

'Absolutely. I would do everything in my power to appease and comfort my lady.' He bent down and kissed her cheeks and then her nose and then her lips. 'And in that vein, I would do much, much more, Joan.'

'You would erase my nervousness?' she muttered, biting her lip. 'Though I am sure it is quite natural in a circumstance such as this.'

'True.' He nuzzled her neck, kissing and nipping from her earlobe to the curve of her shoulder, making her gasp. 'I am sure it will pass.'

'And if it does not?' she whispered.

'Then I shall have to think of something.' He cupped her jaw and tilted her face, kissing her, running his tongue around the outline of her lips, learning again the shape of her mouth and coaxing them apart. He licked and tasted her so deeply, that she felt her knees might give way. He pulled away slightly and gave her a small smile, his fingers caressing her face.

'I shall have to be far more imaginative and help you forget feeling so nervous.'

She smiled, sinking her teeth into her bottom lip, a little swollen after his kiss. 'Ah, now I am very intrigued by the methods that you would deploy.'

'You should be.' His hands wrapped around her waist, pulling her closer to him, and he nipped her earlobe.

'It seems my husband is not only handsome,' she gasped as he sucked the throbbing vein on her neck before nipping her throat, 'but extremely resourceful.'

'I am glad you believe so.'

'But, alas, there is such a disparity between us, Warin.'

He pulled back. 'Oh, how so?'

'Well, you have been married before.'

'I have.'

Oh, Lord, how could she explain? 'Yes, but *this*... this is not something I wish to be in the dark about.'

'Ah, I believe I understand you.' He gave her a reassuring smile. 'We shall soon fix that.'

But, no, Warin did not still seem to comprehend her reservation. This was precisely what Joan felt when she was in a situation that was out of her realm of control. Flustered and unsure, even though she could hardly deny the desire that had flared between them. Still, it made her nervous taking the next step with him—*her husband.* She wished she did not deliberate on these thoughts that whirled through her head endlessly. It was her own failing, not his, even in a situation she had no experience in.

Joan took a deep breath and attempted to make him understand. 'In this light, I can barely see any of you.'

He cradled the back of her neck, his fingers curling around her jaw as his lips, tongue and teeth continued to explore her.

'And should you need to see me?' His voice held a faint note of amusement.

'Yes. After all, you can see me—every part of me.' She grappled with how she could remedy the situation. 'We could blow out all the candles, then we would both be in the dark.' Yes, that could possibly settle her nerves.

A slow wicked smile spread on his lips. 'I believe I have a better idea, if you are willing to consider it?'

Warin turned and strode towards the wooden coffer and retrieved a long length of cloth that had been wrapped and tied around the bouquet of fresh and dried flowers he had earlier presented her with. He walked towards her, dragging the cloth under his nose, inhaling the floral scent deeply.

'Here.' He held out the cloth. 'Tie this around my eyes. It might not be as…er…accessible as turning down the candles, but it is far more inventive.'

She blinked, shaking her head. 'It seems that you are indeed resourceful.'

'It will be just like the game we played in the quadrant of All Hallows Church. But because the cloth is opaque, I will just about see your outline, your silhouette, Joan. In truth, this way we shall *both* see a little of one another. This way, it will cast a warm golden hue that would chase the shadows away. This way, it shall be equal.'

Her heart slammed against her ribs at those evocative words as he reached for her, brushing his fingers down the column of her neck and waited for her to respond. She opened her mouth to answer, but closed it again—the words were stuck at the back of her throat. So she nodded instead.

Joan's hands shook as he handed her the cloth, then gave her a smouldering look before turning around and sitting down on the edge of the bed, with his back to her. She took a deep breath before securing the cream-coloured material around Warin's eyes, wrapping it around a few times and tying it at the back.

'There,' she murmured breathlessly, her voice husky, even to her own ears. 'Does that still cast a sufficient warm glow?'

'Oh, yes, very, very warm.'

He turned back around on the bed, his hands groping about in the dark until he caught her hand, pulling her close gently. Joan moved to stand in between his outstretched legs as he flexed his large hands around her waist until she stood over him and felt his ragged breath against her stomach. One hand trailed up and down her spine, sending a shiver through her. The other reached up to the base of her neck and slowly grazed down her body along every dent, curve and crevice. He made his way back over the curve of her breast, his thumb stroking her nipple over her sheer tunic, again and again, making it pucker. A moan slipped out of her mouth as his hand moved back down, until it reached the dip of her waist.

Her fingers drove into his hair, holding him against her as he began kissing, nipping and licking around her stomach and up the side of her breast through the sheer material, as he slowly slid the tunic up her body using his hands, revealing her little by little. She took a sharp breath in, not knowing whether to concentrate on what his mouth was doing or his hands, which deftly continued to slide the tunic up, whispering against her body as it did so. His hands, mouth, tongue and teeth explored her so slowly that she wanted to scream. She began to sway slightly, the blood in her veins becoming a blaze, melting her. Warin held on to her and before Joan knew what had happened, he had managed to pull her tunic over her head, throwing it to the floor.

Joan had never in her life stood naked, without a stitch of clothing, in front of any other. Yet this was not someone of little or no significance—this was her new husband, Warin de Talmont.

He lifted his head, his eyes covered by a length of material tied around his head, so that he could share with the limitation of Joan's dwindling sight as much as he could. And he had done it for her. He had done it so that she would cease being so uneasy and uncertain. The jolt of realisation made her heart soar. She could only wonder at his selflessness in his attempt to put her at ease. This incredibly gorgeous, brooding, yet kind man.

She cupped his jaw and brushed her thumb over his lips before bending her head to kiss his lips. Emboldened, she copied what he had done earlier and traced his lips with her tongue and heard a low growl escape from his lips before she dipped her tongue inside his mouth and tasted him wantonly.

Heavens, it was all so potent, all so heady and she, God help her, wanted more of this ardour and passion. She revelled in being the one in control, the one who was kissing this big, beautiful man, her hands moving from his jaw down the corded column of his throat and along the wide expanse of his shoulders, finding those scars and blemishes once again.

He stood, towering over her, his breathing ragged, taking her hands and placing them on the ties of his braes.

'Help me undress, Joan,' he whispered.

Her fingers shook as she helped Warin untie the braes that were attached to the hose wrapped tightly around his well-defined legs, but as soon it came apart, one by one the garments fell off his hips and fell to the floor.

Joan's lips quivered helplessly, knowing that he, too, now stood naked before her.

'Take my hand,' he murmured into the crook of her neck before she tentatively placed her hand in his. He gently pulled her to sit back on the bed as he untied the

ties of the bed curtain and Joan was all of a sudden as-
sailed by the waft of lavender flooding her senses. God,
but Warin must have crushed some of the dried petals of
the flower and strewn it on the coverlet of the bed pallet
before. She felt a surge of emotion rush through her, as
she thought of Warin's tender thoughtfulness in all that he
had done to make this first time so special between them.

The bed dipped as he sat beside her and gently
pushed her down on the bed before he moved to lie
down beside her. She blinked and saw that he was on
his side, his arm bent and his head resting against the
tips of his fingers, the length of his body against hers.

Nothing happened for a moment, only the sound of
their breathing and the crackling flame burning in the
hearth. Her chest rose and fell rapidly in anticipation as
Warin hovered over her. She wrapped her hands around
his neck, drawing him closer, and their lips met, his
mouth covering hers—this time they kissed long and
hard, tasting and devouring one another. His hands
moved over her body, learning the shape of her this
time without having the barrier of her tunic in the way.

His hands brushed from her collarbone around her
breasts, over her stomach and all the way down to her
toes and back up again. He palmed one breast, pressing
kisses and licking his way around the soft curve before
taking her nipple into his mouth and sucking it. Joan
wanted to jump out from her skin and scream with the
unexpected sensation building and layering, sending a
shiver through her body. He threw her a wicked smile
before moving to her other breast and repeated touching, licking and sucking as she began to thrash her head
from side to side, unable to contain the mounting need

building in her body. God, but she wanted more—more of this fervour—this madness that was taking hold of her and coursing molten heat through her blood.

Warin manoeuvred himself on top of her, pushing her legs apart, and settled himself in between, draping one leg over his shoulder. She opened her eyes and watched him, blurry and obscure, but still with the length of material tied around his eyes.

'If it is getting uncomfortable around your eyes,' she muttered breathlessly, 'you can take it off, Warin. I want you to be just as you want to be.'

'I find that this is precisely what I would like to do and I must say that it is a revelation, Joan. For me to feel you and use only a handful of my senses is far more exciting then I gave it credit for.'

It thrilled her to have Warin disclose such a thing at that moment. She reached up and touched his face. 'Are you certain?'

He grabbed her hand and placed a kiss in the centre of her palm. 'Absolutely. It heightens everything and makes this a new experience for me, too,' he whispered as he pressed another lingering kiss on her hand before taking her finger into his mouth, making her groan out loud.

'But you know that this—tonight—is not about me, not in the least,' he murmured, turning his head and pressing his lips to the side of her leg, making her gasp. 'It is all for you and I would do a lot more besides…to make you happy, Joan.'

Warin's words bewildered Joan as much as they made her heart sing. She felt so elated with these tender sentiments, but did it mean that he felt more for her than she had assumed? Joan knew he cared for her, but did he feel more? Did he feel as she did? In that moment she wished that she could truly see him—see right into his eyes and determine for herself whether he might possibly love her without actually saying the words to her.

Joan was pulled back into the present by Warin's kissing and nipping her gently along the side of the sensitive skin of her leg. It was then that she lost all coherent thought with all of her so attuned to what her *husband* was doing to her and how he was making her feel.

Oh, heavens above, but how did he manage to evoke such pleasure within her? She felt an inexplicable need inside her that built more and more. His hands took over from his lips and began to stoke her gently along the inside of her legs, making her quiver and arch her back. He leant over her and took her mouth again in another hot passionate kiss, as his fingers moved higher and higher along her legs. He then dipped one of his fingers inside her, moving it in and out slowly, and then added another finger.

Dear God! What was happening to her? What was this man doing to her? How in heaven's name did he make her want more—so much more?

She felt the loss of his fingers as he removed them and pushed up against him. It was then as she moaned and writhed beneath him that she felt Warin push inside her and her breath caught in her throat. He pushed a little more as she dug her nails in his shoulders, holding on to him for support as he slid inside further.

He stilled, not moving, holding his weight on his bent arms on either side of her head.

'This might hurt a little, Joan,' he whispered, kissing her on her forehead. 'But I hope it will be of short duration.'

'No matter.' She reached up and touched his lips, his covered eyes, and delved her fingers into his hair. 'This pain—is one that I never believed I would ever experience. I welcome it with all my heart.'

She could not see his eyes, but his lips stretched into a smile.

'You honour me and never fail to amaze, Joan,' he growled before kissing her open-mouthed and beginning to move inside her again. Then, with a gentle kiss on her brow, he plunged deep inside, drowning out her cry with the heat and potency of his hungry kiss.

Joan's body felt as though it would shatter and break into tiny pieces as Warin moved more and more inside her, quickening his speed as all her senses were suddenly heightened and alive. Sparks burst at the back of her eyes, unlike anything that she had ever experienced before.

It was a moment that she would never forget—not for the rest of her life. This deep connection and complete unity with another. With this wonderful man who had given her so, so much.

She wrapped her legs around him, drawing him deeper inside, and reached out to cup his tense jaw as his body strained above her. He suddenly shuddered and collapsed on top of her.

'I love you,' she whispered as she held on to him tightly, feeling the vibrations of his body, his chest rising and falling rapidly. 'I love you, Warin de Talmont.'

Chapter Twenty

Warin let out a ragged breath and moved his weight back on to his elbows so as not to crush his new bride. He brought his mind back to the words she had just uttered and frowned in bewilderment.

Had she…? Had she just professed her love for him? How was that possible?

It could not be—he must have imagined it in his head. After all his body and mind were preoccupied with the mesmerising woman beneath him, who had captivated him in every possible manner.

Yet she repeated the words.

'I love you, Warin de Talmont…'

Dear God.

It had indeed been a revelation to use only his sense of taste, using his mouth, his tongue and his teeth, and his sense of touch to explore every part of Joan. It had thrilled him beyond comprehension. And it startled him how much he had wanted her—how much he still wanted her—but this was not something he had expected.

Warin knew that there was an amazing connection,

not to mention an incredible attraction between them—but *love*? No that was not something that he had ever considered or particularly wanted. It would expose them both and place a fragile strain on both of them when they had only just wed.

And theirs had not been a union that had been made because of something as fragile as love. Respecting one another and caring for each other was all that was necessary in a marriage, surely? It had to be so when he had given everything—his heart and his very soul—to the ideas of courtly love once before and had lost all that he had ever held dear.

Besides, this had after all been a hastily arranged marriage that had come about so quickly that he could understand why it was easy to get carried away with one's emotions, when neither party had actually been looking for such a union. Mayhap Joan's declaration had been a moment of weakness after the amorous and frankly intensely passionate manner in which they had just consummated their marriage. Yet Warin could not help but feel a little uneasy by what Joan had disclosed, no less since it confounded and unsettled him. It made Warin conflicted and, far worse than that, it questioned his own feelings towards her—something he had no wish to probe.

'Allow me to tend to you, Joan.' He removed the material tied around his eyes and lifted himself off, shuffling to the edge of the bed, before retrieving his hose from the floor, dressing as expediently as he could.

Warin then strode to the antechamber and exhaled the breath he had not realised he was holding on to, taking a moment to compose himself before returning with a large bowl of water and some clean linen towels.

He pushed back the bed curtain and smiled at Joan, who was now sat on the bed with the coverlet wrapped around her body.

Sitting on the edge of the bed, he dipped the towel in the water, squeezing the excess out.

'If I may?' He raised a brow.

Joan frowned as if she was giving due consideration and then, after seemingly making a decision, she released the coverlet slightly, allowing him access. Warin slipped the towel along her legs, wiping and soothing them all the way to the top of her thighs, his hands shaking.

'You must not concern yourself with the sentiment I just blurted out, Warin.' Her voice seemed a little formal, as if she were addressing a stranger. 'I had not meant to embarrass you, especially since you do not return my...what I divulged.'

His hand stilled against her leg and he snapped his head up. 'There is no embarrassment, I assure you. Indeed, I am honoured, truly I am, but this is not what we ought to build the foundations of our marriage on.'

'You are right.' Her smile did not quite reach her eyes. 'But can we cease discussing this further in the hope that we might spare my embarrassment, then.'

'Joan...' he murmured softly, leaning forward so that he could wrap his arms around her.

She jerked back. 'I know that I can never replace her, Warin. I know I can never have that same regard. But I shall try to be a good wife to you.'

Hell's teeth, how had the evening descended to this?

This was precisely why he had such an aversion to the notions of *love*—the damned emotion never failed to complicate a situation. He could not afford the luxury of such an emotion, as it was not just a complication, but prevented him thinking properly and doing his job efficiently. As it had all those years ago, when he failed to protect his first wife, Ada.

'Of that I have no doubt, sweetheart. Just as I aim to be a good husband to you.'

She smiled again. 'I am glad that is settled. We shall talk no more of such sentiments.' She reached under the coverlet and snatched the towel from his hands. 'Thank you for your ministrations, but I think it is done now.'

'Of course,' he muttered, wondering how he could remedy the situation. 'Joan, I would say that...'

She shuffled to one side of the bed and turned to face him. 'I find that I am weary and tired after all, Warin. So, if you don't mind, I wish to sleep now.'

'Yes.' He nodded, unable to think of anything else to say. 'Goodnight, Joan.'

'Goodnight to you, Warin.' She turned away. 'And thank you for...everything.'

'My pleasure.'

And with that inane comment, Warin moved to his appointed side of the bed and attempted to slumber.

Joan woke early the following morn after having a fretful night trying to sleep. In the end she abandoned any further attempts at slumber and resigned herself to being awake. Eventually she rose out of bed at dawn and, after a morning wash, she fetched clean clothes from her coffer and began getting dressed for the day as quietly as possible so that she did not wake Warin. Joan then tidied her hair, securing it under her favourite sheer veil. Her fingers brushed against a handful of the dried lavender flowers and immediately she thought of the night before. She pushed the memory away and dropped the flowers in her small leather drawstring purse instead, tying it to her belt, and looked to busy herself by searching for some repast in the antechamber to break her fast. In truth, it was good to do anything to occupy herself with.

God, what an awful coil Joan now found herself in. She could not counter why she had blurted out her feelings and at such a time and was now filled with a deep sense of mortification and embarrassment. What in heaven's name had she been thinking? Why had she confessed her feelings as she had?

Joan absently grabbed a pewter mug on the small table and poured a measure of ale inside before taking a huge gulp. It was her unruly tongue and impulsive nature that had made her expose herself in that disconcerting manner. If only she could somehow take it back, as if it had not occurred.

'Good morrow.'

Joan swung around and could see Warin standing with his arms crossed, leaning against the wooden doorframe.

'Oh, good morrow,' she muttered, unable to meet his eyes. 'I hope I did not wake you?'

'No, you did not wake me,' he drawled, his stare boring into her.

'Can I fetch you some ale?'

'Yes, I thank you.' He prowled towards the table, his eyes never leaving hers. 'Are you well, Joan?'

'Yes, of course,' she mumbled, frustrated by her sudden shyness, after all the events of the previous night.

'You are not too…ah…sore?' he said in a low voice. 'Mayhap you should rest and I shall see to fetching some food to break our fast together.'

'Thank you, but I am perfectly well.' She turned and gave him a bland smile. 'In truth, I shall break my fast at my brother's abode.'

'You are leaving?' He raised a brow in surprise. 'At this time?'

'Yes, they are all early risers, so I shall not disturb anyone.'

'I am sure you would not, but why now?'

'I find that there are a few of my personal possessions that I forgot to pack.'

Warin stepped towards her. 'Then allow me to go or send a missive to have a serving boy fetch it.'

She shook her head. 'No, I would prefer to go myself. I rather think what I seek might be difficult to find in any case.'

He watched her for a moment before nodding. 'Very well, then I shall be happy to escort you.'

'Thank you.' She fetched both of their cloaks from the other chamber and held Warin's out. 'If we can leave now, I would be very grateful.'

Joan was glad that Warin had decided to fetch his horse from where he had stabled the animal nearby, but remembered too late that she would now have to sit on the saddle pressed closely to his person, wrapped in his huge arms as they trotted through the streets of London. They rode in silence as she recalled his touches, his appealing scent and the feel of his body sliding against hers. It was this awareness of him that had got her into this awkward situation this morning.

She had been so lost in the exquisite moment the night before, swept away in Warin's arms, his unbelievable tenderness and the intensity of his touch, that she had forgotten herself and the vow she had made to hide her feelings. It was not as though she was unaware that her husband did not reciprocate those unwanted sentiments which she had expressed so unwisely.

Why would he, in any case?

Warin might be attracted to her, he might be kind, caring, considerate enough to have brought about this marriage in order to protect Joan, but that did not mean he had not felt obliged to offer for her. He had known that he had little choice and done the honourable thing, despite his protestation to the contrary. And she had misread all of this by adding her own vexatious declaration.

'You are quiet this morn, Joan. I trust that all is indeed well.'

'Thank you, but I believe we have already established that.'

'So we have. Then it must be something else.'

'Apologies, but I can be quite irritable sometimes when I have not broken my fast.'

'Then let us remedy that immediately.'

'That is not necessary, I assure you. We are approaching Tom and Brida's dwelling so we can do so there.'

'No, I insist, Joan.' He pulled the reins, bringing his horse to a stop, and jumped down. 'What sort of man would I be if I could not acquire sustenance for my new bride after being wed for just one day?'

Warin passed the reins to her and strolled a short distance to procure some freshly baked little pasties filled with meat, cheese and herbs from a nearby vendor before returning back. He passed them to Joan and she took a bite of the hot, flaky fare, her stomach making a rumble, welcoming it.

Mayhap all her uneasiness this morning had been due to the fact she had been so hungry. Warin mounted the horse and once again she was nestled against him, her back pressed against the hardness of his chest, making her pulse quicken. Ah, mayhap it had not.

They soon entered the stables at the rear of Tom's house and Warin passed the reins to a groom before helping Joan dismount and taking her arm to escort her inside the courtyard.

'I am sure I can manage from here, Warin. I do not wish to importune you further.'

'I assure you that you are not.' He passed her walking stick to her that he had strapped to his horse. 'Let me escort you inside, at least.'

'I believe I know my way from here, thank you.' She had not meant for her voice to be so sardonic, but it was not as though she did not know her way around her brother's house. Oh, dear, she really was so very irritable this morn.

He sighed, dragging his fingers through his hair. 'Well, since I am not needed here, I shall see to matters that need my attention. Do I need to organise a cart, Joan?'

She frowned. 'A cart?'

'For the many items you left behind.'

'Oh, no, they are small enough to fit in saddle bags.' She rose on her tiptoes and gave him a kiss on the cheek. 'Thank you for escorting me here.'

'My pleasure. That is what I am here for.'

The truth was that, despite knowing that Warin did not love her, it did not mean that this understanding did not hurt Joan deeply. It did not mean that she was unaffected by it or that her heart was immune from shattering into small pieces with this realisation. She attempted to paste a happy smile on her face and turned towards him, hoping that he could not see the turmoil inside. All she needed was a moment of reflection, a moment to compose herself before she could face him again.

'I shall leave you now,' he muttered, kissing her on the lips. 'Take all the time you need. I shall come for you anon.'

Her heart clenched at that touch. Oh, God, she must find a way to protect herself. She must contain and extinguish her love for Warin, otherwise she would always be seeking for something that did not exist. Otherwise, she would commit herself to a life of misery. 'Yes. And thank you, Warin.'

'Until later, Joan.'

She nodded and watched as he left, waiting in her brother's quiet courtyard until she sensed that Warin had walked through the archway and into the stable. It was only then that her eyes swam with tears. She would allow it—her moment of weakness. Just this once.

She could not stay here and be exposed to Tom and Brida's curiosity and scrutiny—Joan could not counter it. She slowly made her way to the front of the building, praying that she would not meet with any of the household, and exhaled in relief as she left with only a handful of the maids and serving boys taking notice of her as they busied themselves before the household rose.

Good. This was precisely the time she needed to gather herself. It was by her own folly that she had found herself in this predicament in the first instance, but it would pass. It must. She would harden her resolve and adapt to her situation as she always had in her life and mask her disappointment. She would quash and suppress her feelings for Warin and resign herself to live with her foolish heart the best way she could.

Joan paused for a moment, her shoulders sagging as she took a deep breath and rubbed her brow. There was nothing for it, she would go to All Hallows—oh, God, how she wanted to be there now. Yes, she would have her moment of contemplation at her haven there.

But Joan never reached All Hallows Church on Honey Lane. For just as she turned into the narrow, cobbled lane, deep in thought, she was grabbed from behind, her mouth covered to drown out her screams, and was bundled into a moving cart before anyone had taken notice of her. But one had noticed. One who had seen the whole dreadful episode—the small fair-haired orphaned maid.

Chapter Twenty-One

Warin left Tom Lovent's stables after retrieving his huge destrier and rode away from the city gates, instead of towards them as he had intended to do. He kept on riding through woods and thickets and over hills, without a clear direction of where he was going until he found himself in the small hamlet of Sheen, nestled next to the River Thames, west of London. With his heart pounding wildly in his chest, Warin made his way to the small church of St Mary Magdalene at the edge of the village.

After paying a young girl for a small posy of fresh flowers, Warin strolled through the wooden archway into the walled churchyard at the side, clutching the reins tightly. There, under an ancient oak tree, was where he had buried his first wife along with their infant daughter. His hand shook as he placed the posy beside the simple wooden cross that marked their internment.

Why in God's name was he here, after all this time? He had no notion why he had come to this place on this miserable grey morn. And yet it had been as though an invisible cord had pulled him back—to the very last place in this kingdom that he wanted to be. But mayhap it was time. Mayhap it was time to finally reconcile himself to everything that had happened in the past with the hope of absolving himself of all his damn failings.

He would never forget her or their infant daughter, Maud... Ah, Maud, the happy little soul, full of wonder and curiosity. God, but how his heart ached after losing her—losing both of them—but Warin knew that it was time to let go.

It was time to rid himself of the guilt and bid farewell to his wife, his child and a future that never came to pass. It was time to acknowledge that his path now lay with another. With a woman who made his blood quicken and his heart sing. A woman who challenged him, questioned him about his perceived notions and who 'saw' the world in her own unique way. A woman who made him smile and whom he desired above all.

Warin dropped to his knees and clasped his hands together as his eyes filled with tears, staring at the unkempt grave. Closing his eyes, he made a silent prayer before finally allowing himself to weep for the wife and daughter he had loved, lost and had failed to protect.

Warin did not know how long he had stayed in the churchyard by the marked grave, but it was many hours later when he found himself back in Tom's stable, passing the reins of his destrier to the stablehand before walking through the arched gateway and into the pretty courtyard, ready to take his wife back home.

Their home—his and Joan's. God, he needed to see her, talk to her and as soon as might be. He, too, had many things that he needed to divulge. Many things that needed to be said. Warin felt as though a huge weight had been lifted from his shoulder and, for the first time in many years, he felt hope for the future. Their future—together.

He stepped inside the hallway and was surprised to find that he was needed urgently by Tom in his private chamber. And as soon as he entered, he found not only his brother by marriage, but Savaric Fitz Leonard, as well as the Chief Justiciar and his liege lord, Hubert de Burgh.

A sense of uneasiness rippled through him. Something was not right.

'Warin, thank God. Where have you been?' Tom strode up to him.

He ignored the man's question. 'What is it? Has new information come to light regarding the Duo Dracones?'

'Are you telling me that Joan is not with you?'

Joan? 'What the hell do you mean? I escorted her here this very morning.'

'Hell's teeth!' Tom rubbed his brow. 'This cannot be.'

Warin frowned, not quite comprehending what he had just walked into. 'Where is she? Where is Joan?'

Tom exhaled in frustration. 'That is precisely the point. I had thought the missive to be a hoax, believing that she was with you. Especially since the last time I saw Joan, I had entrusted her into your care, de Talmont.'

Warin suddenly stilled, dread filling his bones. 'What the hell do you mean—what missive? Are you implying that my wife is no longer here?'

'Despite what you have just told us, Warin, I have not seen Joan today.'

What...?

He felt a trepidation trickle down his spine. 'I do not understand. What do you mean that you have not seen her?'

Tom rubbed his brow. 'I mean that since I have not seen her, she must have left as soon as you escorted her here. It is, as you well know, highly possible knowing Joan.'

'Then I ask again, where is she? What has this missive you speak of to do with Joan?' And why had they all assembled here in this manner. Christ, what in heavens was going on? 'Tell me, Lovent.'

Tom exhaled through his teeth before answering. 'I received a missive early today, with a message claiming that Joan had been taken...by men belonging to the Duo Dracones.'

Dear God. Warin felt as though his knees might give way. Why in God's breath had this happened? None of it made much sense.

Hubert de Burgh placed a hand on his shoulder. 'Come, de Talmont. Won't you sit here?'

He nodded weakly before turning his attention back to Tom. 'Why?'

'We had initially believed this to be a hoax—we believed my sister to be safe with *you*. But now you have returned...without Joan.' Tom Lovent slumped on the stool, shaking his head in disbelief. 'Now I do not know what to believe.'

The tension that permeated the chamber was unbearably palpable, making it difficult to breathe. Just then, Nicholas d'Amberly burst through the door, holding out his hand and revealing a long lock of strawberry-blonde-coloured hair.

'This has just been delivered to one of our informants.'

It was a lock of Joan's hair.

Warin took a sharp intake of breath as he stood, stumbling backwards and falling to his knees. Oh, please, God…no. This could not be happening. Not again. And just as before…a lock of damn hair. Warin felt the blood drain from his face. He might very well bring up the contents of his stomach.

He almost did not want to ask. 'What…what do the bastards want?'

'Silver,' Savaric Fitz Leonard muttered. 'As well as something else.'

'Me.' Hubert de Burgh nodded. 'And preferably my head.'

A buzzing sound started to ring in Warin's ear, drowning out other noises. He dropped his head into his hands. A ransom. Again. God, but it had been the same the last time someone had snatched his woman. It was unfathomable that it was happening again. And the previous time someone had ransomed his wife, he had lost everything. But he could not allow that to happen again—he could not. He needed to be strong—he had to.

He lifted his head. 'What is the plan, then?' His voice was low and steely.

'That is what we need to consider,' Tom answered, looking particularly ashen. 'How to get her back.'

'Right,' he mumbled uneasily, feeling anything but right at that moment.

'Come, we can do this.' Savaric Fitz Leonard pounded his fist on the table, leaning forward. 'Together, as one, we can find Joan. Together we get your wife back where she belongs.'

Yes…yes. Warin had to put his faith and conviction in believing that he would find her. That he would get Joan back. He could not afford to believe any differently or, worse, think of failure.

'Apart from what you have already disclosed, what else have the Duo Dracones demanded?'

'That we arrive at the designated meeting point, just after vespers, with the silver they have demanded.'

Warin needed to think. He needed to formulate a plan to put together with his Knights Fortitude brethren in order to succeed. And to do that, he needed to remain calm and focused.

He ran a shaky hand through his hair. 'And what of you, my Lord de Burgh? How do you come to be part of this?'

'As we had discussed in the Tower, de Talmont, it is *I* whom the Duo Dracones want, or rather my downfall. They have attempted to blacken my name, they have tried to paint me as a traitor by the lengths to which they have gone to pin the problem of the tanners that impacted the whole leather trade on me. But thankfully, you along with the rest of the Knights Fortitude all but scuppered them. Now it seems that nothing will do but my destruction, so it seems that not only do they want one hundred silver marks, but I am to be the sacrificial lamb as well.' De Burgh might have declared this sardonically, but Warin could feel the tension emanating from the man, as well as everyone else in the chamber.

And no more than from himself—but then there was much at stake here.

'What I propose is to have the area of this rendezvous surrounded.' Warin knew it was the only way.

'Yes.' Tom nodded. 'We would wait and take them down before the ransom is exchanged.'

'But we must be prudent and take care. If these bastards have had to resort to this because the Bishop of Winchester, or whoever their master is, has reneged on their agreement, they will now be even more desperate.'

'And far more dangerous.'

'Precisely.'

'Yes, so there is no room for error.'

None of the men present wanted to state what such an error could cost. They all knew what that would mean.

'Are we all in agreement?'

'Aye.' The men of the Knights Fortitude each made their vow to one another—*Pro Rex. Pro Deus. Pro fide. Pro honoris*—and clasped each other's arms.

'Good.'

In the midst of their privy meeting with preparations several hours later, the young mute orphaned maid from All Hallows Church barged inside the private chamber.

'I am sorry, sirs, for this intrusion, but this here rascal ran inside the moment the door was opened and given us jip ever since.' The serving boy caught the girl by the scruff of the neck. 'Come on, you.'

'No! Wait, this child is from All Hallows.' Warin strode across the chamber as the child pulled loose and ran to hide behind him. 'Let her be.'

The servant verified this with Tom, as Warin turned around and knelt in front of her.

'The child seems familiar,' Tom muttered, giving the maid his full attention. 'You have come here before—with Joan, have you not?'

The little girl shrank back a little, despite Tom's voice, which he had intentionally gentled. She managed, however, to respond with a small nod of her head.

Good. They were getting somewhere. Whatever it was that had made the child venture all the way here could only have to do with Joan and her current predicament. Warin was certain about it.

'You must be hungry, little one, since you must have walked all this way.' The girl turned her attention back to Warin and gave him a tentative nod, making him smile. 'Can you fetch some food for the child?' he muttered over his shoulder before returning his attention back to the girl. 'Now, have you come all this way to disclose something about Joan?'

The girl made another slow reticent nod.

'Now, little one.' His heart pounded against his chest. 'Do you think you can tell me?'

The girl made no attempt to answer.

'What is wrong with the child? Can she not speak?'

Warin held up his hand, silencing Fitz Leonard. No, the child did not speak and had not done in a very long time. The only thing he could do would be to coax the answers from her. And as expediently as he could.

'Tell me, did you see the men take Joan?' Warin said, trying to keep his hold of his patience.

The girl nodded again and opened up a small hemp burlap bag for Warin to see that it was filled with the small dried floral heads of lavender. The very same ones that he had strewn all over the coverlet, on their wedding night.

Oh, God, Joan...

'You collected these?' He kept his eyes fixed to the girl as she nodded. 'You collected these from somewhere near All Hallows, didn't you? You collected these because Joan dropped them?'

The girl nodded again.

'Did they travel on foot?' The child shook her head. 'A horse?' Again, another shake of the head. 'A wagon?' The maid smiled.

Warin rubbed his chin. 'So, they travelled by wagon.'

But where to, in heaven's name?

'Do you...by any chance know the direction they travelled in?'

The maid stared at him with those big blue eyes before her lips curled into an impish smile.

The child had not only seen where the wagon had gone, but had followed its slow progress until it had reached its destination by the edge of the quayside near Watling Street, close to London Bridge. It was also close to the deserted wharf where they were due to meet the Duo Dracones after vespers.

Warin stared at the small wooden lock-up shack used for storing goods and wondered whether Joan was still held inside. He clenched his fists tightly against the reins of his destrier. God, but he was tempted to blast through the doors and find whether his wife was there, but knew it was not prudent to do so, especially since they had everything planned meticulously to get her back soon. He looked down at the child who stayed anxiously close to him and squeezed her shoulders to reassure her. He could ill afford to put any of their lives in danger.

Later…yes, later he would have his reckoning with the bastards who thought to take Joan away from him.

Joan tried to suppress the feeling of trepidation which had gripped her ever since she had been abducted. She was in a dark, dank, musty space with many goods stored in huge sacks dotted around, but now the space was plunged in near darkness. The man with the scar on his face whom she remembered from the night at the Tower and his accomplice had brought her here, dispatching a ransom to her brother, from the snippets of conversation she had managed to hear, which made her feel far worse than being stuck here.

God, but once again she had been a nuisance—so aggravating to put her loved ones through more vexation and all because of her tempestuous impulsiveness. Again. If only she had not heedlessly rushed out of her brother's home, none of this would have happened. It was all entirely her fault—because of her foolishness. She wondered whether her trail of lavender had possibly been observed—but then it was grasping at very little on London busy roads whether anyone would have seen them or even cared. By now, however, her brother, if not Warin, would have noted that she was missing.

Oh, God… Warin.

The thought that she might never see him again, that she had thoughtlessly put their lives in danger, filled her with despair.

Joan had to get out of here herself. She had managed to loosen the rope tied around her feet, but to what avail? She could still not get very far with her hands bound tightly to a wooden post, and even then, her poor sight would let her down. But she would do it. She would do everything in her power to save herself. All she had to do was to wait and bide her time until the moment was nigh.

Warin could not put his finger on it, but something did not seem as it should on this eventide as he waited, hidden under an archway, blowing his breath in between his hands. The temperature had plummeted as it sometimes did at this time of year, with a slight dampness in the air and mist rising from the surface of the Thames, adding to the eerie atmosphere in this secluded bend of the quayside.

Mayhap it was the anticipation laced with a palpable feeling of dread, as he waited for events that the Knights Fortitude had planned to unfold. But even so he could not help the feeling of uneasiness trickling down his spine.

He pushed his mind back to the task at hand and trying assuage his concerns about this night and the implications if they failed... It would not serve Joan well if he was unable to do his job. He had to allay his fears and stay strong.

Even now d'Amberly was in position by the quay dissembled as a drunk beggar, while Warin and Fitz Leonard were hiding in the shadows with their quivers filled and their bows strung against the arrows, ready to take aim. And Tom stood with two huge saddlebags stuffed full of silver beside a man pretending to be Hubert de Burgh, wearing a cloak with a deep hood covering his head. Tom made a few covert signs with his hands and nodded in Warin's direction.

It was time... His heart beat a rapid tattoo as he realised the sequence of events was about to commence imminently. He blinked and wiped his clammy brow as two figures walked towards the designated meeting place, with the filmy mist sweeping at their feet. He watched them—one man and the other evidently Joan, who also wore a cloak with a hood covering her head, as they ambled closer towards Tom.

Warin frowned as Joan and her abductor stopped a distance in front of Tom, who began to speak with the man. Something was not right. He leant forward, studying the pair, but it was too dark to be able to see properly. His frustration grew as his visibility was preventing him from seeing anything that would confirm his suspicions in the damn darkness.

It was then that Warin realised that he needed to use his intuition—he needed to trust his senses, his convictions—*just as Joan would do*. Just as she had shown him time and time again. His clever, beautiful, wonderful wife.

Without another thought he moved forward quickly and with purpose, dropping the bow and arrow and drawing out his sword from its scabbard. He caught the pair off guard as he charged at them and, with a few swipes of his sword, had them pinned against a stone wall, with the blade of his sword against the cordwainer's neck. Hell's teeth, he wasn't even the man with the scar.

Damn.

'This is not Joan,' he growled, removing the hood off the woman's head, confirming his suspicions. 'But I know where she is and, by God, when I find your accomplice he'll wish he was never born. D'Amberly, take over from here. Fitz Leonard, come with me.'

His fellow Knights Fortitude brethren swept to his feet in a flourish, his whole demeanour changing as he took charge of the situation.

Warin turned on his heels and strode away with Tom and Fitz Leonard following behind.

'How the hell did you know for certain that the woman was not Joan?'

'Because she did not have Joan's walk. It should have been far more assured, as Joan's would have been, but this woman stumbled on her feet since she was unused to having her eyes covered. And I knew for certain once I approached the fray—her scent was also not my wife's either.'

'That was an almighty risk, Warin.'

'No, I would never have risked Joan's safety,' he retorted, glaring ahead. 'I knew, Tom. I knew for certain.'

'As you are regarding where she is now?'

He nodded. 'That, too.'

The heavens opened as they ran along a series of roads and pathways that eventually lead to a narrow lane opening out to the isolated quayside timber lock-up shack that he had visited earlier that day with the young maid from All Hallows. He opened his mouth to speak when a shrill scream rang out from inside the building as a woman—Joan—rushed out of the shack, closely pursued by the man with the scar face. Warin,

Tom and Fitz Leonard raced towards them, as the man grabbed Joan by the neck and threw her against the stone wall. That was the very last thing Warin remembered before a red mist descended over him. He lunged at the man, tearing him away from Joan, and hurled him to the ground. He was on him, punching him again and again and again. Over and over until he heard Tom's voice as the rain thrashed against him.

'Enough. We need the man alive.'

At that moment, he did not care. 'The bastard thought to take my wife away from me. He thought he could take her away and hurt her.' Warin continued to beat the man with everything he had.

'Stop, Warin. He is not worth having his death on your conscience.' Joan's beloved voice penetrated his senses. Thank God, she was here with him once more.

Warin swung around and after tentatively touching her face to check that she was real, he wrapped his arms fiercely around her. They stayed like that for a long moment in the pouring rain as his Knights Fortitude brethren apprehended the man with the scar, pulling him to his feet, but somehow the man managed to wriggle free. And before either Tom or Fitz Leonard knew what had happened, Joan's assailant and member of the Duo Dracones stepped back and dragged a blade across his own throat and fell to the ground in a pool of his own blood.

Warin pulled Joan against him, turning her away from the scene. The man might be dead. They might still know very little about the Duo Dracones, but Warin did not care.

'It is over,' he murmured in relief. 'Thank God, it is over.'

And thank God he had Joan in his arms. Safe. Unharmed. And yet the danger had loomed far too close. He felt her knees give way and caught her, pulling her into his arms and carrying her away from the harrowing scene.

'I thought I had lost you,' he whispered against the top of her head. 'I thought I might never see you again.'

'I knew how it would be and how you must have felt…after what had happened to you before.' She pulled away slightly, a frown burrowed in her brows. 'I am sorry for putting you in that situation, Warin. I am sorry for causing you pain.'

'No more than me, sweetheart.'

'How did you know where to find me?'

Trust Joan and her inquisitive mind to get straight to the point. 'The young maid from All Hallows. She followed your lavender trail from the wagon.'

'I was lucky that it was moving, but I cannot believe she came to you afterwards.'

'I told you that her tenacity reminded me of you. Talking of which, I was hoping you might agree if she came to live with us?'

'Truly?'

'Only if you think it would be the best for the maid.'

'Oh, I do.' She hugged him tightly. 'I do, thank you.'

'Good, I am glad that is settled.'

'In which case I would also like to add my heartfelt gratitude to you for coming to my aid. I really do not know what would have happened otherwise.'

'Hush, that is not worth thinking about, my love. It

is and always will be my duty to protect and care for you. I would go to the ends of this world for you, Joan de Talmont,' he muttered softly. 'And never again will I lack the courage to disclose what I feel for you.'

She blinked in surprise. 'What you feel? For me?'

'Indeed.' He bent his head and pressed a firm kiss to her lips. 'I love you,' he stated simply, unable to say more but knowing more was needed. It had all been his fault and he had almost lost her. 'I love you, Joan. It just took me longer to recognise it, even though it was glaring in my face, but it was always there from the first.'

'You cannot mean this?'

'But I do. You have captivated me, Wife—body and soul. And I would do everything in my power to be worthy of you. And to be worthy of a second chance at happiness—with you.'

'Oh.' She blinked as her eyes filled with tears. 'I love you, Warin. And you should know that I intend to make you very happy.'

'I am glad to hear it.' He smiled. 'I intend to do the very same. Now and always—until I draw my last breath.'

With that he kissed her once more.

* * * * *

*If you enjoyed this story,
be sure to read the other books in
the Protector of the Crown miniseries,
coming soon!*

*And, while you're waiting, why not check out
Melissa Oliver's other great series
Notorious Knights?*

The Rebel Heiress and the Knight
Her Banished Knight's Redemption
The Return of Her Lost Knight
The Knight's Convenient Alliance